THE RULES OF HEARTBREAK

BOOK ONE: THE HEARTBREAK SERIES

BRITTANY TAYLOR

THE RULES OF
Heartbreak

To Lisa
For being the mother I didn't know I needed,
and for encouraging me to always keep going for what I want in
this life.
I love you for your strength and for your unwavering belief in me.
Especially in the times I had trouble believing in myself.

PROLOGUE

Sloan

Death is a beast that wears many masks.

Some deaths cut deeper than others. Some barely leave a scratch.

My mother's death was the latter of the two.

She's been dead for years. Well, that's not entirely true. She's only been dead for the past four months, but the amount of time my mother has *actually* been dead doesn't make a difference to me either way. It may sound harsh, but she never gave me any reason to think she cared for me at all. For years, I've accepted the cards I was dealt in my life—a mother who had no interest in her daughter.

It was easier to believe she was dead than it was to believe she was the shitty mother she was in real life. I simply didn't allow her choice of abandonment to ruin my life. It's nearly impossible to allow yourself to be hurt by something you've never had. How can you be sad about something you never lost in the first place?

Still, my mother's actual death had nothing on the other kinds of death I've experienced. Those were the ones that tore the life I had built to shreds. Those were the ones that made my decision to move to Austin an easy one.

And this time, I'll be ready for any heartbreaks or deaths that come my way.

RULE #1

When you catch your fiancé having an affair with your best friend, start your life completely over.

CHAPTER ONE

Sloan

"It's so fucking hot." I tip my chin up to the clear blue sky and squint my eyes against the bright sun. Sweat drips down my face, sliding its way down the back of my neck. My back aches and my skin heats with the mid-June sun scorching across every inch of my body. I swipe the back of my hand across my wet skin.

My chest has transformed to a light shade of pink, highlighting the faint freckles dotted across my skin, and my hair is saturated with sweat. I inhale a deep breath and crack my eyes open, dreading the last box I need to finish loading into my house. I don't even bother picking it up. Instead, I stick my foot out and scoot it across the threshold of the front door. The box scrapes against the pavement before sliding across the hardwood of the front entrance of my mother's old house. Or, I guess I should say my new house—a fact I still haven't been able to wrap my head around. I leave the box sitting on the floor with the rest of the boxes I've already stuffed inside.

"Exhausted?" Liam passes me with his arms wrapped around a box, carrying it inside. His eyebrows arch across his forehead, the corner of his mouth curling.

"A little." I smirk, wiping my hands on the front of my shorts.

Liam walks back outside, headed for the truck parked in my driveway. I lean against the door jamb and stare outside, taking in my new neighborhood. My eyes dance across the street, taking it all in. It's surprising to me that up until three months ago, I never knew my mother lived in a place like this. In fact, I shouldn't be surprised at all. I never knew a single thing about her, not even so much as her hair color, until her lawyer showed up at my doorstep. It's funny how in the twenty-four years since she gave birth to me, she never made any effort to get to know me. Instead, she decides to leave me her house in Austin, Texas. Nice touch, Mother.

In a way, my mother's dying wish to have me inherit her house has become a blessing. I didn't realize how bad I wanted to get out of Minnesota until the opportunity presented itself.

Life in Minnesota was colder and more isolating.

Not here.

The hot Texas air warms my body, burrowing itself deep in my bones. The people here seem to be happy. It feels as if I've transported myself to a whole different world, away from the life I was living, opening up the possibility to start a new one.

I cross my arms over my chest and rest my head against the door frame of my new home. The sun shines across my driveway as my brother steps out of the back of the moving truck.

He rakes his fingers through his damp hair. "Are you sure this was a good idea, Sloan?"

"What?" I ask him, faking a smile. It's the thousandth time he's asked me this question. "Liam, we've already loaded every-thing into the house. There's no way in hell I'm taking it all back out even if I wanted to."

"I know, I know." He holds his hands up. "I've probably asked you too many times."

"Only about a *thousand* times."

He dramatically sighs, following it up with a shrug. He moves past me and bends down to pick up a box labeled *Kitchen*, carrying it down the hall.

I don't follow him. I'm enjoying the view of my street too much from where I'm standing. The neighborhood is nice, definitely a few steps up from the cabin I grew up in back in Minnesota.

The exterior of the houses are covered in brick, each one a different shade than the one beside it. The yards are large, giving each house a good amount of separation. Even though the grass has turned a light shade of brown under the scorching summer sun, the neighborhood is still beautiful. The two-story houses are full of life, home to families of all kinds. An older couple walking their dog passes by. They smile and wave before continuing on their way.

Liam returns from the kitchen a few minutes later. This time his arms are empty. He catches my attention, and I glance over my shoulder long enough to see him walking down the hall.

"I'll never stop asking you if you still think this was a good idea," he says with a heavy breath. "This place is fucking hot as hell."

I laugh, pointing at his clothes. "It is when you're dressed like that. Leave it to the man from Minnesota to still be wearing jeans and a long-sleeved t-shirt when it's nearly a hundred degrees out." This time I give him a genuine smile.

"Hey, I'm not the one who decided to move to a different state where they know absolutely *no one*." Liam arches his eyebrows, sarcasm dripping from his tongue. I let his comment slide, knowing how hurt he is that I've decided to leave Minnesota.

I look down, keeping my arms crossed over my chest. I frown, dragging the tip of my sandal across the concrete. "There's nothing left for me up there, anyway."

"That's not exactly true." Liam frowns. "But I can understand how you would feel that way."

I can sense part of him is still angry about what happened between me and my ex. He's always been protective of me. While Liam's anger still boils, mine has been reduced to a mere simmer. To some degree, I still feel what he did. Don't get me wrong—finding my fiancé fucking my best friend on our dining room table was enough to make me carry an entire life of hatred, but I decided to move on, to attempt to start a new life. The past few months have allowed me to transform the knots twisted in my chest into nothing but loose unraveled tendrils. My old life has now become a memory, a recollection of what used to be. The pain doesn't cut me the same way it did when I found out about Cole's affair. I've simply learned to live with it.

Liam's eyebrows knit, sadness pooling in his irises. "You still have me and Mark."

Liam is my brother, but not in the traditional sense. His mom married my dad when I was three years old and Liam was four. Since we were so young when our parents married, I don't remember a time when he wasn't in my life.

I nod but can't bring myself to look at Liam. I'll miss him and his husband, Mark, but I know deep down this was the right choice. For the first time, I feel like I'm finally grabbing my life by the horns, directing it exactly where I want it to go. Which is here, in Texas.

"I promise, this is where I'm supposed to be. I may not know anyone yet, but I will. I have plenty to do around the house, and I'll start looking for a summer job to pull in extra money. I'll be good, don't worry." I cross my arms over my damp chest and nod my head back toward the house.

"I'm sorry I keep asking you." He sighs. "I'm just going to miss you, that's all. I'm glad you were able to find a job quickly."

"It wasn't too difficult to get certified here in Texas. I'm just thankful I was able to snag the third-grade teaching position in this school district. My commute doesn't seem too awful."

This coming school year is the first year I'll be teaching out of college. It was only a week after graduation when I found out about Cole and Brenna's affair. As horrendous as it was, Cole's indiscretion came at the most opportune time. Finding a job such as this one in Austin is nearly unheard of for a teacher fresh out of college, and I consider myself lucky—lucky and relieved. I truly am starting my life over in every sense.

"That's good." Liam nods, pressing his lips into a thin line. The corner curls into a smirk. "Plus, you're right about this place. You'll have plenty to do around here. It's missing that Sloan Montgomery touch."

I shrug. "I'll see what I can do. She might not have had the best taste in design, but this is a nice house." I clear my throat. "At least it's one thing I've learned about Ellie that I didn't know before. In fact, it's the only thing."

"You have a good point." Liam nods in agreement.

I narrow my gaze, attempting a smile. Standing here with Liam has become more weighted and emotional than I expected it to be. "The offer still stands, you know. You and Mark are always welcome to move down here. I bet Mark would love it here."

"Maybe." He frowns, considering the idea. His eyebrows dip and the thoughts clearly swirl in his eyes, but disappointment fills his expression when he tilts his head. "I don't know, Sloan. It's a big deal. I'd have to talk to Mark."

I nod, unraveling my arms and sliding my hands into the front pockets of my shorts. "I understand, but you will both have to at least visit. I won't accept anything less." I smile, hoping this offer cheers him up.

"Are you kidding me? Of course we will." He grabs my hand and holds it between us. Tears well in his eyes. After a heavy sigh, he clears his throat and releases his grasp. He bends down to pick up another box, but I stop him.

"You don't have to do any more, Liam. I've got it from here."

He straightens his back, swiping his hand across his forehead the same way I did a few moments ago. "It feels like you're trying to run me out of here."

"I'm not, but I know Mark needs you back at home, and you only have about two hours before your flight leaves." I place a reassuring hand on his shoulder. My fingers stick to the sweat on his back, and I immediately regret placing it there. I move it away and wipe it across the front of my shorts. Liam's eyes follow my hand before he looks down at his shirt, scrunching his nose.

"Do you mind if I take a quick shower before I head out? I don't think I should be going on a plane when I feel and smell like this." The corners of his mouth dip in disgust.

I laugh. "Of course you can."

"Okay." He gives me a small smile and runs out to the truck to grab his bag. When he comes back inside, he heads for the stairs but stops when he lands on the second step. "I can still reschedule my flight. I can leave tomorrow instead." He's grasping at straws.

Liam and I both drove down here in the moving truck, my car attached to a trailer behind it. We made it just in time for his return flight home. The longer he stands here, the more I realize how much I'm going to miss him.

"Seriously, Liam. I'm fine."

A dot of sweat slides down his cheek, or maybe it's a tear. I can't tell at this point.

He clears his throat. "Right." He doesn't offer up any other reasons for me to question my move here before he disappears upstairs. Once I hear the shower running, I start to dig through one of the boxes piled in the front entrance. I start with the easy box, labeled *Blankets*. I lift all of them out of the box and carry them to my bedroom.

Not only did my mother leave me her house in her will, she also left me everything inside of it as well. This includes her bed. Part of me feels odd using it, not knowing a single thing about the woman who slept in it. The same applies to every bit of furniture in this house. Eventually I'll replace it all with my own furniture, but I don't have a choice tonight, at least not until I have the time to take a trip down to the mattress store. Cole kept ours after our breakup, and I've been sleeping in Liam's guest bedroom. It will feel good to have a bed of my own. For tonight, this will have to do.

On the way back downstairs, I avoid looking at the pictures lining the wall in the upstairs hallway. There are only a handful framed and nailed to the wall and only one containing a picture of my mother. The other pictures are all scenic. Mountains, palm trees, beaches, you name it. It's an odd, eclectic collection of photographs, but so was my mother it appears. The one picture of her is the only time I've ever come close to seeing what she looked like. Her head is tilted back in laughter, leaving only half her face visible. Although her eyes are closed, it's her smile I notice first. I only know the woman in the picture is my mother because it's the same as mine. I stare at the photograph as a pit grows in the bottom of my stomach. I take a deep breath then walk away, hoping the feeling will pass.

When Liam is finished with his shower, he finds me sitting on the couch in the living room. I have my feet propped up on the coffee table, and I've been scrolling through social media on my phone, the reality of my new life staring me directly in the face. He grabs a glass from one of the boxes in the kitchen and fills it with water from the tap without speaking a word. We both know it's time for him to leave.

"Are you all set?" I carefully ask him. Even though Liam and I are adults, it still saddens me to know he won't be a quick five-minute drive away anymore. We've never lived so far apart.

"I think so." He smirks, glancing around at all the boxes scattered throughout the first floor of my house. "Are you?"

I follow his gaze and study each box, taking in all the work I have ahead of me. There's no denying there's a lot for me to go through and set up, but part of me is looking forward to it. I'm building a life of my own, one without anyone else. I look Liam in the eyes and nod. "I am."

"Good." After grabbing his bag, he tosses it over his shoulder and heads to the front door. I follow him out to the driveway and catch up to him. He wraps his arm around me, keeping me close. We walk quietly, listening to our feet drag across the pavement.

Once we make it to the truck, Liam opens the door but abruptly stops. I wince when his elbow jabs into mine, his stare focused out on the street. "Oh my god." His jaw drops and I follow his gaze, trying to see what he's looking at.

"What?" I ask him, scanning the yards across from mine.

"Is that your neighbor?" he asks me, his eyes open wide. His voice is a sharp whisper. "He definitely wasn't out here earlier, and there is no way we would have missed him."

My eyes widen when I spot the man Liam is talking about. In fact, he's hard to miss. His wet brown hair dips across his forehead as he bends down, digging into what looks like a tool bag. The muscles of his bare back stretch with every movement, his tan skin glistening under the sweltering sun. His faded jeans are worn, covered in several grease stains and torn across his knees. The man doesn't look up, focused on working on the motorcycle parked in his driveway. He carries the wrench over to the bike and bends down again. Liam is right—there's no way we wouldn't have seen him out here earlier.

Liam jabs me with his elbow again. "Maybe moving here wasn't a bad idea after all," he mutters under his breath, acting as if the man can hear him from where we're standing in my driveway.

I roll my eyes at his comment. "You're married, Liam."

"Hey, that man is *gorgeous*. Don't lie and tell me you don't see it too. And being married doesn't mean I can't still appreciate an attractive man when I see one." He points his finger at me. "And you can too."

I shake my head. "I don't think I'm ready to jump into that pool. Not for a long time, anyway." I'm still staring at the man, studying his profile. He looks around my age, maybe a bit older. His eyes are intently focused on his bike as he twists the wrench, music playing from the phone halfway stuffed into his back pocket. My eyes make it back up to catch the features of his face. There's a sharp plane to his nose, stopping above his full lips. Sweat drips down his jawline, slithering down the tan skin of his neck. I swallow and press my lips together, heat rising up my throat. Maybe Liam has a point. There is no denying that my neighbor is obnoxiously good-looking, but I have rules and promises I've made to myself.

"You will be at some point." Liam finally breaks his gaze away from my neighbor. His eyes sadden again when he pulls me in for a hug. His strong arms wrap around me, and I bury my face against his chest. He smells clean, and although he took a shower here, he still smells like home.

I scoff and roll my eyes. My brother's optimistic outlook on my love life is quite the opposite from mine.

"Wait." I pull back, keeping him at arm's length. "I just got my sweat all over you."

"I don't care." He shakes his head and chuckles.

I smile, pulling him back toward me. "Call me when you land."

"I will." He kisses the top of my head and hops into the truck. A tear slips down his cheek, and this time I don't have to wonder if it's sweat. I know he's truly crying.

I swipe away a tear of my own as Liam starts the engine and begins backing out of my driveway. I don't move to go inside the house until Liam turns and drives out of my neighborhood. In a way, his absence brings out two different feelings. A weight lifts off my shoulders and I feel ready to take the next step in my new life, but the other piece of me aches for my family. I know I'll miss them, but I also know it'll fade with time. This is now my new home, and I intend to do everything I can to make it feel that way.

I stand in the middle of my driveway until the sweat starts to run down my cheeks the same way it did earlier. I peer up at the sun, squinting. It may be hot, but I can feel the sunshine pouring into my soul. I've never felt the sun this way before, at least not somewhere I call home. The only other time was when I took a vacation to Florida with Cole for spring break our junior year of college.

I look down at my feet, already noticing how my skin has started to tan. I smile, but my eyes widen when I catch the ring of sweat around the collar of my tank top. Dots of sweat bead my chest, and I frown. The frayed ends of my shorts cling to my thighs. I wrap my hands around my neck and sigh, tipping my head back in exhaustion. I trail my fingers across my skin, attempting to wipe away the sweat gathered there. The sun dips behind the trees lining the street. It's getting late, and a shower and bed sound like the perfect way to finish out my first day in my new home.

I spin on my heel, ready to head back into my house, but

quickly stop. My feet tangle, the tip of my sandal scraping across the pavement. I stumble forward, reaching my arm out toward the hood of my car. My hand slaps against my black vehicle, catching me before I fall flat on my face. My neighbor, the one who was too busy focusing on fixing his motorcycle to notice me and Liam, is now staring directly at me. His dark eyebrows slant, studying every inch of me. It's as if I can feel his stare burning a hole through my chest.

My breath catches in my throat and I stare straight back at him. I stand, clearing my throat, wondering what about me has caught his attention.

He's standing beside his bike, running a rag across the palms of his hands and through his fingers. Black smudges streak across his sculpted arms, all the way down to his wrists. Sweat drips down the front of his chest. He's still shirtless, his bare chest exposed for all the neighborhood to see.

The music is still playing from the phone in his back pocket. I swallow, my throat starting to dry from the intense heat. At least that's what I'm telling myself.

My cheeks blush, mostly from my embarrassing stumble in front of this stranger.

Great first impression, Sloan.

The man's eyes don't move, and his expression catches me off guard. He doesn't smile and he doesn't wave. He does nothing. His face and body are still, as if he's been caught in a trance. He simply stands in his driveway with a blank stare.

I stare back at him with confusion. I don't know this man and have never seen him, but I can't help feeling like my heart might burst out of my chest. All from the intensity of his stare. The awkwardness of our situation leaves me clueless as to what to do. I start to think of all the reasons I know moving here was a good idea. I'm determined to start this new life of mine off on the right foot. I take a step forward, ready to walk over to him to introduce myself, but then I stop. Nerves rise inside me, my stomach fluttering. I'm covered from head to toe in sweat, and from the expression on his face, my neighbor doesn't appear too eager for me to walk over to him.

Instead, I stupidly lift my hand and wave, giving him the largest grin I can muster. "Hi." My voice wafts across the sweltering air between us. There's a considerable distance as we're both standing in the middle of our driveways. For a second, I'm unsure if he heard me.

But the heat in my cheeks intensifies when the man lifts his hand and swipes the pad of his thumb across his bottom lip. His eyes narrow and his jaw tightens. He doesn't respond to my greeting, at least not verbally. Instead, he turns around and walks back up his driveway. His boots beat against the pavement as he makes his way to his front door, shutting it behind him.

I awkwardly stand in my driveway, trying to decipher what just happened. Why was he staring at me? And how is it that I could feel his stare burrowing its way into me as deep as the sun's rays have been?

My first interaction with my neighbor isn't quite what I expected. I hope my new co-workers won't react the same way.

I turn around and head back into my house, refocusing on building this new life of mine. The second my eyes land on the mountain of boxes still piled in the entrance, I groan. I walk past them and slowly head up the stairs.

I take a quick shower then throw myself onto my mother's old bed, and before I'm able to even think about the million things I still have to do, I close my eyes and let sleep take me away.

CHAPTER TWO

DALLAS

"I TOLD YOU ALREADY, I'M NOT INTERESTED." I SIT ON THE edge of my bed and rest my elbows on my knees, catching my breath. The tingling in my legs has already started to dissolve, the rush of last night fading away.

"I don't see what the big deal is." Her voice is slow, her hot breath dancing across my back as she moves behind me. Her hand slides across my bare shoulder, the points of her long sharp nails digging into my muscle. "It's just coffee," she adds, as if that's enough to convince me to change my mind.

"I said no, Kate." I glance over my shoulder and shrug her hand away. I look her in the eye, letting her know how serious I am when it comes to this topic. Her black mascara is caked around her eyes, and her pink lipstick is smudged across her bottom lip.

She stares at me wide-eyed, her mouth open. She's resting back on her heels, her knees pressed into the mattress, and her eyebrows knit as she stares at me in disbelief, clenching her jaw. "My name is Kylie."

"Whatever." I roll my eyes and sigh, standing up to face her. "This was never more than what it is. You know that."

"Yeah," she says, crawling off the bed. "Well, maybe I hoped you would eventually change your mind."

"Nope." I roll my head to the side, avoiding her piercing stare. "We agreed to fuck. That was the deal. Nothing more." I leave Kate—shit...*Kylie* in my room and head toward my bathroom. I turn on the shower, allowing it to heat up.

I walk back out into my bedroom, checking my phone for the time. Perfect; it's still early enough for me to get Kylie out the door and make my morning run.

"I just don't understand why you're always rushing me out of here so early in the morning." She's standing at the foot of my bed, crossing her arms over her bare chest. She still hasn't bothered to get dressed. Her breasts pop out from her arms, my teeth marks still visible on her flesh. "It's still dark out."

"You understood that was the rule when you came over here," I tell her. "If you have a problem with it, so be it. Doesn't matter to me either way."

"What the hell is wrong with you?" She quickly snatches her sequined top and slides it on before gathering her long brown hair into a ponytail. She swipes her tongue across her mouth, wetting her lips.

It's hard for me to believe her mouth was wrapped around my dick only a few minutes ago. Her tongue slid across my length, her lips puckering around my tip as she swallowed my cum. I fight the way my dick begins to perk up with the memory. The last thing I want is to bring Kylie back to my bed. She needs to leave.

"You think I care what you think about me?" I ask her, already tired of this conversation. The longer she stands here in my house, in my bedroom, the more anxious I get for her to leave. We agreed to sleep with each other, not deal with all this extra bullshit.

"Wow." She nods, quickly stepping into her mini skirt. "Fuck you, Dallas."

"Been there, done that." I sneer. "And trust me, it isn't that great."

I'm lying. The sex was pretty fucking awesome, but at this point, I'm ready to say anything to push her out the door.

Kylie finishes the zipper on the back of her skirt, her face frozen as she stares at me in silence. I couldn't care less about the way she looks at me. It's better to have her look at me with hatred than with longing, hoping to be anything more than what we are. No amount of mind-blowing sex is worth even something as insignificant as a coffee date. Not anymore, at least. Sex with any woman this past year has been meaningless, and as far as I'm concerned, this conversation pretty much sealed the deal on any more nights with Kylie. This is only the third time I've brought her back to my place, but I've decided it's already been three times too many.

She wants more than I am willing to give.

She only blinks once before she storms out of my room without another glance in my direction. Her footsteps echo down the staircase followed by her slamming the front door.

Once I see the headlights of her car pass across my window and I'm certain she's gone, I step into the shower. It's steaming, and I welcome the sting across my skin. As always, I only stay in the shower long enough to rinse off before heading out for my usual morning run. I always take a full shower when I get back, but there is something to be said about jumping in long enough to wash away the choices I made last night.

After I finish in the shower, I quickly toss on my running shorts and head for the front door.

The morning is my favorite time to run. The city hasn't woken up, and when you live in one as big as Austin, you value the silence the darkness offers. Texas summers have always been nearly unbearable, so I take every opportunity I have before the sun decides to leave its mark across the city.

The sky is still black, an orange, purple shade slowly emerging from behind the house across the street. The same car that's been there the past week is still parked in the driveway, the moving truck gone. I don't know who moved into Ellie's house, and up until a week ago, I didn't know if anyone would. There was never a For Sale sign pitched in the front yard, and as far as I knew, Ellie didn't have family.

But as for the other day, the woman standing in Ellie's driveway was someone I wasn't expecting. She was gorgeous even with sweat covering every inch of her pale skin. She clearly wasn't from Texas. Not only did her skin look as if it had never seen the light of day, the license plate on her car said she was from Minnesota.

Her dark brown hair was swept into a ponytail, the ends dipping into the beads of sweat collecting along her back. At first, I couldn't ignore how her ass cheeks were peeking out of the bottom of her cutoff jean shorts. Then she saw me. It was as if I couldn't break my eyes away from hers. She was staring at me like a deer caught in headlights, her round eyes softening under the simmering summer sun. There's a story to the woman who now lives in Ellie's house—a story I have no interest in digging into. If I am going to stick to the promises I made to myself the past year, involving myself with my new neighbor isn't anything I am interested in.

I turn my attention to the road, following my usual route out of my neighborhood. The trees sway in the morning breeze, the wind beating against the brick exteriors of the endless number of houses lining my street.

As soon as my feet hit the pavement of the road, I start to pick up my speed, clicking through my playlist until I find the song I'm searching for. The music blasts through my headphones, drowning out the sound of my heavy breaths and weighted footsteps. This is my favorite part of the day. It's easy to block out the thoughts running through my mind. Running is a new habit I adopted along with not attaching myself too closely to anyone. As evidenced by what happened with Kylie this morning. I've developed a few good habits and a few bad ones, depending on how you look at them, but I don't give a fuck anymore. There is no reason to. I like to call it balance.

I've barely made it twenty seconds into the song when it suddenly stops, indicating I have an incoming phone call. I slide my phone out of my pocket and swipe the green button the second I see the name flashing across my screen.

"Dude, what the fuck?" Colton's husky voice travels through my headphones, his voice too loud for someone calling me so early in the morning. He's clearly still pissed at me for flaking out on him. In his defense, I have been a terrible friend and business partner lately. I haven't held up my end of the bargain, so there is a small piece of me that can't blame him for being upset with me.

I take a few steady breaths and turn onto the next street before answering him. "Look man, I'm sorry. I couldn't bring myself to go up there, so I dipped out early."

Colton and I opened our bar a little over a year ago in the center of downtown Austin. As far as the food and drink are concerned, we are considered a success. The entertainment side of it, not so much. I know summer is setting in, and every day our sales are climbing with students off for summer break. Music is a sure-fire way to attract more customers. Colton knows it. I know it. It's part of owning a bar in one of the most popular cities in Texas. No matter how much I know my playing would bring in customers, I still can't bring myself to do it. And that's where Colton's five a.m. complaint comes in.

"If this is how it's going to be every time I ask you to play a set at the bar, the least you can do is tell me the truth." He sighs. "Not give me this constant bullshit runaround."

"Can we talk about this later?" I ask him, breathless. I'm dodging this line of conversation. The thought of playing music again or even picking up my guitar makes me physically ill.

"I guess...but I'm just letting you know I'm looking to hire a couple extra bartenders and servers for the summer. With UT on summer break and tourist season ramping up, pretty soon it's going to be more than we can handle."

"Fine." I quickly agree with Colton. I may not have the motivation to play on stage, but I'm capable of talking about this side of the business.

Colton and I have been friends since our sophomore year at the University of Texas here in Austin. He majored in business, and I majored in music. Over the years, Colton tried to convince me we could open a barbecue restaurant and bar here in the center of the city. For most of our senior year of college, he turned into Bubba and I became Forrest Gump, but instead of shrimp, Colton was convincing me to run a barbecue restaurant.

"What happened to you last night anyway?" he asks.

"Nothing." I shake my head even though he can't see me.

"Oh, no." He chuckles under his breath. "Please don't tell me you left with Katie again."

I laugh under my breath. "Kylie."

"What?"

"Her name is Kylie, not Katie."

Colton pauses. "Right. Anyway, you left with her again, didn't you?"

"What if I did?" I don't know why I'm suddenly feeling defensive of the choices I've made lately. It's not like it's any of Colton's business who I sleep with. "It's not a big deal."

I swipe my arm across my forehead. Sweat has started to drip across my eyebrows, the corners of my eyes stinging with the salty liquid. I turn back down the main road and run along the sidewalk, watching the sun peek out at the end of the endless stream of streetlights.

"I figured you would say that."

"Whatever." I brush him off. My chest starts to tighten, the effect of my run beginning to wear on me. I look down at my watch. I've only made it a quarter of the way through my route. I still have to run through the park before swinging back to my neighborhood.

"I know you, Dallas," Colton says, hesitation filling his voice. "Every other night for the past week, Kylie has stopped in at the bar, and you always seem to dip out on me not long after she leaves. From what I can tell, the chick really likes you."

"Well then, I guess I dodged a bullet with that one." I smirk, happy to have ended it with her this morning. I'm not interested in dating a woman. Haven't been for the past year.

"Don't be like that, man."

"Like what?"

There's a long pause on Colton's end of the line, and for a moment I think I've lost him. Then I hear his heavy breath through my headphones. I can feel the tone of our conversation start to shift. I'm already hating where this is going, but I give my best friend the benefit of the doubt.

"I know you're still hurting after what happened with Hailey."

"Don't. Don't go there, man." My chest twists and tightens again, but this time I know it isn't from my run. I wish I had ended our conversation minutes ago.

"I'm not," he quickly says. "I'm just saying. Ever since, well, you know...and with what happened to Ellie recently...you haven't been yourself."

"You're right, I haven't." I chew the inside of my cheek until the stinging becomes nearly unbearable. I don't want to talk about Ellie, and I sure as shit don't want to talk about Hailey. I watch the cars passing me on the road as I turn into the park outside my neighborhood. There's no one else out here aside from me. That's the way I like it. Colton is slowly killing the craving I had for a peaceful run.

"Dallas, I'm sorry. I didn't mean to bring this up. I'm just worried about you." The tone of his voice has dramatically changed since I answered his call. It's always the same when I talk to anyone about Hailey. Their voice suddenly becomes timid and hushed as if they're afraid I'm going to break. It's fucking frustrating.

"Don't be worried about me. I'm twenty-six, Colton. I can take care of myself, and I'm happy with where I'm at in my life right now." I'm not entirely lying, but I'm not entirely telling the truth either.

I pause, allowing myself to catch my breath. I don't like talking about Hailey, and Colton knows it. Why he decided to bring her up is beyond me. But he's right—I am a different person from the man I used to be. My life will never be the same, and I've come to accept the fact that I will never be that Dallas again. It's easier to detach myself from the person I used to be. This life is simple and less complicated.

"It's fine." I run my hand down the side of my face. Sweat collects along my palm. There are streams of perspiration dripping down my chest and back, but I revel in the sense of calm it gives me.

"Are you sure?"

"Look," I tell him, too exhausted to continue this call, "I-I have to go. I'll see you tomorrow night."

I hang up and quickly press the play button, resuming the song I had playing when I first started my run. The music blasts in my ears as I turn it up as loud as it will go. I hate to admit it, but Colton's gotten under my skin. I was looking forward to this run, ready to start the day fresh once I got back to my house. The day hasn't even officially started, but I find myself wishing it were already over.

I start running down the main road leading into my neighborhood. The houses are still quiet, most of the cars still parked in the driveways and along the street. The sun has turned from a rich orange to a bright yellow behind the trees. My chest burns, thirsty for air. Each breath I inhale is sharper than the last as I approach my street. I'm nearing the turn when I start to think of what work still needs to be done on my motorcycle before my shift tomorrow night at the bar. I'm hoping Colton will forget all about our conversation by then.

My calves begin to ache, the muscles stretching with each furious step I'm taking. Colton's words leave me stewing inside, taking it out on each step I take, carrying me home. I hate thinking about Hailey, because thinking about Hailey makes me think of love, and that love turns to hate. Then hate transforms to regret, and regret is one ugly, evil son of a bitch.

My house is only about a hundred feet away, and the frustration of the past twelve hours is still burning a hole through my chest. I close my eyes, inhaling deep breaths. I keep running, not caring that I'm on the wrong side of the street from my house or if I even pass it. My feet slam against the sidewalk, each step faster and harder than the one before it.

I snap my eyes open the second a sharp pain hits my chest and I fly backward onto the sidewalk. My head hits the concrete and I crack open my eyes in pain, the morning sun nearly blinding me.

"Oh, shit."

Those two words don't fall from my mouth. Instead, they come from the person lying on top of me. Her lips are parted, and puffs of her minty-scented breath flit across my face as her eyes stare back at mine. The sun is shining bright behind her, creating a nearly white glow around her round face.

She's the woman I saw a week ago, the woman who is now living in Ellie's house.

Her cheeks are flushed, but I'm unsure whether it's from the fall or if it's from embarrassment at the predicament we've both found ourselves in. Her long brown hair is tied back into a pony-tail, the ends resting against my bare chest. Her palms are pressed flat against me, gliding up and down with the movement of my breathing.

She looks down at her hands as if she's trying to understand what happened and how we ended up lying in the middle of the street, her on top of me. Her eyes move from her hands, and I can feel her stare burning every inch of my chest up to my throat, then all the way across my face before she stops, matching her eyes with mine.

And then, as if her words have suddenly awakened me, she asks, "Are you okay?"

CHAPTER THREE

Sloan

When I decided to start my life over in Texas, I was certain it wouldn't involve falling in front of my new neighbor twice.

Nope. Not once.

Twice.

Only this time I didn't fall in front of him. I literally fell *onto* him.

My hands are pressed against his bare chest and my mouth is hovering above his. Our scattered breaths bounce between our lips, never quite deciding where to stop. My heart pounds against my chest, against his. His golden skin is glistening with sweat under the morning sun, and the entire front of my body is saturated with it. My eyes find his the second I realize what's happened. Now that I'm substantially closer to him than the first time I saw him from across the street, I study his eyes. They're two ice blue orbs, the color swirling and blending with the morning sunlight, heavy and guarded like a shield made of iron.

He hides those icy eyes of his as he lifts his hand to his head. He squeezes them shut as he exhales a hiss between his teeth.

"Are you okay?" I ask him, wincing.

"I don't know." His statement comes out more as a question, as if he's unsure how to answer me. His voice is husky yet smooth. The sound travels down his neck and to his ribcage, vibrating against the palms of my hands. This is the first time I've heard him speak. He lifts his hand and presses his palm to the side of his head. A hiss escapes between his perfectly straight teeth, the corners of his mouth creasing as he winces in pain.

My cheeks blush with heat and embarrassment, unsure of what to do. I don't realize until this moment that neither of us has bothered to move.

I'm still on top of him. He's still under me. My leg is still wedged between his thighs, my knee pressed into the street. His body relaxes under me for a moment as he sighs. After a few seconds, he opens his eyes again, staring directly at me. I press my lips together and swallow when his body stiffens, his blue eyes turning cold. They narrow, darkening as he studies me.

I quickly look down at my hands, knowing I've been lying on top of him far too long. "I'm so sorry." I back up, lifting myself off the man below me. Embarrassment fills me once again, and heat blooms in my cheeks. "I guess we should stop meeting this way."

"What?" He grunts as he stands. He bends down, picking up his phone from the spot where we fell on the street. There's a set of headphones plugged into it, and he yanks the cord out and places both back into his pocket. He plants his hands on his hips, his chest rapidly rising and falling as if he's still attempting to catch his breath.

I try to laugh off our situation. There's never been a more embarrassing time in my life. "You know, because of the other day when I was moving in, and I tripped? I saw you working on your motorcycle in the driveway." I point to his house. His motorcycle isn't in the driveway like it has been nearly every day since I've been here. He must have moved it into his garage.

He glances in the direction of his house then his eyes move past me to my house behind me. We're both standing at the end of my driveway where it meets the street.

"Right." He swipes his tongue across his bottom lip then takes a step back onto the street.

I can sense his eagerness to escape our fiasco, but I can't help myself. I could blame it on my first rule, starting a new life, but really, it's the desire to not feel completely alone in a strange house in a strange city in a strange state.

"Sloan." My name sputters out of my mouth, quickly stopping him before he completely turns around, leaving me alone at the end of my driveway.

"What?"

"My name...my name is Sloan."

"Oh." He nods once, pressing his smooth full lips together. "Good to know, Sloan."

He tries to leave again, but I stop him. "Wait. What's your name?"

He pauses, considering me for a moment. His blue eyes narrow slightly, and the corner of his lip twitches. "Watch where you're going next time."

He attempts to leave again, but I take a step forward, stopping him—again. I can't explain the pull I feel to this man, the neighbor I'm unable to put a name to who has a ridiculously gorgeous face. The more he pushes me, the more I want to push back, even though I know he stares at me as if my very presence annoys him. Nerves shoot through me, my heart rate picking up.

"Excuse me?"

"Yeah." He breathes out. "You should watch where you're going. You're lucky you ran into me and not a car. What were you doing out here this early anyway?"

I cross my arms over my chest, frustrated by his artificial concern for my well-being. Not that it's any of his business, but I couldn't sleep last night. I haven't been able to sleep all week. I can't stop the constant thoughts clouding my brain. There are a multitude of changes I want to make to the house for it to feel officially mine, but I don't know where to begin. The list is long and endless.

The bushes in the front yard look like they haven't been trimmed in years, and the flowers are completely dead. Each window in the house is draped in thick mustard-colored fabric. The velvet couch in the living room is the color of eggplant, and all my mother's pots and pans are painted vomit green. It's as if her house is straight out of the seventies. It doesn't make sense considering these houses weren't built until the nineties, a fact I learned from my mother's lawyer.

Although the decorations in the house are odd, that isn't what had me tossing and turning all night. It was the thought that although this house was a gift from my mother, it also feels completely foreign, not a trace of me in sight other than stacks of brown cardboard boxes scattered throughout each room.

It feels as if I have transported myself to a completely different world. My mother truly was a stranger to me. She was a stranger even to my own father. I don't know what she did for a living. I don't know where she was born or what her favorite food was. Pieces of my mother are scattered through the house, and each piece has a story, a story I've never read before. There are so many things I don't know about my mother, and I lay there in her bed coming to terms with the fact that I might never know.

Even now, standing on the sidewalk with my neighbor, I feel even more out of place and unwelcome.

I still have my arms crossed over my chest, deciding the best way to answer him. Humidity lingers in the air as the sun rises, drying out the morning dew. My arms are sticky, and my skin is covered in a thin film of sweat. The loose ends of my messy bun cling to the base of my neck.

"Does it really matter why I was out here? This is my house, and you were the one who ran into me." I swallow the echo of my words as soon as they leave my mouth. I have yet to officially meet anyone I can even remotely consider a friend, and it doesn't seem as if I'm off to a good start, but I can't help it. I don't understand where this man's contempt for me comes from. None of his actions toward me make sense.

In all honesty, I am having a difficult time staring at my mother's belongings, wanting to get a jump start on making her house my own. I began with the small things, the pieces of her life that didn't matter. That included changing out the hideous mustard-colored curtains. The store doesn't open for another four hours, so I decided to start the transition by tossing the curtains in the trash before the garbage truck comes for its weekly pickup. That was when I was knocked down by the mysterious neighbor who also happens to inexplicably dislike me.

I search his face, digging for any hint or clue as to why I annoy him. His ice blue eyes pierce me as he continues to watch me. Maybe I remind him of someone he once knew, someone who hurt him in the past. If that's the case, I can relate.

I open my mouth to break the awkward silence between us, but I stop when his eyes catch the pile of yellow fabric at the end of my driveway. He slowly walks over to it and picks the curtains up from the ground. He carries the thick cloth over to my garbage can and tosses them inside. I don't quite understand his reaction, but I can't bring myself to break my eyes away from him. There's something about the way his eyebrows turned downward at the sight of my mother's hideous curtains.

"Did you know my mother?" I ask him. I don't know why it

didn't occur to me until now to ask him if he knew her. Maybe I was slightly afraid of his answer, or maybe it was because he made it incredibly difficult to strike up casual conversation.

I'm thinking it's a combination of the two.

His expression has softened, but it doesn't last long before settling back into his usual scowl. "Your mother?"

I nod, hitching my thumb and pointing behind me. "Ellie Roberts. This used to be her house."

He pauses, moving his gaze over my shoulder. He frowns, three creases forming in the corners of his mouth, followed by a shake of his head. "Not really."

"Oh." I look down at my hands then take two steps backward. I fight the need inside me to press him for more information, unsure if he's being honest. I can't explain it, but his answer wasn't what I was expecting. Neither is my reaction. I guess I was hoping he knew her. Maybe then he could have told me more about her than what I already know: hideous décor and poor motherly instincts.

However, I couldn't help but notice his eyes shift the second I mentioned my mother's name. Maybe he did know her, but this man is a stranger, and there really isn't any reason I shouldn't believe him.

"Well..." I clear my throat. "Sorry about running into you."

"Yeah." He closes his mouth, pressing his lips into a thin line. He rests his hands on his hips, and his long, slender fingers press into his perfectly sculpted flesh.

Seriously. It's as if his hips were molded from smooth clay. The surface of his tan skin is polished and unflawed. Beads of sweat drip down his skin, effortlessly gliding onto each of his fingers. His abs are prominent, raised on top of his torso. This must be how he's managed to look the way he does—by running at an ungodly time of day.

I close my mouth and swallow down the rabbit hole I seem

to have gotten myself into. It's not that staring at my neighbor's abs has me considering dating again. Not starting a relationship with any man is not only one of the most important rules I put in place for myself; I'm also not ready to take that leap.

He catches me staring, dipping his head just enough to draw my gaze up to his. "It's like I said—next time, watch where you're going."

I unravel my arms, taken aback by his attitude. I don't understand him. The other day he stared at me without speaking a single word. Today he runs into me then plays it off as if it's my fault. Every move he makes toward me is confusing.

I open my mouth to call him out again, but this time he doesn't give me the opportunity. He turns around and quickly jogs across the street to his house.

When he disappears behind his front door, I silently walk back inside my house. The cool air inside hits me like a brick wall, almost immediately drying my sticky skin. I slowly walk over to my mother's eggplant-colored couch. I must hand it to her—it may be ugly, but it's surprisingly comfortable.

I tip my head back and stare at the ceiling. It's vaulted with large wooden beams stretching from one end to the other, a black fan mounted in the middle. I watch the blades slowly spin in circles. My mind wanders to my neighbor and our literal run-in with each other a few minutes ago. I still don't know his name, but I can't get the image of him out of my head. The way the corner of his top lip curled at the sight of me. The way his firm abs contracted with every deep and weighted breath. I bite back the tingling sensation between my thighs. I don't need or want to think of my neighbor that way.

Blowing out a heavy breath, I swipe my phone and car keys from the coffee table. I need to get out of this house. I need to think of curtains and appliances and furniture, anything that doesn't involve my mother or the neighbor who can't stand me.

CHAPTER FOUR

Sloan

THEY SAY EVERYTHING IS BIGGER IN TEXAS. WHEN I HEARD that phrase in the past, I always thought it meant the size of the state or the size of their steaks. Apparently, it includes their prices as well.

"Are you kidding me?" I stare at the cashier behind the counter with my jaw dropped.

"No." He shakes his head and frowns. "I'm sorry. We have to charge a separate delivery fee for the mattress because that one comes from a different supplier."

I groan, sliding my debit card out of my wallet. "Fine. Do you mind taking off the delivery fee for the desk and lamps? I can take those in my car."

"Sure, but they won't be available for pick up until the end of next week."

I resist the urge to roll my eyes at the kid. I keep calling him a kid in my head, but he's most likely the same age as me, maybe a year or two younger. Either way, I'm thankful for the savings I've managed to build up the last twenty-four years. It's now offered me the opportunity to afford new furniture.

Once I've paid my monstrous furniture bill, I step out onto

the sidewalk of downtown Austin. The sun beats across my skin as I slide my sunglasses down from the top of my head, shielding my eyes from the bright rays. I am enjoying this weather. I can feel it deep in my soul. I feel lighter when I stand underneath it. If the sun ever wanted to swallow me whole, I'd let it, as long as it made me a promise to never allow me to go back to the cold air of Minnesota.

There is a small part of me that allows myself to feel a sense of accomplishment about my day, but I'd be lying if I didn't acknowledge the fact that I am still thinking about my run-in with my neighbor this morning. There are so many pieces of our conversation I've rewound in my head, playing back the way it felt when I touched him. The way his blue eyes sparked as I stood there with my arms crossed, my breasts swelling against the pressure. Then the way his face shifted when I spoke of my mother. I've only been living in Texas for one week, but the only person I've come to know in this short time frame is him. It's been hard for me to understand how the only person I've talked to here can't stand me. It's still driving me crazy that he couldn't even be bothered to tell me his name.

The frustration growing inside me propels me forward. I'm still wearing the same leggings and crop top I was wearing this morning, but I don't care. If I am going to get through another eight hours of sifting through my mother's belongings, I need something to eat. It also wouldn't hurt if there were a large margarita sitting next to my plate.

I drive around the city, looking at the sights before deciding to turn onto a street downtown. I'm not a fan of the traffic, but it doesn't bother me. There is no one I have to answer to and no one to check in with. I don't want to go home and deal with my neighbor or the enormous list of chores I have.

The midday heat beats against my skin the second I step out of my car. Trees line the streets between each of the buildings.

A large group of people pour out of one of the buildings, their voices drawing my attention in their direction. Down at the corner of the street, there's a large green neon sign hanging above the door of the bar: Dallas' Barbecue and Brew. I find it funny and a bit odd that there's a restaurant with the name Dallas in it located in the heart of Austin.

A small group of people exit the bar when I finally make it up to the door, their laughter and shouting carrying out to the sidewalk. I'm surprised they're so energetic when it's just past noon. I guess that's part of living in a college town, especially one as big as this one. I study the outside of the building. It has a vintage feel to it, the black-painted brick on the outside contrasting with the neon sign hanging above. Music booms from inside, and when I make it to the door, the smell of barbecue immediately hits me. My stomach grumbles, and I know I've come to the perfect place to sit down and finally get a feel for this city.

I walk inside, and the dining area isn't nearly as busy as I expected it to be. Nonetheless, there are quite a few people packed into the small space. A long bar stretches across the right side of the restaurant while nearly a third of the space to the left is scattered with tables. I step farther inside and decide to take a seat at the bar.

I place my wallet on top of the bar and look around while I wait for the bartender. Near the back of the room is a stage, a single microphone placed in the middle, a guitar case resting against the beige wall.

"I apologize for the long wait."

I snap my head in the direction of the voice to find a woman smiling back at me from behind the bar. Her long brown curly hair is pulled back into a ponytail and her lips are painted a bright pink. She's wearing a black shirt with the Dallas' Barbecue and Brew logo on the front, a red flannel shirt tied around her waist. She tosses a coaster with the same logo in front of me.

"It's okay. I just sat down."

"Oh, good. This is always the busiest time of day," she adds with a thick southern accent. "I keep tellin' Colton he needs to hire more people." She shakes her head, clicking her tongue against her perfectly straight white teeth.

I notice she's already started to make me a drink, and I widen my eyes at how big the glass is. Correction—it's not a glass, it's a goblet.

She continues talking to me as she pours liquid from one bottle before reaching for another. My drink goes from clear to yellow to a pale green in a matter of seconds. I'm mesmerized by her movements. It's like watching a duck swimming in water. Half the time she isn't even looking at the bottles she's using.

"Anyway," she says, sliding the glass toward me. She tosses in a lime wedge followed by a bright purple straw. "I hope you like margaritas."

"Um..." I clear my throat and stare at the enormous goblet in front of me. "This is perfect."

"Cool." She doesn't move from her place behind the bar, reaching down into the sink in front of her. She washes a few glasses, placing them on a rack to dry.

I take a sip of the drink, placing the purple straw between my lips.

Wow. This margarita is fucking amazing.

The woman nods toward my drink, the corner of her mouth turning up in a smile. "It's good, right?"

"This is the best margarita I've ever had." It's the truth. I don't think I've ever had a margarita taste as smooth as this one.

"You aren't from here, are you?" she asks me, genuine curiosity written all over her face.

I shake my head and take another sip. "No. I'm originally

from Minnesota." I wipe the corner of my mouth and slide the menu out of the plastic holder sitting in front of me on the counter. I start reading through each item. All of it sounds delicious, and I don't know what to order.

The bartender's hand grips the top edge of the menu. She pulls it down, diverting my gaze to hers. "If you like the drink, you'll love our food. Here." She pulls the menu out of my hands and places it back in the holder. "I know just what to order you."

Her hazel-colored eyes sparkle in the light of the neon bar signs hanging on all four walls. There's a chalkboard behind her, drink and food items scribbled from one corner to the other.

"Thank you." I give her a large grin. It feels good to have finally met someone who doesn't look at me with annoyance. It feels good to be sitting with someone who actually wants to talk to me.

She walks over to her register and taps on the screen a few times before she refills a drink for a man sitting at the opposite end of the bar. Afterward, she walks back over to me and reaches her hand out. "I'm Vada."

"Sloan." I return her gesture and shake her hand over the counter.

"Nice to meet you." Vada then leans over and crosses her arms on the glossy wooden bar top. "Minnesota, huh? I've never been there." It's slowed down a bit since I sat down, and I guess she feels comfortable enough to stop long enough to make small talk with me. I'm thankful for her company.

I grin, glad to have walked in here. "Well, there are a lot of trees and a lot of lakes."

She smiles back. "So you're saying it's quite a bit different than Texas."

"Yep." I laugh.

"How are you liking it so far? Living here?"

I wince, leaning down to take another sip of my delicious

margarita. It's almost empty. Vada notices and straightens her back, ready to make another. She grabs a fresh goblet.

"Ouch. I'll take your silence as your answer that it hasn't gone too well so far."

"It's a long story, but basically my mother died a few months back and left me her house." I scrape my fingernail across the wood and avoid looking up at Vada. I don't want or need to go into the brutal details of how, up until her death, my mother acted as if I never existed. It's strange for me to be sharing such personal pieces of my life with a stranger, but something about her makes me feel comfortable enough to do so.

"I'm sorry to hear that." She sticks out her bottom lip, frowning.

"It's okay." I wave her off. "Living in her house has actually been great considering that I didn't mind leaving my life back in Minnesota. But apparently, my neighbor doesn't seem to feel the same way I do about me moving in."

"What do you mean?"

This time I look up at Vada. She's already placed my second drink in front of me and taken my empty. Damn, she is good.

I sigh, swirling my straw around inside my glass. "I don't know. I've run into him two times since I moved here, and I don't know how to explain it, but it feels as if he hates me. I mean, shit." I scoff, thinking back on this morning. "He wouldn't even tell me his name."

"I must say this guy sounds like he's making us Texans look bad. We're known for being super friendly."

"Well, apparently he's the exception." I roll my eyes.

"Maybe he's into you," Vada suggests with a casual shrug of her shoulder. She walks over to a small window opening to the kitchen and grabs a basket full of food sitting inside the pass-through. She places it in front of me.

There's a large sandwich that looks like it's stuffed with

pulled pork and a mound of fries underneath. It smells amazing. I pick up a fry and bite into the end of it.

"Yeah, right." I snort, baffled by her assumption as to the reason for my neighbor's behavior.

"I mean, I wouldn't blame him. You're super-hot." She turns around to the register and cashes out another person at the bar sitting a few seats down from me. "Are you single?"

I straighten my back in my seat and clear my throat. "I am, but I'm not looking to date anyone right now."

"Who knows." Vada wags her eyebrows at me a few times. "Maybe you'll change your mind." She sounds as optimistic as Liam was the last time I saw him.

"Nah." I shake my head, picking up one half of my pulled pork sandwich. I hold it with both hands, ready to take a bite. "Not any time soon, at least. I have rules, and you know what they say about those."

"That they're meant to be broken?" she asks, laughing.

I'm about to explain my reasoning but stop when her eyes shift to the front door.

"Oh, shit," she says loudly, her expression morphing into one of annoyance.

I follow her gaze to see a man walking through the front door and behind the bar. His black-rimmed glasses are perched on his sharp nose, and a serious, worried expression spreads across his face as he charges toward Vada.

"What the hell, Vada?" the man says. "I was in the middle of a statistics class when you were blowing up my phone."

"Look," she says, holding her hands out. "We were slammed, and I had absolutely no one here to help me. Brandon is back there handling the food, and I'm responsible for everything out here."

"Doesn't look so bad now," he says, quickly looking over the restaurant.

"Duh, Colton. That's because the lunch rush is over because...well, it's *past* lunch." Vada crosses her arms over her chest, and I can't help noticing Colton's eyes catch her movement.

The whole situation reminds me of what happened this morning with my neighbor.

"I get that you're taking extra classes for your master's degree," Vada says, her cheeks reddening, "but you also have a business to run."

Colton pinches the bridge of his nose, nudging his glasses higher than they were before. "We shouldn't be talking about this out here." He sighs then adjusts the black frames. His eyes catch me staring at him and Vada. "I'm sorry," he says to me. He grabs her by the elbow to move their conversation to the back, away from spectators.

"It's fine." She shrugs, nodding her head in my direction. "This is Sloan."

"Hi," Colton says, offering me a quick smile before shifting back to his argument with Vada.

"Sloan just moved here from Minnesota. She's my new friend." She grins, sticking her chin up in pride. I return her smile, relieved to have met someone kind for a change. It's been a while since I've felt like I've had a true friend. Brenna and I had been friends since we were thirteen, but somehow that didn't matter to her when it came to fucking my fiancé. The way Brenna betrayed me left me cautious of any new friends, but a part of me wants to put the past behind me, one step at a time. Vada isn't Brenna, and she seems nice enough.

"Sloan, this is Colton. He's one of the owners."

"It's nice to meet you." Colton holds out his hand, and I give it a shake before pulling back.

Vada's smile fades when she turns back to face Colton. "I keep saying you need to hire someone. It's only going to get busier each day, and I can't keep working like this. It's too stressful."

I don't understand the depth of their relationship, but from what I've gathered in the two minutes they've been going at it back and forth, their connection cuts deeper than a typical boss-employee relationship.

"Don't worry, Vada. I know we need more employees. Besides, I talked to Dallas this morning and he agreed we need more help, so I'm on it." Colton reaches for one of the clean glasses behind the bar and fills it to the top with soda. He takes a long gulp before placing it down on the bar top. "I'm also thinking about hiring a performer to sing and play guitar every weekend and maybe a few nights during the week."

She pauses, taking one step closer to Colton. I can tell the weight of their conversation has shifted. Apparently, this is the first time Colton has brought this topic up.

"Does Dallas know about this idea of yours?"

Colton winces, sliding his glasses up with the tip of his finger. "Not exactly."

"Colton." She tilts her head to the side and crosses her arms over her chest. "I don't know if he's going to like that idea."

"What am I supposed to do? You know how it's been lately, and we need a new bartender and performer. I can't keep waiting for Dallas to make up his mind."

"You know," I interject, glancing between the two of them, "if you're looking for someone to start right away, I might be able to help."

"Really?" Colton asks, his dark eyebrows arching above his glasses.

"Yeah—I mean as a bartender, not the performer." I pause, feeling both of their stares searing me with their deep expressions of hope, as if I'm saving them from misery. It's not that I can't sing—in fact I can, but I have never performed in front of a crowd before, and I don't intend on starting now. I clear my throat and straighten my back, sitting up in my chair. "Anyway, I'm a teacher, but since I'm not working right now, I happen to be looking for a summer job. This would be perfect. It's been a while since I've worked in a restaurant, but I know the basics."

It's true. The past two years were full of student teaching and wedding planning. I didn't have much time when it came to working a side job. The last time I worked in a restaurant was at one of the lakeside resorts my father managed back in Minnesota. For the first two years of college, it paid for my food and gas.

"You're a teacher?" Vada asks. "That's fucking awesome."

I laugh, my cheeks warming with her compliment. I can't wait for the school year to begin and for me to be inside a classroom full of students. Until then, I need something else to keep me distracted. A summer job working as a bartender in one of the most popular bars in downtown sounds perfect.

"Well?" Vada plants her hands on her hips and stares at Colton, waiting for him to make a decision on if he should hire me.

"Shit." He rubs his forehead with his fingertips. I can tell he's stressed about this whole situation. "Dallas usually does the interviews for new employees, but..."

"So, you're worried about what Dallas will think about you hiring someone to play a few nights a week but not about hiring a new bartender without interviewing them?"

Colton narrows his eyes. "Whatever, Vada." There's a hint of a smile hidden behind his hardened expression.

"Trust me." She waves him off. "Dallas will only care that you found someone so quickly."

Colton rolls his eyes. "You're only saying that because you're relieved to finally have someone to split the workload with."

"You're damn right I am." She laughs as she pops the cap off a beer bottle for another person sitting at the bar. She slides it across the top then turns to me.

"Who's Dallas?" I ask.

"He's the other owner," Colton says. "I mostly deal with the back of the house, and he manages the front. That's why I say he usually does the interviews."

"Oh." I nod.

"Does that mean you're hiring Sloan?" Vada asks Colton.

I trade glances between the two. So far, today has been a mix of emotions. Between the run-in with my neighbor, spending a fortune on furniture, and now suddenly the perfect summer job seeming to land in my lap, I'm not sure if I should consider myself lucky or not.

An hour ago, I was reconsidering my move to Texas. I was far from home and far from the life I once knew. Living in Texas is vastly different than Minnesota, but ever since I walked inside this restaurant, I finally feel like I belong somewhere, as strange as it sounds.

Colton reaches across the bar and holds out his hand. The corner of his mouth is slanted, and I can already see the slightest bit of relief flicker in his eyes. "You're hired. Can you start right now?"

CHAPTER FIVE

DALLAS

I haven't seen Sloan since she was lying on top of me yesterday morning. I also haven't been able to stop thinking about the whole situation between us in general.

It's fucking ridiculous.

I don't know anything about her other than that she's Ellie's daughter from Minnesota. It's not that I'm interested in getting involved with Sloan—far from it—but I also can't deny how sexy she is in her crop top or how my dick perked up when she landed on top of me, even when my head hit the pavement.

But my quick erection faded the moment we stood up and she started asking questions. She was pushing me for details about her mother. It was there, written on her smooth, gorgeous pale face. Her dark blue eyes sparked at the thought that I might tell her any detail about Ellie, anything at all.

But I couldn't.

I couldn't tell her about her mother, a mother she clearly had no interest in until her death. Why does she suddenly care now?

I know it's shitty to lie to someone you barely know, but it didn't occur to me to bother telling her the truth.

Sloan is a mystery, and I've spent the past hour of my morning run trying to understand where she fit into Ellie's world and why in the past two years that I knew her, she never mentioned having a daughter. Did she and Ellie have a falling out before her death? That would explain why I never saw the house up for sale. Maybe she inherited it.

The clouds fill the sky today, and I'm thankful for the momentary reprieve they offer. Thunder rumbles in the distance, the darker clouds moving closer. The puffy edges touch the outskirts of my neighborhood, and I'm glad I was able to get my run in before it starts to rain.

My feet hit the asphalt of my street, bringing Sloan's house into view. Sweat drips down my bare back and chest, soaking into the waistband of my shorts. I slow down, watching as she paces in front of her bushes. Her long hair is tied back into a high messy bun. She's wearing a similar crop top to the one she wore yesterday, only this one is a bright blue. I stop when she bends down, her spandex shorts riding up on her thighs, accentuating her curves.

Fuck.

I start to wonder whether she lives here alone, or maybe she's in a relationship. I've considered the possibility that she might be. There was a man with her the day she moved in, helping her carry boxes inside her new house, but I haven't seen him since.

I shouldn't care. I don't want to. Whether or not Sloan is in a relationship doesn't change how I feel about being in one.

I step backward onto the sidewalk in front of my house and remove one of my earbuds. My playlist still plays through the one I've left in, the music fading and blending with the sounds of the impending storm.

Sloan hasn't seen me. She's too involved with her bushes. I

tilt my head to the side when I watch her walk into her garage and come back out with a large pair of shears in her hands.

I rest my hands on my hips, curious to see what she plans on doing with them. The blade is nearly as long as her thigh, and each bush is taller than the windows spanning across her house.

Ellie neglected her yard in the last few weeks before she died, and I didn't have the time to take care of it since I was working on opening the restaurant.

She groans and drops the shears onto the grass then walks back into her garage. She comes back out a few seconds later, carrying a small ladder. It isn't nearly the size she needs to be able to reach the top of the first bush. She uses it anyway.

She still hasn't noticed me watching her, and I'm sure if she were to catch me staring, she'd think I was a creep. But this is too good to miss, and I'm not about to stop her from wanting to work on her own house.

She begins to step up the small ladder, staring at the top. "Stupid fucking bush."

I stifle a laugh, covering my mouth with my closed fist. It's ridiculous, really. I don't have time to stand here, watching Sloan attempt to trim her unruly bushes. I need to get back to working on my motorcycle since it's been out of commission for the past two weeks. I also need to clean up and head over to the restaurant.

There is humor and amusement in watching her, and I can't break my eyes away from her. She obviously doesn't know what she's doing.

She stands on the top step, lifting her heels to reach higher. The shears wobble in her hands as she reaches for a branch. Her calves flex as she lifts one foot off the step, balancing herself with the tip of one foot.

This isn't going to end well. I already know it.

As if the universe read my thoughts, my phone pings inside my pocket.

Sloan snaps her head to the side at the sound, catching me watching her from across the street. "What—" It's the only word she manages to get out before the ladder starts to topple over, her feet flying out from under her. The shears fly in the air above her as she falls backward. She quickly shields her face with her arms and falls against the mulch in her garden bed.

Before I even realize what's happened, I'm already running across Sloan's lawn.

When I reach her, she's lying flat on her back with her eyes squeezed shut. The shears landed a few feet away from her, thankfully.

"Are you okay?"

Her eyes crack open, staring up at me. She groans then closes them again. "Oh, great." She rolls to her side, slowly moving to stand. "It's you."

"What the hell were you thinking?" I point to the ladder now resting on its side in the grass.

"What do you think I was doing?"

"Looked like you were trying to kill yourself to me."

"I was *trying* to trim the bushes." She brushes the dirt from her legs and huffs, stomping over to where the shears landed, not once bringing her eyes in my direction.

"Maybe you should be a little more careful when you're standing on your tiptoes while holding twenty-four-inch scissors."

Her full bottom lip pops out from her teeth, her chin dropping slightly. "You are unbelievable."

I challenge her, staring back at her with as much annoyance as she's dishing out to me. I don't know where this feeling is coming from. I somehow get a rise out of pushing Sloan to the edge.

"You're the one who can't seem to keep both of your feet planted on the ground."

"Look," she says, brushing hair away from her face, "I'm alive and still in one piece. You can go back to doing whatever it is you were doing before you ran over here."

Her fingertips ghost across her smooth full lips, brushing away a few specks of dirt. Her eyebrows knit together as she stares up at me, her dark eyes clouding over under the dark grey sky.

"Fine." I hold my hands up. I don't need to put up with her brush-off. I'm the one who rushed over to make sure she wasn't severed in half by a gardening tool. I start walking back to my house then hear the sound of metal clanking. I stop and turn around. She's climbing the ladder again.

"What are you doing?"

"I told you," she says, continuing to reach for the branch. She's only made it to the first step on the ladder. "I'm trimming the bushes. I have work later, and they've been bugging the shit out of me."

"Sloan, stop." I reach for her hand, stopping her from taking another step. I don't know what's come over me. A part of me doesn't want her risking another fall, and another part of me wants to ask her where she works, but I stop myself. I don't care enough to question her about it.

Her blue eyes widen and fall to where my hand is holding on to hers. I follow her gaze, just as surprised as she is.

I quickly pull my hand back and reach for the shears.

She yanks them back, her eyes narrowing to two thin slits. Her long black eyelashes nearly brush against her skin. "What are you doing?"

"I'll trim it for you."

"What?" A laugh erupts from her mouth. She nearly snorts as if she can't believe I'm offering to help.

"Come on." I roll my eyes and tip my head back, urging her to step down from the ladder. "I'm taller and can reach the branches in the back."

"Oh." She giggles. "You're serious." Her well-manicured eyebrows arch above her dark blue eyes. Her mouth still has that subtle curve to the corner of it, thinning her full lips just enough to make me want to know what it might feel like if my teeth were to ever graze them.

"I am serious." I fight the twitch beneath my running shorts, my dick perking up at this new idea of mine.

She thinks about it for a moment, considering if she should take me up on my offer. I can tell she's surprised by it. She props her hand on her hip and tilts her head slightly to the side. Her mouth follows suit, the corner twisting in a way I haven't seen. Her eyes spark at the idea, but then her expression changes. The corner of her mouth relaxes, falling back into its natural place, and she straightens her gaze on me.

"I think I can handle it." She tentatively steps back. I don't miss how her eyes roam over my body. She not-so-subtly tucks her bottom lip between her teeth, taking in my outfit. Her eyes stop on my bare chest. "I wouldn't want to keep you from your morning run." There's a bit of sarcasm laced into her voice. She pauses, letting her words linger between us before she shifts her eyes back to mine.

"Sure." I don't bother telling her I've already finished my run and that's when I found her attempting to trim her bushes.

Instead, I simply nod then leave her to deal with her yard on her own. I'm not going to argue with her, no matter how much I might be enjoying it.

IT'S ONLY BEEN two days since I've been down to the bar, but Colton texted me yesterday telling me he already hired a bartender to help for the summer. Usually, I would be upset about him hiring someone without me knowing, but given our current circumstances, I don't give a shit. We need the help, and I'm not in a position to care about the details. It's a relief, and I feel a bit less stressed than I have for the past week.

When I walk into the restaurant, I find my sister, Vada, behind the bar sitting on a barstool. She's leaning over the counter, laughing as she scrolls through a few TikTok videos.

"Hey." I walk past her, flipping a chunk of her curly hair. "Nice to see you working."

Her smile fades when she closes her phone and turns to me. "We don't open for another hour, and I could say the same about you." She tilts her head to the side, studying me. "It feels like you haven't been here in a while."

"What are you talking about?" I pull a bowl of limes from the small refrigerator and begin slicing them. "I was here the other night."

"I guess." She stands beside me and leans her elbow on the counter. I continue cutting without looking at her. "But you weren't here for very long. Didn't you promise Colton you were going to play?"

"Leave it alone, Vada," I warn, tossing a few slices of lime into a separate bowl. What is it with her and Colton wanting me to perform again?

"Okay." She nods. She doesn't push me, and I'm thankful for it. I decide to change the subject.

"Colton told me he hired a new bartender."

"He did." She immediately perks up, her grin widening. Vada and I were never very close growing up. Although she's only three years younger than me, we never went out of our way to spend time with one another. We had separate groups of friends, and when I was in college at UT, she was still stuck back in Texarkana with our mom.

A few years back, I was surprised when she told me she wanted to follow the same path I took by going to the University of Texas, only she decided to major in English literature.

My sister was well on her way to becoming editor in chief at *The Austin Daily News* when I called her to tell her about what happened to Hailey. She didn't hesitate to put her promotion on hold to help me here at the bar. Sometimes I feel guilty that she hasn't gone back to the newspaper full time, but then another part of me has enjoyed her company the past year. In a way, it's brought us closer. I know she wants to go back at some point, but she hasn't mentioned when. Until then, I plan on enjoying having her here while it lasts.

"I was the one who introduced her to Colton." She decides to start helping me and grabs a lime from the bowl. "It was perfect, actually. She came in here for lunch yesterday and was sitting here at the bar when Colton stormed in complaining about how I was texting him too much when he was in class." Her voice tenses at the mention of Colton.

There is a history between Colton and Vada, one I don't understand. I'm sure neither of them talks to me about it for many reasons, one being that they're my best friend and sister.

"Anyway," she continues, "I was talking to him about how we needed an extra bartender when she just offered. She said she just moved here and only needs a job for the summer since she's a teacher."

"Huh." I nod, amazed how coincidental it is that our new bartender came in here when she did. I think back to Sloan and how, like our new employee, she just moved here as well. I just hoped this new bartender isn't as accident prone as she seems to be.

"You know, she told me she's single." Vada nudges me with her elbow before she walks over to the sink to wash her hands.

"No." I shake my head. What is it with her and Colton wanting me to start dating again?

"Oh, stop." She dries her hands then grabs a washcloth. She starts wiping down each of the chairs lining the bar. "It wouldn't hurt to give her a chance. Not only does she have a stable career, she's fucking gorgeous. Plus, she's only working here for the summer."

"Vada, I said no." I feel like a parent scolding their child for asking to buy them a toy for the hundredth time, only we're siblings who are twenty-six and twenty-three. "You know I have no interest in dating, and I don't want to."

"I don't see what the difference is. You've been out with Kylie a few times. You left with her the other night."

I roll my eyes, annoyed by this conversation. "I never went out with Kylie, and it never went that far."

"Yeah, but—"

"No. No 'but'." I sigh, finishing off the limes and placing them in the caddy of drink garnishes. "I really fucking wish you and Colton would drop this. I don't need to date. I'm fine. You don't see me prying into your love life, do you?"

She pauses, stopping her hand mid-wipe. Her green eyes cloud over with sadness. I already know what's caused them to shift. It's the same reason Colton's voice changes when he talks to me about dating. "No." She clears her throat. "You don't."

"Okay then. Stop trying to change what can't be undone."

I stop and stare at my sister, hoping she understands where I'm coming from. She presses her lips together then continues with her wiping down of the counter. I reach my hand across the bar and stop her, forcing her to look up at me.

"I get that you want to help me move on," I tell her. Her

eyes line with tears threatening to spill over. "But I'll figure it out on my own. Okay?"

"Yeah." She nods.

"Good." I pull my hand away from her and turn around to open the register.

"Colton said he's looking to hire a performer to start playing every weekend."

"What?" I stop counting the cash and turn to see Vada standing on the opposite side of the counter.

Two dark royal blue eyes stare back at me, freezing me in place. It's been storming all afternoon, the rain starting not long after I left Sloan alone to trim her bushes. Water drips down her face, soaked into her hair and t-shirt.

"Sloan," Vada says, crossing the dining area to meet her near the entrance. She stops and trades glances between the two of us when she catches us staring at one another.

"What are you doing here?" I ask her.

"What? You work here too?" Sloan whispers, the same confused expression as mine written across her face. She isn't wearing her usual crop top or skintight leggings. No. She's wearing cutoff, frayed, denim shorts and a t-shirt. Printed on the left side of her chest, directly above the perfect swell of her breast, is my name and the logo of my restaurant.

It takes my mind several seconds to catch up with what I'm seeing. "You—" I point to her. "You're our new bartender?"

"Wait," Vada interrupts, wagging her finger between us. "You've met Sloan before?"

"She's my neighbor. She just moved into the house across from mine." I keep my eyes glued to Sloan, even though I'm answering Vada. I don't understand why she's here, in my bar.

Sloan's eyebrows immediately dip and her cheeks flush. It's the same expression she had this morning when she found me standing above her and the toppled-over ladder: annoyance.

"Well..." My sister sighs, walking back over to the counter to finish her cleaning. She leaves us standing in the same places we haven't moved from. "Small world, huh Dallas?"

"Dallas?" Sloan asks, cocking her head to the side. "You're Dallas?"

"That *is* my name," I tell her. "I own this bar."

Her eyes move past me, over my shoulder, to the brick wall behind me. In thick white letters, my name and logo are painted across the black background.

She moves her eyes back to mine. Her pink painted lips curl to the side in a smirk, and her dark blue eyes shimmer under the golden lights above.

"Nice to meet you, Dallas. Looks like you're my new boss."

RULE #2

Don't, under ANY circumstances, get involved with another man—no matter how tempted you may be.

CHAPTER SIX

Sloan

THE HITS JUST KEEP ON COMING. IF I WANTED TO, I COULD make a list of all the embarrassing moments I've had with my new neighbor since the first day I saw him, the same new neighbor who also happens to be my boss—my incredibly gorgeous, rude boss named Dallas.

I haven't spoken to him since my shift started three hours ago. I'd say it's because I don't want to talk to him or vice versa, but I haven't had much of a chance. Once I spoke to Dallas when we saw each other, he disappeared into the back of the restaurant while Vada and I finished setting up to open for the dinner shift, and ever since, the place has been packed.

That's not to say I don't want to talk to Dallas. I'm just not sure I want to talk to him right now. I still don't understand if he likes me or not. Most of our interactions are seeded in snide comments and brush-offs. The only exception was when he offered to trim my bushes for me. Although it was a sliver of kindness extended on his part, there was a part of me that didn't want to give in to him. I didn't want to give him the satisfaction. Instead, I finished trimming the bushes on my own. Luckily, I was able to stay on the ladder this time.

I'm three hours into my shift and I know I've already made more money than I have in a long time. As soon as one of the customers sitting at the bar leaves, I clean the counter as the next person fills it. Vada's been serving most of the tables all night, moving just as smoothly out on the floor as she did at the bar when I met her yesterday.

She spent the entire night training me last night, and after the first few groups of guests, I learned the drink and food menu well enough for us to split up. Although I was glad to be making money, I was also nervous to be working the bar on a busy Friday night.

Music booms and bounces off the brick walls, drowning out the loud chatter. A man takes a seat at the barstool in front of the spot I just cleaned. I toss the rag aside and greet him with the best smile I'm able to muster. I toss him a coaster as his eyes scan the chalkboard menu behind me.

"Welcome to Dallas'. What can I get for you?"

The man shifts in his seat as he tucks his mid-length hair behind his ear and leans forward. He rests his forearms on the glazed wood, offering me a grin. "Hi, can I get a whiskey sour?"

"Sure." I look down and grab a small glass from the rack. It doesn't take me long to whip up my new customer's drink. When I finish it off, I place it in front of him.

"Thank you." He leans forward on his arm, attempting to yell over the music in the restaurant. "What's your name?"

He sits back in his stool and picks up his glass, bringing it to his lips as he stares at me over the rim.

"I'm Sloan," I yell back.

"Sloan." He repeats my name, a dimple appearing on his cheek with how wide his smile is. "I like it."

"Thanks?" I ask him with a smirk. It's not that this guy doesn't seem kind, but I can tell he's being a bit forward, clearly interested in more than typical casual conversation. I don't bother asking him for his name. I don't need it or want it.

He laughs then leans forward again. This time he crosses his arms over the counter. "I was sitting over there with a few of my friends when I saw you." He tilts his head in the direction of a table near the front of the restaurant. There's a group of six people surrounding a pitcher of beer and three different plates of ribs.

This guy is full-on, hands-down flirting with me. His eyes move along my body before finding my face again. He leans back again and shrugs. He's arrogant as fuck. I can tell in the way his back hits the back of the barstool, dripping with confidence. He picks up his drink without lifting his back from his chair and stretches out his arm. He lifts the glass to his mouth, finishing off the rest. "I figured I'd come over here and see if maybe you were interested."

"Interested in what exactly?" I ask him loud enough so he can hear me. I'm not interested, not in the slightest. Not only is it because of the rules I've clearly laid out for myself, it's also because I have absolutely no interest in the man sitting in front of me. He wears his arrogance like he wears his cologne— entirely too much all at once.

He leans forward, sliding his empty glass to my edge of the counter. "Anything really. Dinner and a movie out?" He shrugs, lowering his gaze. "Or in?"

"Sloan?" Vada calls my name as she quickly walks behind the bar. She passes by me from behind, walking over to the cooler to grab a handful of napkins and silverware. "Do you mind grabbing three light draft beers and taking them to table twenty-two?"

She doesn't stop before she leaves the bar, disappearing back into the crowd. I turn back to the man in front of me. "I'm sorry. I have to go." I nearly stumble on my words, silently thanking

Vada for her interruption of a situation I didn't know what to do with.

The man taps his fingers on the counter, inhaling a deep breath. He doesn't say another word as he stands. He's still wearing the same amount of arrogance as before, only this time he walks away a bit more deflated than when he sat down. He gives me a simple nod then heads back to rejoin his friends.

I shake my head and grab three beer glasses to start filling for Vada's table.

From the corner of my eye, I find Dallas at the end of the bar for the first time tonight. I knew he was here, working the crowd and making his rounds interacting with his customers, but this is the closest I've been to him all night. There's no one standing between us.

He's talking to one of the customers down at the end, gripping the edge of the bar top, flexing his arm. It dawns on me that this is the first time I'm seeing him with a shirt on. Every other time he was either running or working on his motorcycle. It's strange to see him like this. He's wearing a black t-shirt, the sleeves stretched across his biceps. His hair is pushed up, the ends dipping slightly with every move he makes. They hover above his ice blue eyes as he glances around the room before his eyes stop on me. He stares at me for a few seconds before turning his attention back to the man in front of him. The way his eyes narrowed when he saw me was enough to keep me moving—anything to distract me from the thoughts swirling in my brain. I need to focus on work. I need to focus on getting these drinks out.

I walk halfway down the length of the bar and stop in front of the beer taps, filling the first one. I glance to my right, looking over at Dallas. Then I start to fill the other glass. I take another glance at Dallas. This time he's moved farther down the bar to talk to another customer. He's narrowed the space between us, but he's still a considerable distance away.

He's listening to the couple seated in front of him, scratching at his chin with the tips of his fingers. They graze across the light stubble along his chin, and then, as if I'm seeing it for the first time, he smiles. A real, genuine smile. Not too big, but enough to crease the corners of his cheeks and make his eyes spark under the golden lights of the bar.

He finishes his conversation and spins around, grabbing a basket of wings from the kitchen window. He carries it down the bar to the end and places it in front of a customer before grabbing a bottle of beer from the cooler. He reaches into his back pocket for his bottle opener, popping the top off before setting it on top of the bar.

"Um, you might want to wipe the drool dripping from your chin there."

I snap my head to the left, catching Vada standing beside me.

"What are you talking about?" I turn my attention back to the beer glasses, and one is overflowing, foam spilling down the sides. "Shit."

She laughs, reaching for the glass and dumping the entire contents down the sink. She hands me a new one. "I thought you said my brother is an asshole."

"He is." It's true. I did tell Vada her brother is an asshole. After Dallas disappeared to the back of the restaurant after he found out I was his new employee, she asked if I could elaborate more on the details of our interactions since moving here. I called him an asshole because I feel like that's all he's been since I've met him.

"Well, you aren't looking at him like you think he's an asshole." She smirks, grabbing the now full beers from me. I internally sigh with relief, thankful to have not spilled it again.

She swiftly circles around me, and suddenly I'm feeling defensive. I can't explain it, but her words have sparked something inside me.

"I know what you're thinking, Vada."

She shrugs, raising one shoulder. She's still inching her way out from the bar, carrying the beers as if she has more than two hands. "By the way, I won't hold this against you." She adds a smirk, her brown curls bouncing as she takes a step backward, lifting her arms just enough for me to know she's talking about how long it took for me to make the beers.

"Thanks." I laugh. "Wait a minute—you implied I have a thing for him, which I don't," I yell back. "Besides, you know I have my—"

"Rules." She nods, finishing my sentence for me. "Right." She doesn't give me another chance to respond before she disappears into the crowd out in the dining room.

"What rules would those be?"

I straighten my back and swallow. I turn around to find Dallas standing within inches of me. He's so close I can smell his cologne, a mixture of pine and cedar. It reminds me of the times I would go camping on the lake back in Minnesota. The scent sends chills over my body. It's either that or how close Dallas is standing to me. My face is in line with his chest. I make sure to tip my chin up, staring directly at his face. He looks down, meeting my eyes with his. His expression is dark, his eyes clouding over as dark as the storm clouds that rolled in this afternoon. There's a grey tint to them, dulling his usual piercing glare.

He crosses his arms over his chest and grins. It isn't the same grin he was giving the guy at the end of the bar. This grin is more mischievous and more amused. "Huh." He scratches at the stubble lining his jaw. "I think I'd like to hear more about these rules."

I plant my hand on my hip and stare up at him, more confused than ever. This man is the poster model for confusion. "Now what makes you think I would tell you in the first place? Up until now, you haven't exactly been open to sharing."

"Maybe I'm not the man you think I am."

I can't help but snort. I'm thankful for the booming country music playing through the speakers above, but my snort is still loud enough for Dallas to notice.

"Somehow, I doubt that," I tell him.

He crosses his arms again, waiting for me to crack. His muscles retract and his jaw ticks as he stares at me. Why does it always feel as if Dallas and I are in some staring contest?

"It's nothing." I sigh, not sure where this conversation is going. "Don't worry about it." We both need to work, and if I am going to make any kind of money tonight, it sure as hell won't be done standing here talking to Dallas. There is no way in hell I am going to tell him the rules I set for myself when it comes to my dating life. I didn't even want to tell Vada, but after our initial meeting yesterday and the comment I made to her about my rules, she coaxed them out of me. I didn't go into too much detail, glossing over the fact that I caught my fiancé cheating on me with my best friend. Instead, I only told her he had cheated on me.

I step forward, trying to walk around Dallas' large frame to get back to work. I still need to take the drinks to my table. He towers over me, the warmth from his body radiating into the empty space between us.

He reaches out with his arm, stopping me. His hand lands on the top part of my stomach below my breasts, and I would be lying if I said it didn't send a tingling sensation straight to my core. I don't want it to. I've sworn off all men since Cole, promising myself not to get too close to another man, both physically and emotionally. But as Liam told me before, it doesn't mean I can't still be attracted to them.

My heart is pumping against my chest to the same beat as the music up above. Dallas is making me feel things I swore I wouldn't allow myself to feel for a long time. My heart rate speeds up and my thighs tense. I inhale a sharp breath.

I hate that Dallas effortlessly pulls this part of me out. I don't want to react to him. I don't want to be imagining the way it might feel if his fingers dragged down the rest of my stomach and slid between my thighs. Because men like Dallas always know exactly what they're doing. Regardless, the small flutter in my stomach where his fingers are resting is hard to ignore, no matter how strict I am to sticking to my rules.

"I have to tell you..." Dallas says, clenching his jaw. He lets his hand fall away, and I hold my breath, waiting for him to finish what he's about to say.

The bar is dark. Every inch of wall and ceiling is painted black, the golden lamps casting Dallas' face in shadows. Although it's dark and impossibly loud, I can still see the way his eyebrows dip and his lips press together. His mood has visibly shifted.

"If you take more than five minutes to deliver drinks again, I'm going to have to fire you."

The storm that was brewing in his eyes before is now replaced with the familiar ice blue tone I'm used to. I've heard if darkness clouds one's eyes, it usually means anger. With Dallas, it seems to be the opposite. The more irritated he is, the icier his eyes become. They're two piercing shards, cool and distant.

I swallow down the lump forming in my throat. I don't know if Dallas is being truthful in his words or not, but I need this job, and despite him being my boss, I still want to work here.

I tip my chin up and give him a small grin in understanding. "Of course."

I leave Dallas where he's standing and walk back over to the same two glasses I've been trying to make for the past five minutes. There's a small pool of water in the bottom of each glass, and I pick them up, tossing the ice into the sink again.

Dammit.

I fix the two glasses and take them to my table as quickly as possible. Once I drop their drinks off, I take their order, put it in the computer, and then greet the next table.

By the time the dinner rush has passed, exhaustion slams into me. My shoulders ache and there's pressure building behind my eyes. Dallas closes all the tables, leaving only half the bar open for the rest of the night. There are only a few people left sitting at the bar. A small group of people sit at one end, chatting while slowly sipping on their beers. On the other end, the same woman hasn't moved from her spot for the past three hours. I also can't help noticing that she hasn't stopped watching Dallas for those whole three hours.

She rests her chin in her hand and tilts her head to the side, stirring her drink with her straw.

Dallas is near the back of the dining room, turning the last few chairs upside down and placing them on top of the small square tables. I tilt my head and study him. I've never seen an owner so involved in the running of their business before. Back at the lake resorts in Minnesota, I would never catch my boss out front cleaning the tables or serving drinks. I would either find them out front talking to the guests or back in the office pretending to sift through paperwork.

Dallas loads the last chair onto the table and makes his way toward the front end of the bar where I'm standing, waiting for the glasses to finish.

The woman at the end of the bar immediately perks up,

sensing his movement, but he ignores her again, stopping on the other side of the bar from where I'm standing.

"What do you have left to do?" he asks me. There's a softness to his voice, a stark difference from the tone he used when he spoke to me earlier. It's confusing and my mind is too muddled to decipher which Dallas is the honest one. He brushes his fingers through his hair then leans forward, gripping the end of the counter.

I grab a handful of straws and organize them into the cup in front of him. He watches me. "I'm waiting for this last batch of glasses to finish, and then I was going to wipe down the counters."

"Okay." He nods, pushing off the bar. "You can leave when you finish up with those two things."

"Are you sure?" I ask him, shrugging. "I don't mind sticking around and helping out a bit more."

He glances around and stares out the front windows for a few minutes, considering my offer. He rubs his chin then turns back to face me. "That's up to you."

I stare into his eyes. Yellow flecks contrast with blue irises, and I try to read his expression. I still don't know if he even likes me—not necessarily in a romantic way, like more in a basic, decent, courteous kind of way.

"Okay." I croak out the word, the letters scratching at the back of my throat. I hadn't realized how much I had been yelling all night with how incredibly loud it was when we were slammed earlier.

Dallas taps his fingers on the back of the barstool in front of him then backs away, disappearing into the kitchen. I follow him with my eyes, watching as he pushes through the double doors.

The dishwasher beeps, signaling it's done. I start loading them into the cooler while Vada greets a guest down at the end of the bar that's still open and serving guests. Once I'm done with the glasses, I grab a clean rag and begin wiping down the counter. The empty stage in the back catches my attention. It hasn't been touched all night.

"It hasn't been used in about a year."

"Really?"

Vada stands beside me, her hands resting on her hips. Her eyes are glued to the stage like mine were. This is the first time I've seen her all night that she isn't making a drink or carrying a basket of food in her hands. They're empty, and I can tell she's having a hard time standing here without a task in front of her.

"Yeah." She sighs, wiping the same spot on the counter I did only seconds before. I was right—she can't stay still. "Dallas used to play guitar and sing every chance he got. Before he opened this place, he would travel to different bars and clubs in the area, anywhere that was willing to hire him for a gig."

"You're kidding." I'm shocked. I don't take Dallas for the performing, artistic kind. There's a shadow lingering over him, one he casts out on nearly everyone he encounters. It's hard to imagine him up on stage, singing to a crowd, wooing them with poetic lyrics. Although, I am suddenly curious what his voice sounds like when he sings.

She sighs, her eyes brimming with tears at the memory. "He was incredible."

"What happened to make him change? I can't imagine Dallas singing on a stage."

She turns to me, sniffing. Her tears haven't spilled over, but her cheeks blush pink as she inhales a steady breath. She hesitates and then frowns, considering how to answer me. I can tell it's a weighted question. "It's been a rough year on all of us." That's all she says before she walks away to the end of the bar to check on her customer.

I want to agree with her. It's been a rough year for me, and apparently, it's been a rough one for Dallas as well.

I look back at the stage and the lone microphone standing in the middle of the platform, wondering what Dallas' voice must sound like when he performs. But even more than that, I wonder what made him cut music off completely.

Maybe we do have more in common than I thought.

While I've spent the last three months trying to find the person I want to be, Dallas has spent the past year attempting to lose the man he used to be.

Our end goals might be different, but our pain is just the same.

CHAPTER SEVEN

$$Sloan$$

It wasn't a difficult decision to move to Texas, far away from Cole and Brenna. Heartbreak has a way of motivating you to change the pieces of your life you haven't necessarily been satisfied with.

It's safe to say I am using my new job as a diversion. I'm avoiding working on my house, working nearly every night of my first week at Dallas' bar. At first, I convinced myself I was holding out on sifting through my mother's belongings because I simply didn't have the energy, but in all honesty, I know deep down it's because I'm afraid of what I might find. As the days pass, I find myself wanting to be at work more than my new home.

I don't feel connected to my mother because, for nearly all of my twenty-four years of being on this earth, I was raised to believe she was a horrible woman, the kind of woman who willingly gave up her child for her own selfish reasons.

Even though I'm avoiding rummaging through my mother's things, I'm running out of excuses not to. Not only has Dallas given me today off from the bar, I also received a call that my new desk came in and is ready for me to pick up at the store.

While I am happy to have received a small glimpse into the kind of woman Ellie was, I don't care if I replace her belongings with mine. I avoid the boxes in her attic, surely stuffed with details about her, pictures and items documenting the life she constructed without me. Instead, I continue with the same idea I had when I started with the curtains.

I've been standing in front of my mother's desk for the past ten minutes. I don't know why I keep staring at it. I know it isn't going anywhere until I move it. Her desk is sitting against the farthest wall in the office, a thin film of dust coating the top. Eventually I want to clear this room for school supplies and shelves of every kind of book imaginable, everything from children's books to romance. If it has words typed out onto pages, I love it.

The first step is removing my mother's desk and replacing it with the one I am scheduled to pick up in an hour.

I step up to the desk and release a deep breath, grabbing the handle of the front drawer. The painted wood sticks before it finally pulls free.

I gasp, surprised to find hundreds of sheets of paper stuffed into the drawer. At first, I think they must be grocery lists or to-do lists. For all I know, my mother was a hoarder, never bothering to toss out her trash. I pick up one of the pieces of paper and read the words written.

BLUE WATERS *by Ellie Roberts*
> *I dream of the day*
> *When I've seen the tides*
> *From the blue water on the bay*
> *It never ends*
> *No matter how deep it bends*
> *I dream of the day*

When I've seen the tides
~~*The blue water*~~ *Of the blue water rise*

I DROP the first poem and pick up another.

PIECES *of You by Ellie Roberts*
  Everywhere I look
  There are pieces of you
  The pieces, the pieces are scattered
  Like torn pages from a book
  I try to find them
  And put them back in order
  But sometimes I'm lost in the sea of pages

I DROP the page back into the drawer and quickly fan through the rest.

They're endless, one after the other, a hundred poems my mother wrote. I sit down on the chair in front of the desk and hold the pieces of paper in my hands.

I spend the next few minutes reading every word written on the pages. Here I was, afraid I would find a piece of my mother inside, and I was right. Pieces of my mother's soul are written on these pages, and surprisingly, I'm not upset to have found them. I feel relieved.

It's as if I've been gifted a tiny glimpse into the kind of person she was. She was a writer. A poet. A lover of words.

My hands shake and tears threaten to spill. I'm staring at my mother's words written in her own handwriting. The words start to blur with the tears, and then it hits me. I was hesitant to find out more about my mother because I was afraid of liking her. I spent my whole life believing she hated me, and opening up to the possibility of liking the person who hated me is like asking for heartbreak. I've already had enough of that in my life than I care to.

I dig into the drawer and gather the rest of her poems, straightening them into a neat pile. I place them on the seat of the chair then clear out the rest of the supplies resting on top of the desk. I don't waste any more time getting rid of it. The wood creaks and wobbles as I grip the edges, dragging it across the carpet.

"Come on." I grit my teeth. I manage to pull it out into the hallway, a few feet in front of the door, before I feel myself getting tired. My arms ache with the strength I've been using to move the monstrous desk. For a moment I consider walking across the street to ask Dallas if he could help me carry it the rest of the way to the curb, but my pride overrides that option. There is no way in hell I will crack and ask for Dallas' help. It always seems as if I am caught in some damsel-in-distress moment and he is my reluctant knight in shining armor, only I'm not the damsel in distress and he sure as fuck isn't my knight in shining armor. He is broody and acts as if my presence is inconvenient.

I swipe my arm across my forehead, convinced I'll be able to pull it the rest of the way. I open the front door and start to drag it across the floor, lifting it slightly to slide across the threshold. Half of the desk is still inside; the other half is sitting on the concrete of my front porch. I wrap my fingers tightly around both sides of the desk and pull. I dig my feet into the concrete, gritting my teeth as I tug on it harder. The hot midday sun beats across my back and I immediately start to sweat. I'm thankful I'm wearing a tank top, but these sandals weren't the best fashion choice when attempting to dispose of a desk.

My feet slide across the pavement with every attempt I

make to pull it out. The ends of my toes push past my sandals, grating against the concrete.

I've nearly made it out the door when two hands reach around me, caging me in. I can immediately feel him behind me. His chest presses against me, his shirt clinging to the sweat beading across my back. I inhale a sharp breath, staring at his hands as they grip the edge of the desk.

Dallas lowers himself, nearly resting his chin on my shoulder. I can tell it's him because he's wearing the same black leather bracelet he's worn every day since I've known him. His mouth hovers above my ear. Hot wafts of breath breeze against my skin, sending chills down my neck and arms, the heat between my legs spreading farther down. It's already a thousand degrees outside, but Dallas has managed to make it even hotter.

"Need help?" His voice moves across me in waves, shooting straight between my legs. I fight the tingling sensation once again, knowing I'm already wet between my thighs simply because he spoke two words. I hate it.

It's strange the way our interactions have shifted over the past week. It's not as if him being my boss suddenly changed the dynamic between us, but I can tell there is a piece of Dallas that wants to get to know me better, and I would be lying if I said I didn't want to know more about him too. He asked me what my rules are, clearly interested in what it could mean.

I also can't stop thinking about what Vada said that night at the bar, about how Dallas used to sing and perform on stage. I still can't wrap my mind around it and whatever happened to make him cut it completely from his life.

Dallas' secrets follow him around like a shadow. He is just as much of a mystery to me as my mother. Regardless, Dallas and I have spent most of the past week avoiding one another and keeping our conversations to a minimum. The man is an enigma, a puzzle I can't quite piece together. I don't know how I feel about it other than the annoyance I feel toward him always finding me in the worst possible moments.

I let go of the desk and stand up, straightening my back. "What are you doing here?"

Here he is again, appearing out of thin air as my knight in fucking shining armor.

"It looked like you were struggling so I figured you needed some help." He peeks around me at the desk, still sitting outside my front door. "And it appears I was correct."

I rest my hands on my hips and stare up at him. "Why?"

"Why what?" he asks, that all-too-arrogant expression written across his face.

"Why do you always show up at the worst time?"

He frowns, crossing his arms and scratching at his chin. "Actually, I think I happen to show up at the perfect time."

"Have you always been like this?" I don't care what Vada said about Dallas changing over the past year. I want to ask him because I can't imagine him any other way. There's a darkness to Dallas, a veil surrounding him. I don't know what is fact and what is fiction. I also don't understand how thin that veil might be.

His ice blue eyes narrow, and he considers me for a moment.

"Okay." He sighs, taking a step back. He holds his hands up in surrender. His fingers are covered in black grease, and his white shirt is smudged with black streaks. His motorcycle is parked in the driveway the same way it was the first day I moved here. "I won't help you then."

I watch him start to cross the street and step onto the curb in front of his house. I turn back to the desk, imagining how I'll have to drag it the rest of the way. Then I turn back around, catching him before he takes a seat on the stool he has sitting next to his motorcycle. "Dallas, wait."

He stops and turns around.

My shoulders sag as the bright sun shines into my eyes. I crack and ask for help. "Do you mind helping me?"

I point to the desk as if he has no idea what I need help moving.

He doesn't hesitate before crossing the street again, his boots landing hard against the asphalt of my driveway. There isn't anger written in his expression, and there isn't arrogance either. It's a blank expression, one I'm having a hard time reading.

He walks around the desk to the end still sitting inside the front entrance of my house and grips the edges. "Ready?" he asks. Sweat drips down the sides of his face, the beads sliding across the sharp curves of his jaw. He raises his eyebrows, waiting for me.

"Um…" I clear my throat, grabbing the desk. "Yeah, sorry."

"Try not to trip this time."

I can't help but smile at Dallas' comment. Maybe Vada was right and there's more to him than I know. I don't know what to feel about it. All I know is the feeling I get when he stares at me like this, like he's reaching into my chest and jumpstarting it with his piercing blue eyes. We both lift the desk and start carrying it out to the sidewalk. I glance over my shoulder, watching for where I'm going to step, then turn back to Dallas.

"So why are you getting rid of this desk?" he asks.

"I bought a new one and I have to pick it up this afternoon. This one is kind of falling apart, and I don't really have anywhere else to put it."

"Was it your mom's?"

I swallow, thinking back to all the poems I found stuffed inside.

"Yeah."

"Huh." He nods once then sets his end of the desk down. I

follow behind him and am thankful I cracked and asked for his help.

I plant my hands on my hips. Dallas hasn't moved from his side of the desk. He lifts his hand back to his chin and scratches at his scruff once again. A black streak of grease runs from the top of his cheek to the bottom of his lip.

"Well, thank you for your help." Unlike every other time I've been with Dallas, I'm not eager to leave him standing on the sidewalk.

He isn't being kind. He isn't being nice. That simply isn't Dallas, but there is more to him than the way he's been toward me for the past week. I haven't seen him much at work, and the guitar and microphone still stand at the bar untouched and unused. We only worked two other nights together after that first day of seeing one another, and most of it was spent on opposite sides of the bar with minimal conversation.

I don't believe Dallas simply had a change of heart toward me. I can still see the subtle glimpses of irritation in his eyes at the sight of me, but there is also a bit of intrigue, like he wants to know more about the new neighbor who also happens to now be his new employee. Either way, I don't know what he thinks of me. Does he hate me? Does he like me? Or does he merely put up with me because I am his neighbor and employee?

He's still standing on the other side of the desk from me as he lifts his hand, threading his fingers through his sweat-soaked hair. He pushes it up and off his forehead, exposing his tan skin.

"Do you work tonight?" I ask him. It's a stupid question, really. I already know the answer.

"No."

I narrow my eyes against the beaming sun, looking away from Dallas. I focus at the end of our street where it opens to the main road then turn back to Dallas. "Do you mind helping me with the new desk?"

He considers me for a moment, pulling a rag out of his back pocket. He slowly wipes each finger. "I guess I should go just to make sure you don't break a bone or something."

Maybe he doesn't hate me.

I grin at the same time he looks up, stuffing the rag back into his pocket. "I guess so." I hitch my thumb over my shoulder. "I'm going to grab my keys and then we can go."

He stays on the sidewalk, and when I step back outside, he's already standing beside my car. He's leaning against the passenger side with his legs crossed at the ankle. His phone is perched in one hand as he drags his thumb across the screen. He chews on the inside of his cheek, twisting his mouth to the left. Three lines crease the corner of his mouth, disappearing into the scruff lining his jaw.

"Ready?"

He looks up from his phone, sliding it into his pocket. "Yep." He pushes off the side of my car then tilts his head in the direction of his house. "Come on. We'll take my truck."

"You're kidding." I cross my arms, surprised he's offering to drive.

"Does it sound like I'm kidding?" He shoves his hands in the front pockets of his jeans. His boots scrape across the pavement as he spins around, not waiting for me to follow him before he's already walking away.

"Not exactly, but why does that not surprise me?"

He scoffs as I lift my purse strap over my shoulder and jog to catch up with him at the end of my driveway.

Along with his motorcycle, I know Dallas owns a truck. I've never seen him ride his motorcycle, and the few times I've caught him coming and going to work he was in his truck. I wait at the end of his driveway while he pushes his bike into the garage.

I watch him as he effortlessly hops into his truck, and the

engine roars to life within seconds. He backs out of the garage and stops before hitting the curb, allowing me to climb into the passenger seat.

And by climb, I mean literally climb. In the past, I never considered myself a short woman, but Dallas' truck has me questioning the whole idea. I step up onto the running board and reach up for the 'oh shit' handle above me. I can feel Dallas' eyes on me, watching as I pull myself up and slide into the seat with entirely too much effort, way more than should be necessary when getting into a vehicle. The interior of his truck is black, the seats wrapped in leather. The back of my thighs stick to the seat as I adjust and strap on my seat belt.

Once I'm situated, I glance over at Dallas. He's still watching me. His eyes roam over me, searing every inch of my body. I can't explain it, but unlike any time before, there's a heat coming from his intense stare, blue flames raging inside his eyes. And from what I know, blue flames are the most dangerous.

"You ready?" He smirks, turning his attention back to his rearview mirror.

"Your truck isn't exactly the easiest to get into."

He shrugs, a smug grin appearing on his all-too-perfect mouth. "It's not a real truck unless it's the kind you have to climb into."

I roll my eyes. "Right."

"Besides, you're in Texas—nearly everyone has a truck."

"I doubt that's true." I shake my head. "I don't know anyone who has a truck."

He scoffs, reaching into the center console and pulling out a pair of sunglasses. "You just moved here. Plus, you know me." He raises his hand to his chest, keeping one arm outstretched with his fingers wrapped around the steering wheel.

I wince and lift my hand, turning it halfway over before going back the other way. "Sort of."

Dallas glances at me before turning his focus back to the road. His long fingers flex against the steering wheel, his knuckles turning white. He clears his throat. "What do you want to know?"

I straighten my back against the seat, shocked he's asking me such an open-ended question. This conversation just took a drastic turn.

I prop my elbow on the door, resting my head in my hand. I watch Dallas, intrigued by the possibilities laid out in front of me. I decide to ask him the first question that pops into my head.

"What's your favorite color?"

His eyebrows shoot up across his forehead, arching perfectly over his frosty blue eyes. "That's your first question?"

"It's a legitimate one."

He shakes his head, attempting to rub away the small smile forming on his mouth with his finger. He shifts his gaze to mine. "Blue."

"What, like your eyes?"

"No." He shakes his head. "A deep, dark blue. It's the same shade of blue the water on the lake turns when the moon shines across it at night. That kind of blue."

"Huh." I bite down on my bottom lip, satisfied with his answer, though it only makes me more curious.

"What's yours?" he asks me.

"Green." I grin. "But not bright green, more of a Kelly, Irish green."

He gives me a small nod and doesn't respond to my answer, waiting for me to toss my next question at him.

"How long have you lived in Texas?" It's a question I'm genuinely curious about. Vada hasn't mentioned how long they've lived here, and I assume with the kind of name Dallas has, he must have been born and raised here in Texas. I'm hoping his answer will give me a tiny bit of information on why he is the way he is.

We head off the highway, and once we hit the intersection at the end of the ramp, we get stuck at a red light. I shift my body toward him, resting my elbow on the center console. He's still wearing his black sunglasses, shielding his eyes from me. The corner of his mouth twitches before he opens it to answer my question.

"I was born in North Carolina, but my mom moved us out here when she was pregnant with Vada." The light turns green, and Dallas pushes down on the gas, turning onto the street where the furniture store is. "My mom was a huge R.E.M. fan when she was growing up. When she was a teenager, she would find a way to get tickets to their concerts and sneak out."

"Your mom sounds like she was a bit of a rebel." I grin.

"She was." He clears his throat, continuing. "My mother had a rough childhood, so the concerts were a great escape for her. That's where she met my dad. R.E.M. has this one song called Texarkana, and ever since my mother heard it, she made a promise to herself she would move there one day. She and my dad were going to run away together, but their plan didn't work out when she found out she was pregnant with me. Even though she was only sixteen, my grandparents supported both my parents when I was born, but when my mom got pregnant with Vada a couple years later, they cut them off. They were extremely old fashioned in their beliefs. They thought my dad was a piece of shit who knocked up my mother twice. I mean, they were right, he was a piece of shit, but that's beside the point." He inhales a heated breath through his nose and sets his mouth into a firm line. "My mom packed me up and moved to Texarkana a month before she had Vada. That's where we grew up."

"Wow. I'm sorry your dad didn't stick around. I kind of

know a little about that." I'm still resting my elbow on the center console when I curl in my bottom lip, biting down on the tender flesh. It's odd to be sharing a piece of myself with Dallas, let alone having a conversation such as this one with him.

His mouth twitches again, much like it did at the start of our conversation. He parts his lips, opening his mouth far enough for me to think he's about to say something, but he doesn't. He keeps his hand on the steering wheel, passing through one intersection after another.

"So, what made you move to Austin?"

"We're here." Dallas pulls into a parking spot next to the front door of the furniture store. I didn't even realize we'd turned off the main road. He doesn't answer my question as he throws his truck into park.

"Oh." I sit up, removing my elbow from the center console. Dallas quickly steps out of his truck and shuts his door behind him.

I grab my purse and meet him on the other side. His black sunglasses are still perched on his nose, shielding his blue eyes. He doesn't speak another word until he opens the door to the furniture store.

"Come on, let's get this over with."

CHAPTER EIGHT

DALLAS

I shared more information with Sloan than I intended. I don't know what to make of my situation with her. It's not as if I don't see the woman enough as it is. She's not only my neighbor—she's my *employee*. And since she is my employee, I shouldn't be fucking looking at her the way I am right now.

I follow her as she walks through the furniture store, passing living room sets and rows upon rows of mattresses. She's walking in front of me in probably the shortest shorts known to man. If they were any higher up her thighs, I'd consider them to be underwear more than anything. Her once pale skin is now sun-kissed, glistening like gold under the bright white lights. I start to imagine what it would be like if I pulled her onto one of the hundreds of mattresses we've walked by and wrapped my hand around the back of her neck, pressing my lips to hers. I push away the thoughts and try to hide the temptation to give in behind the sunglasses I still have perched on my nose.

Sloan walks all the way to the back, stopping at the largest desk. "Hi," she says. "I'm here to pick up a desk I ordered. I was told it was ready for me."

"Sure." I don't miss how the man's eyes shift between me and Sloan, his eyebrows dipping. Maybe he's wondering what she's doing with a man like me, or maybe he's wondering if we're together. When his eyes shift back to Sloan, I don't miss how they travel all the way down her small frame, pausing on the cleavage she's clearly leaving on display for this stranger to see.

I press my lips together and grind my teeth. If this man doesn't move his eyes from her chest to her face in the next few seconds, I might not be able to stop myself from jumping across the desk and allowing my fist to knock the stupid grin off his face.

"What's your name?" he asks her, his eyes still roaming over her.

"Sloan Montgomery."

He taps his finger on his tablet a few times, finding her order. "Found it. It's in a fairly large box, so I'll wheel it out from the back and meet you up front."

"Thank you."

He shifts his gaze to Sloan's chest one more time before leaving his tablet on his desk and disappearing to the back.

I keep my eyes trained on the man until he's completely gone. It isn't my place to speak up about the way anyone looks at Sloan, much less on whether she wants the attention or not, but something in me tells me she didn't even notice. There are still so many things I don't know about her other than her favorite color is green and she is eager to toss out her mother's belongings as if they were riddled with disease.

"Dallas." Sloan's voice pulls me away.

She's already started walking back to the front, standing a few feet behind me.

I tap my finger on the desk then start to follow her. This time she waits until I'm beside her. Her steps fall into line with mine. She tilts her head, trying to catch my attention since she can't see my eyes behind my sunglasses.

"Are you okay?"

"I'm fine." I brush her off. I don't want to let her know how our conversation from earlier has stayed with me since we stepped out of the truck. I've never been big on talking about the relationship between my parents or the choices my mother made. Every choice has a ripple effect, and Vada and I were left to suffer the aftereffects of those very choices. Not very many people know the kind of dysfunctional relationship my sister and I were raised in, how my mother's inability to let go of her first and only love was a constant burden that fell on me and Vada.

Sloan is the first person I've told since Hailey, and the sudden realization of what I shared doesn't sit well with me. I push the front door open and lean against the wall. I shove my hands into my pockets and stare up at the sun. I close my eyes even though my glasses are blocking most of its brutal sunlight.

I open my eyes and roll my head to the side, feeling her stand beside me. She leans against the wall in much the same way I am. Her breasts are pushed up, the swell of her flesh rising well past the deep V of her tank top. There are three buttons in the front of her tank, but she's left the top two open.

She's unraveled her braid, the long ends cascading across her shoulders and down her back. Red strands peek through her brown waves, catching in the sunlight. She's fucking beautiful, and I hate the way it feels when I look at her. She swipes her tongue across her mouth, and I'm nearly convinced she's doing it on purpose.

It's easy to see why she gets the attention she does. The man inside the furniture store isn't the first one I've seen looking at her, hoping to even get the slightest bit of her attention. Sloan's second night at the bar, my first night working with her, I caught her talking to a customer longer than usual. Normally, it wouldn't be odd for her to be talking to someone ordering a drink, but I could tell he wanted her in the way he was looking at her, not to mention I'd overheard him earlier in the night talking about how he thought the new bartender was fucking hot. But as far as I could tell, she never showed any interest. She never noticed and she never cared.

She tips her head back against the brick wall and squeezes her eyes against the sun before rolling back to my direction. "Vada told me you used to sing and play guitar."

A stinging sensation pricks at my chest, and a lump immediately swells in my throat. I cough, hoping to rid myself of the feeling. I don't want her to see how talking about my music affects me. I severed that part of my life along with any sort of serious relationship. "My sister talks too much."

"She only told me because I asked her about the empty stage at the bar. I could tell it hasn't been used." Sloan tucks a lock of hair behind her ear. "Why did you stop playing?"

I inhale a sharp, heavy breath. The prickling feeling in my chest has only worsened. The tips of my boots scrape against the sidewalk as I push off the wall. I spin around, catching her interrogative glare, her eyes zeroed in on me. She knows this is a touchy subject for me. She knows there is a story about why I don't play or sing anymore. I rub my chin, scraping the tips of my fingers along my jaw.

I spin around and step closer to her, narrowing the space between us. "Tell me what your rules are."

It's driving me crazy that I don't know what Sloan's rules are. It would be easy to write off her conversation with Vada the other night, the one where she mentioned having rules, but I know there is more to it than what was on the surface. Even if she does tell me what her rules are, there is no fucking way I am going to tell her why I don't play music anymore, no matter how many times she asks. It may sound fucking harsh, but so is life. Talking with her this way is worth it. The satisfaction I'm getting from this moment is too good to pass up. I don't quite understand what I'm doing in this moment or what my end goal might be. All I know is that the closer I stand to her, the harder my cock becomes.

Her eyes form two narrow slits as she stares up at me. "What?"

"It's my turn to ask the questions." I take a step closer. "Tell me what your rules are."

"That's not how this game works. You didn't ask a question, and you can't just demand answers. They have to be given willingly." She tips her chin higher in defiance, keeping up with the level of my gaze. She presses her hand against my chest, preventing me from stepping any closer. I stop her by quickly lifting my hand and wrapping my fingers around her wrist. Her smooth lips part the second my hand is on hers, a deep blue fire igniting behind her eyes. It takes everything in me to not let go and move it to a different part of her body, one that would bring her closer so I could possess that gorgeous mouth of hers.

"I didn't realize we were playing a game," I admit.

"Well, we are."

"Okay, I have a different question for you then." I give her a smirk, hoping if she won't answer my question about her rules, this one will at least give me a hint. "Did you notice the way that man was looking at you inside?"

She considers me a moment, narrowing her gaze on me. "How was he looking at me?"

"Like he wanted to rip those tiny shorts of yours to shreds and fuck you right there on his desk."

"He was not."

"Trust me. He was."

She swallows, her cheeks flushing bright red. "I don't really care how he was looking at me."

"Why is that?"

"For one, that's his problem, not mine. And two, I'm not interested."

There it is, the clue I was looking for. I can't explain it, but her voice shifted the moment those words left her pretty little fucking mouth. They held more conviction than anything she's ever said before. She meant it.

I keep my fingers wrapped around her wrist, holding her hand against me. My focus flickers between her blue eyes and her smooth, full lips. I don't know which part of her to focus on more. My heart pounds in my chest, nerves shooting down my spine. I'm sure she can feel it beating beneath her small palm.

"Are you not interested in him, or are you simply not interested in anyone?" I reach my other arm out, pressing my palm against the wall beside her head. I'm halfway caging her in. Her large blue eyes widen, disguising themselves with innocence, but I know better.

Her body shudders and she nervously swipes her tongue across her lips before swallowing. Deep down, I can see the battle raging inside her. She doesn't know if she wants me to stay or go. I keep my hand wrapped around her wrist and my other arm pushed against the wall beside her head. I know I'm on to something.

There's a battle inside me too, but I stay silent on that subject and my music.

She opens her mouth, ready to answer me, but we're interrupted. Our attention immediately shifts to the front door.

I push off the wall and away from her, taking a few steps back.

The asshole from earlier emerges, pulling a large flat cart behind him. Three large boxes are stacked on top of it.

"Alright, here you go. One of the boxes contains the top part of the desk. The other two have the legs and hardware. If you show me where your vehicle is, I can help load them up for you." The man points to the boxes. He's strictly talking to Sloan, acting as if I haven't been standing beside her the entire time we've been here.

I'm almost positive he wants to fuck her.

Fucker.

"We're parked right here," I tell him, pointing to my truck, which is in the closest spot possible.

"Oh," he says, his eyebrows arching across his forehead. He gives a nervous smile then starts to pull the cart around to the back of my truck.

I open the tailgate and lift one end of the box, propping it onto the edge before sliding it in. The man bends down to pick up the next one. Honestly, I could have loaded everything by myself, but I stay silent, not wanting to make it a big deal. I just want to get the fuck out of here and back to Sloan's.

Once all the boxes are in the back, I shut the tailgate and spin around. Sloan is already standing by the passenger side door, reaching for the handle.

"Thank you for your help." She waves to the man, leaving him to walk back inside without another ounce of attention from her.

He nods and gives both of us a tight-lipped smile before going back inside the store.

Good.

I run my fingers through my hair, wondering how the rest of the day with her will go. I'm not entirely sure she wants me to help her set up her new desk. She's independent, but she can also be stubborn. It's great she's willing to do things on her own, but I want to help her.

I climb into my truck and turn the key to start the engine.

My truck roars to life. I place one hand on the steering wheel as I slide it into reverse. She's been silent ever since we've been back in the truck. I glance over my shoulder, watching to make sure I'm clear behind me. I chance a quick look at her then focus on my rearview mirrors.

"It's a good thing we took my truck. There's no way we could have fit those boxes in the back of your car."

"You're right." She glances over her shoulder quickly before turning back around to click in her seat belt. "Thank you." Her voice is quiet, a stark contrast to the way she's been talking all day. She rests her elbow on the door and closes her eyes. I take it as a sign that she wants to take a break from our question game. Maybe it was the conversation we had before the furniture salesman came out with her desk.

I'm glad she doesn't press me any further on my music and why I've stopped playing. Opening up about my music is also opening up about my past. I only gave her a tiny sliver of it, one that won't have her looking at me in a different light. The other reason I'm holding back is because I don't talk about that part of my life. Ever.

Sloan is no exception.

Once we make it back to her house, I back my truck into her driveway then step out to start unloading the boxes. Sloan unlocks the front door then meets me near the back of my truck.

"I can carry them in."

I stop sliding the box out, keeping half of it hanging off the back of my tailgate. "What?"

"Seriously, you've already helped me enough, Dallas. I'll take them in and then you can go." She steps forward, her breasts bouncing with her movements. It's hard for me to not stare at her round hips or her subtle tan skin.

I stop her, holding my arm out like a barricade. "No. No way."

"Dallas." She firmly plants her hands on her hips, narrowing her usual round eyes.

"Sloan." I say her name sarcastically, mocking her. "We're seriously right here. I don't mind carrying them inside for you." I had a feeling she would pull this move on me. Like I said, she is independent and fiercely stubborn. It only makes my desire for her grow.

We spend the next few seconds in a staring match, daring one another to break and give in. There is no way she is going to break me, and I won't give in.

Annoyed, she presses her lips together in a huff. "Fine. You can leave them in the living room before you leave."

She spins on her heel before disappearing inside her house.

I don't care that she's upset with me. The more she pushes me, the more I push back. I am probably acting like an asshole, but it doesn't matter.

I give a smile of satisfaction at winning and I turn back around to grab the boxes from the back. I carry them into the living room as she requested. I try not to pay too much attention to the inside of the house, but with Sloan's new décor, it's hard to ignore. It's been three months since the last time I was in here, and it feels like a completely different house.

The walls are still painted a pale lavender color, but the mustard curtains are now replaced with thin white fabric, and paintings are hung on the walls of the living room. After sliding the last box against the wall, I cross the room, one of Sloan's pictures catching my eye.

It's of her and the man who was with her the day she moved in. It looks like the picture was taken at an outdoor festival. There are crowds of people surrounding them, groups sitting on blankets. Behind them, out of focus, is a large stage. Their arms are wrapped around each other, and he's kissing Sloan's cheek while she grins.

I'm still staring at the picture when she emerges from the kitchen with two bottles of beer. She holds one out to me. "For helping me with the desk."

I stare at the beer in her hand but don't take it. I run my fingers through my hair, sliding my palm across the side of my face. Here I am being an asshole again, but I can't take another minute of standing inside Ellie's house. It feels wrong to be here, especially when I can't decide which is the better choice to make—wrap my fingers around her waist and possess her mouth with mine or simply walk away.

I take a step back. "I have to go."

Her eyebrows knit, confused. I don't know who is worse when it comes to indecision, me or her.

CHAPTER NINE

Sloan

I DON'T WANT TO THINK ABOUT DALLAS IN ANY WAY OTHER than my boss and neighbor, but it is becoming increasingly difficult the longer I stay living in the house across the street from him.

Indecision lingers under my skin, just beneath the surface of the way I have decided to live my new life.

Dallas is quickly becoming a bad habit I can't shake. Just when I thought he was starting to change toward me, he pushed his cold shoulder on me once again. Admittedly, I would do the same in return.

When he brought up the fact that the furniture salesman was clearly flirting with me, something inside me triggered, sparking like the flash from a freshly lit match. I don't want to be in a relationship. Cole's affair left a bitter taste in my mouth, and love is out of the question, or even anything remotely resembling love.

But that doesn't mean I don't still get wet at the sight of Dallas working on his stupid motorcycle or that my throat doesn't swell when he's standing within inches of me. Truthfully, I want him to kiss me. I want to know what it feels like to have his strong hands grip the sides of my waist, making me bend to his will. My mind is in a constant battle between if I want him to touch me or never talk to me again.

Human attraction is a bitch.

"I wrote this article for *The Chronicle* the other day about all these upcoming festivals in Austin. I thought maybe we could check a few of them out this summer." Vada's standing beside me behind the bar with her arms crossed over her chest.

We've just gone through the lunch rush, and we're now in the sweet spot between lunch and dinner where there's hardly anyone sitting at the bar. She's bored, and I can tell.

I need to stay busy. I've been cleaning the counter for the past ten minutes with the same rag, watching Dallas from across the dining room. He's standing on top of a booth, changing out one of the light bulbs above the table. The muscles on his arms tighten and flex as he stretches them out.

"Sloan? Are you even listening to me?"

"What?" I don't move my eyes away from Dallas.

He steps down from the booth, and when he turns around, he catches me staring. I don't care that he does. My cheeks flush pink, but it isn't from embarrassment. It's from anger that I've allowed myself to feel even the slightest bit of attraction toward him.

My heart thrashes inside my chest, and the all-too-familiar lump swells in my throat.

Dallas moves his eyes to the side, briefly looking at me before he walks over to the next table. His eyes are firm, his mouth set into a thin, stubborn line. I can see the thoughts clearly written in his expression. Something between us shifted yesterday, and he doesn't know what to make of it. Neither do I.

I shamelessly watch him as he steps onto the next booth, reaching up to change the next bulb. The bottom hem of his t-shirt rises, displaying his firm, sculpted hip bones. He's angry with me, yet I'm not sure why. I also don't understand why it bothers me if he is.

"Sloan." Vada repeats my name, and this time her tone is enough to pull me away from staring at Dallas. "What is going on with you?"

"Nothing," I tell her, shrugging. I don't want to deal with her interrogation or her questioning. I quickly walk through the back of the bar, heading toward the kitchen to grab another bag of clean rags. She follows me.

"You're clearly distracted. I thought you would be excited about my idea since you're new here."

"Excited about what?" Colton peeks out from behind the kitchen counter. One of his black-glove-clad hands is wrapped around the handle of a very large butcher knife, the other gripping a brisket. He drags his knife through the other end, loading the slices into one of the many warmers set up in front of him.

She crosses her arms and rolls her eyes. "I don't think it's anything you'd be interested in."

Colton's eyebrows dip behind his thick-framed glasses. He lifts his hand to his chest, holding it out far enough to not touch his shirt. "Ouch, Vada. You've really hurt me with that one."

She pauses, biting down on her bottom lip as she stares daggers back at Colton. There's clearly something not settled between them. They always converse as if they hate each other.

"Anyway..." She rolls her eyes back to me. "You've been distracted today."

"I'm not distracted." I pull the bag of rags free from the closest and lift it up to show Vada. "See?"

Passing Vada, I start heading back toward the front, leaving her and Colton behind. I don't want to get into this conversation with her. She doesn't know about my trip to the furniture store with Dallas or how he tested the waters with how close he could get to me. My main reason for not telling her is because I don't know what to make of it myself, hence the obsession with the need to stay busy. The other small reason is because I am hesitant to share any information with her. To be honest, it isn't entirely fair to her to leave her completely in the dark. I long for the days when I felt I could trust someone enough to tell them my deepest thoughts and secrets, but I am also afraid. I know Vada is the closest person I have to a best friend. She was the first person to welcome me to Austin with open arms. I can't discredit her for that, but after Brenna, I can't help holding my cards close to the vest. I've been burned before. I'm hesitant, afraid it could happen again.

I shove through the door leading to the front and drop the bag on top of the cooler. I tear open the top, tug a rag free, and immediately start folding it. Dallas is no longer changing out the light bulbs above the tables. Instead, he's sitting at the far end of the bar, flipping through a stack of what looks to be invoices. He keeps glancing from the paper in front of him to his phone sitting on the table beside him.

"Something happened that you're not telling me." Vada reappears beside me. She reaches inside the bag and pulls a rag free. There's still only one customer sitting at the bar, and his drink is nearly full. Dallas must have gotten him a refill while Vada and I were in the back.

We fold the first few rags in silence, but the guilt starts to set in for not sharing a single piece of information with her. The pressure from the secrets I've been keeping is starting to boil over.

"I found a ton of poems my mother wrote when I was emptying out her desk." The moment my confession falls from my mouth, I internally sigh with how relieved I feel to finally tell someone. I hadn't been able to talk to Liam lately since he's so busy with work back in Minnesota. Between his schedule and mine, we just haven't had the opportunity to talk like we used to.

"You're kidding?"

"No. I just pulled the drawer open and there they were. When I say there were a ton, I mean there were *a ton*."

Vada drops her hands, stopping mid-fold at my confession. She knew about the lack of relationship my mother and I had before I moved here and how she left me her house with absolutely no warning. So, her reaction to this news doesn't surprise me. She knows I've been both hesitant yet eager to know more about the person my mother was. This is simply one small puzzle piece added.

"That's pretty awesome. How does that make you feel though?"

"I'm not sure. It's one thing to live in a house with her furniture. It's another to see something she wrote at one point in her life, if that makes sense. It's like watching an actor in a movie and then meeting them in real life. One feels more alive than the other, more real, and I'm not sure I was ready to feel that just yet."

I shrug, thinking back to the words she scribbled across hundreds of torn pieces of notebook paper. When I went inside to grab my purse before Dallas and I headed to the furniture store, I gathered all the papers together and stuffed them into one of the kitchen drawers to get them out of sight until I'm ready to sift through them again. I don't want to lose them, knowing they are a piece of my mother's soul written with ink, a piece of her soul she likely didn't share with anyone before.

"I get what you mean." She nods, continuing to fold the rag in her hands.

"Hey." Colton walks up behind me and Vada, grabbing our attention.

"What's up?" I ask him, glancing over my shoulder, giving

him a warm smile. Over the past week I've worked here, I've come to grow fond of Colton. He's always kind to me even though he spends most of his time either in one of his graduate classes or tormenting Vada. I'm not entirely sure which one he seems to get more enjoyment out of.

Colton clears his throat and runs his fingers through the strands of his dark hair. "I talked to Dallas about performing again, and he's still not budging."

"I told you I didn't think he was ready." Vada's voice is soft, the same tone that's usually used when anyone discusses what to do about a way to incorporate live entertainment. "Plus, why do you always seem to bring this up to me when Dallas isn't in the conversation?"

Colton tentatively shifts his gaze to Dallas before looking away. He dips his head and whispers, "It's not like I leave him out of the decisions, Vada. It's just that every time I bring it up to him, he changes the subject. He's basically left it up to me to figure out, and I really think we need to give this a try. Basically every other bar within a three-block radius is doing it. We're the only ones who aren't."

Vada sighs. "You've got a point."

"Wait a minute," Colton says, a sly grin slivering across his mouth. "Did you just admit I'm right?"

"I never said that." Vada shakes her head.

Colton crosses his arms in satisfaction before circling back to our conversation. "I would hire someone, but I don't think we have it in the budget right now since it was always supposed to be Dallas."

"I'm sorry," I say. "I don't know anyone who would be able to perform. You guys are the only ones I talk to." I laugh it off. I'm happy with the small circle I've built in the time I've been in my new hometown.

"Wait." Vada perks up, pointing at me. "Didn't you say you can sing?"

"Oh yeah." Colton perks up too. "You did."

I trade glances between the two of them, stunned by their suggestion. Blood drains from my cheeks at the thought of singing to anyone but myself. "Well," I scoff. "I did, but I've never sung to anyone before, much less on stage."

"You should try it," Vada says, wrapping her slim fingers around my wrist. Her brown curls bounce with her excitement. "Come on, isn't this what you moved down here for? A chance to build a new life, to experience something new?"

"I don't know." I shake my head, shifting my gaze to Dallas. He still hasn't spoken to me all day, letting his silence settle in between us, delivering his message loud and clear. He wants us to keep our distance, and so do I.

"We could try it on a trial basis," Colton rushes to offer. His round eyes are hopeful, and suddenly I can tell he's looking at me as if I've suddenly rescued him. "You can sing one night, see how you feel. If you hate it, that's okay. I'll crack and hire someone."

I consider the idea for a few seconds. I chew on the inside of my cheek then shift my eyes to the empty stage, imagining what it would look like with me standing in the middle of it. I imagine the dining room packed with customers, their eyes trained solely on me while I hold the microphone in one hand, nerves rattling through me.

"What music would I be singing to?" I ask Colton. I sure as hell don't know how to play any instrument. The only songs I've ever sung to were when Liam and I would take short road trips in college between Minneapolis and our family cabin in northern Minnesota. Liam was the only person who has heard me sing, and he begged me for years to enter one of the many ridiculous singing competition shows on TV, but I never wanted to make a career out of it. I wanted to teach, and that's what I went to school for.

Colton stops to think, rubbing his fingers on his chin. He quickly snaps his fingers with a smile. "I have someone in my economics class who told me he plays the guitar. I'm sure he wouldn't mind helping at least for the one night. I'll see if he can come in the day before so you guys can work out a couple songs. Maybe I can find some cover songs for you to play if that makes it easier."

"Are you okay with this?" Vada asks.

I want to tell her and Colton no. I want to tell them I didn't agree to add singing to my list of duties when I started working here as a bartender. Regardless, here I am, looking at a desperate Colton and an overly intrigued Vada. She looks way too thrilled at the prospect of hearing me sing.

"Okay." I give Colton a small smile and continue folding the rags. When I look over to where Dallas was working on paperwork, he's no longer there.

"What's going on?" I hear his voice coming from behind me. Convenient how he shows up at the precise moment I check to see where he is.

When I turn around, he's standing two feet behind me, leaning with his hand against the edge of the bar. I breathe in, trying to calm my thoughts. He smells like a mix of cedar and the grease from his motorcycle. He must have been working on it again this morning. I don't know why I'm more nervous around him today. Maybe it's because I'm nervous about what he might think about me being the one to perform instead of him. Or, it could be that up until this very moment, he hasn't spoken a word to me all day. Either of those could be a real possibility.

"Nothing," Colton interjects, saving me from answering

Dallas. He locks his eyes on me before finally moving on to Vada then Dallas. "We were just talking."

"Hey," she says to Dallas. "What do you think about checking out some festivals this summer?" She grins, raising her eyebrows.

"Like music festivals or…?" Dallas' question trails off.

"Yeah, some of them." Her expression falls. Her once hopeful demeanor is now replaced with anticipated disappointment.

His eyes shift back to me as his jaw ticks. My heart pounds in my chest so loud I think he might be able to hear it. Shit, the entire bar probably can. I don't know what's going on with Dallas. One minute he looks at me like he hates me, and the next it looks like he wants to throw me up against the wall and slam his mouth against mine. My imagination flies away with me, thinking of all the things Dallas could do with those strong fingers that are gripping the edge of the wooden bar.

Again, his stare pours into me like water breaking through a dam. It rushes in, hitting me at all once.

Then it clears and calms the second he switches back to Vada.

"Count me in."

"Really?" she asks, stunned. In fact, we all are. Colton's eyebrows dart up his forehead, above his glasses. I drop my shoulder and quirk one eyebrow.

"Yep."

"Cool." A ghost of a grin appears on Vada's mouth.

Colton chimes in. "Nice. Maybe we can all four go one time. It'll be awesome. Oh, and good news." He taps Dallas on the arm. "I figured out what I'm going to do about the nights we want live entertainment."

I immediately glare at Colton, wishing he hadn't brought it

up. I'm still not entirely sure it's a good idea or if I even want to do it, but alas, here I am.

I'm surprised when Dallas' lack of reaction to Colton's news ends up having me feeling relieved.

"Great." Dallas places his hand on Colton's back in appreciation before leaving the three of us standing behind the bar completely confused.

Good. At least I'm not the only one.

CHAPTER TEN

DALLAS

My motorcycle is finally back in working order. It took me nearly a month to get the one part in and nearly two weeks for me to be able to fit the time in to replace the broken part enough to get it back up and running. I don't allow anyone else to touch my bike, so taking it to a shop was never a thought. The one part of my father I always appreciated was how he taught me the important things in life. My mother was more nurturing. She was a hopeless romantic to a fault, always allowing her emotions to get in the way of seeing the more rational reality of the life surrounding her. My father on the other hand was the practical, logistical kind. He wasn't big on emotion or sharing his feelings. If he was, they were always hidden behind a stern, cold face and long beard. In a way, I think I'm more like him now than I was before, when I was with Hailey.

Although he wasn't around too much growing up, a few of the things my father taught me managed to stick with me through the years, one being how to work on any kind of vehicle, including motorcycles.

I've just finished my morning run, walking the rest of the

way down my street to cool down. The storm clouds from last night finally cleared out, leaving the perfect weather to go for a ride on my motorcycle. I'm hoping to fit in a ride before heading into work tonight.

In truth, I am finding anything and everything to take my mind off Sloan. The indecision regarding how I feel about her is starting to irritate me. Relationships are still considered an immediate write-off to me, but I can't get over how even the slightest of Sloan's movements brings a reaction out of me.

At first, I thought it was the way she wears those fucking crop tops or the way she seems to bite down on her bottom lip when she's concentrating. But I know my attraction to her is more than that. The biggest thing is her stubbornness when it comes to accepting help. Her defiance and insistence only make me want to push back harder. It only makes me want her more.

I've been fighting the same battle in me ever since we went to the furniture store last week. I keep my interactions with her short, only speaking to her when needed. But then when I'm home and I pass by her on my daily runs, it's difficult to suppress the thoughts that constantly run through my mind. Most days, I end up thinking about her when I'm in the shower, hoping the scalding hot water will help.

My morning runs only hold off the tension building in me for a short amount of time. All of this is temporary.

When I make the turn onto my street, I pull my phone from my pocket to check for any messages. There's one from Kylie sitting in my inbox. I hover my thumb over the keyboard, deciding if I should reply to her. It's been weeks since I've spoken to her, not since that morning she stormed out of my house calling me an asshole.

I still don't care what she thinks of me. Even though I know I am never going to be able to give her what she wants, I consider the possibility of seeing her again. Maybe she's changed her mind. After all, if she knows I never want to make our relationship anything more than a good fuck, why is she still taking the time to text me?

Refusing to give in to Kylie, I ignore her text and slide my phone back into my pocket. No amount of frustration is worth that mess.

I've nearly made it to my house when I slow my steps. Sloan is in her front yard, mowing her lawn. This woman has truly spent an exorbitant amount of time working on her house. One day she's trimming bushes, the next she's shoving desks out of her front door.

Sloan can't hear me, the sound of the lawn mower drowning out the sounds of the neighborhood. I don't stop to watch her like I did the day I watched her trimming the bushes in her front yard. Instead, I keep walking toward my house, but she's hard to ignore. I find myself glancing over my shoulder more often than I should.

She wipes the back of her hand across her forehead, the sweat dripping down the smooth skin of her face. The end of her ponytail dances across her back with each step she takes, and the golden highlights in her hair match the tone her skin has taken on since she moved here. The Texas sun has kissed her, giving her its signature golden color. After wiping her forehead, she runs her hand down her cheek, sliding her fingers across the curve of her jaw. Her fingers grip the back of her neck and move to her collarbone.

Sloan hasn't noticed me walking by, even when I make it to my front door. In truth, I'm relieved she didn't see me. My cock is hard as a fucking rock, begging for relief. I jog up the stairs and head straight for my bathroom, quickly turning on the shower. I don't bother waiting for it to heat up. I quickly step out of my shorts, kicking them aside before stepping in. The ice-cold water shocks my heated skin, rinsing away the thick film of sweat.

I grasp my bottle of body wash, squeezing way too much into the palm of my hand, but I don't give a shit.

I hate that this is what I have resorted to: fucking myself in the shower after my morning runs, thoughts of Sloan's golden sun-kissed legs wrapped around me. I hate how I imagine her pink lips sucking on the same skin where my fingers grip. I tighten my fingers around the base of my cock, sliding my hand up and down. I move it faster, and the subtle numbing sensation traveling down to my toes is almost too much for me to handle. I lean forward, pressing my free hand against the tiled wall for support. It doesn't take long for me to cum. I lean forward and rest my head against the wall of the shower, catching my breath. I watch as my cum swirls down the drain, mixing with my soap. The now hot water scalds across my back, and thoughts of Sloan still haven't left me. The relief is immediate, yet it only lasts for so long.

After I finish the rest of my shower and get dressed, I head downstairs to my kitchen, hoping I can find something to eat.

"Hey, how do you not have any coffee?"

"Oh, shit." I quickly stop when my sister pops out from behind the door of my refrigerator. "Vada."

"I'm serious," she says, holding an energy drink in her hand. She slides one to me, her expression filled with disapproval. "These things aren't exactly healthy."

"What are you doing here?" I grab the drink off the counter and snap open the top. The carbonation pops and sizzles before I take a long gulp.

"I came by to check on you." My sister has had a key to my house ever since the day I moved the rest of Hailey's belongings out of the house. There are still pieces of her scattered throughout my house. Those pieces I can live with; the rest deserved to be somewhere else.

Since she has a key, I'm not entirely surprised to see her here.

"How long have you been here?" I leave her standing across from me at the kitchen island and pull the package of eggs from my fridge. I start cracking them into a bowl.

"Not long," she answers behind me. "Long enough to realize I should be sure to bring coffee with me whenever I come over here because you will never buy any."

"Well, you don't live here, so..." I'm thankful my sister hasn't been here long enough to know I just spent the past twenty minutes in the shower, jerking off to thoughts of her new best friend.

"You're right, I don't. Are you still thinking of selling this place?"

After whisking the eggs in the bowl, I pour the mixture into the pan. It bothers me to my core that she's asking me this question this early in the morning. She's nonchalant in her delivery, not caring why I'm considering selling it in the first place.

"I haven't decided yet." I run my spatula through my eggs, watching as they slowly solidify.

"Okay."

"I hope that's not why you came over here so early in the morning, to ask me if I've decided to give this all up." I wave my spatula in the air. I still haven't turned around to face her, using my cooking as a distraction. I'm still reeling from my thoughts of Sloan earlier and what it was like to see her this morning.

"No, that's not the only reason," she says. She moves out of the kitchen and sits down on the couch in the living room, now facing toward me. "Sloan asked if I could help her paint her living room today. She's finishing up mowing the lawn, but I told her I'd be over here until she was done."

"Shit. Sounds like she'll never stop working on that house."

"What do you mean?" Vada sits up, pulling her back away from the couch. She's suddenly more interested in this conversation now that I've brought Sloan up. "How do you know she's changing it so much?"

Shit. I forgot I never told her I knew Sloan's mother and have been inside her house more times than I can remember. She and I grew apart once we both graduated high school. After I went off to UT, I was too wrapped up in my own life to bother going out of my way to talk to her outside of the usual holidays. Up until I lost Hailey, she never knew much about my life. I never told her the kind of relationship I shared with Ellie.

"Well..." I shake my head, sliding my eggs onto my plate. "She's always out there either working on her yard or leaving a piece of furniture on the curb. I can only assume."

I sit down at my dining table and start to eat my eggs. She stands up from the couch and takes a few steps closer to me. The kitchen is between us, but I can feel her stare burning the right side of my body. I prepare for an interrogation.

"Huh." She crosses the living room and the kitchen before sitting across from me at the table. Gold streaks peek out from her curls as the morning sun shines against her brown strands. She looks just like our mother, barely a trace of our father in her. I'm glad. The asshole didn't deserve Vada.

She rests her elbows on the table, placing her chin in her hands. Her palms cup her jaw as she stares at me.

I drop my fork. "What?"

"Nothing." She sits back, and her hands fall into her lap. "Have you talked to Colton lately?"

I pick up my fork again and stab a chunk of egg. I lift one shoulder as I chew. "Not since yesterday. Why?"

"No reason." She chews on her thumbnail then drops her hand again. She gives me a reassuring smile. "We were just supposed to go to a movie last night, but he never texted me. At least not until this morning to apologize. He said he fell asleep studying."

"He's been busy with his classes. I don't think he has many left, so he shouldn't be as busy."

"Right." Her shoulders rise as she inhales a deep breath. "I was going to talk to Sloan about this but figured I'd mention it now. There's a festival next weekend we could check out."

"I'll see."

"You will see?" Her eyebrows arc across her forehead. "The other day you were all about going. You said to count you in."

I scoff. "Not all of us have our entire month planned out, Vada. I'm not sure."

"I figured as much." She tucks her hair behind her ear and leans forward, crossing her arms on the edge of the table.

"What does that mean?" I stand up and drop my plate into the sink then turn around to face my sister.

"Exactly what you think it means."

She's right. I do know exactly what she means. For the past year, I've found it extremely difficult to follow through on anything. Relationships, family, business. The part of myself that once was has been drowning, but I don't give a shit if I toss it a life raft or let it sink to the bottom of the ocean like an anchor. It's easier to let the past fall away and hope to forget it than it is to deal with it and hope to make it out on the other side.

"Look, Vada, I'm handling the restaurant fine. I've been working on my bike again." I wave toward the front door. "I even helped Sloan pick up her new desk the other day from the furniture store. What more do you want from me?"

"You what?" she asks, her eyes widening.

Shit.

I pinch the bridge of my nose and sigh. "It's not a big

deal." I'm a big, fat liar. It was a huge deal. There is no denying that me offering to spend my time with a woman outside of my bed sheets is a big deal according to everyone who knows what my life has been like recently. "She was struggling to get her mom's old one out the door, and when she told me she was on her way to pick up the new one, I couldn't let her do it on her own. Knowing her, she'd likely have broken her ankle or tripped just carrying in one of the boxes."

"Sure." There's a sparkle in Vada's eyes, a hint of amusement at my story.

"Stop." I hold my hand up to her.

"I won't say any more about it." She holds her hands up and leans back in her chair, crossing her arms. "But I know how you are, Dallas." There's hesitancy lingering in her expression as she shakes her head, raising her shoulders. "And Sloan isn't that kind of woman."

"How do you know what kind of woman she is? And who says I'm into her that way?"

My own questioning doesn't even convince me into believing I'm not into Sloan. I want to fuck her. There isn't any other way around it. The proof is in the way I thought of her in the shower only thirty minutes ago.

Vada's expression shifts, showing me she knows me all too well. She can see straight through my thin veil of artificial ignorance.

"I'm just letting you know, Dallas. You shouldn't get involved with Sloan."

"You're being ridiculous."

"Oh," she scoffs, rolling her eyes. "Sure I am."

"But now you have me wondering why. Why should I not get involved with Sloan?" Here I am again, pushing to find out what Sloan has against men. I lean against the kitchen counter and cross my legs at the ankle. I shove my hands into the pockets of my shorts and look down at my feet.

"It's not really my place to say, but I'll just tell you her mother's death was only one of the reasons she was so quick to move down here from Minnesota. You're both complicated, but in different ways."

"Oh." I don't know why, but Vada's words feel like a fist hitting me in the chest in one blow. Even though she said we're complicated in different ways, there's a brief moment where I imagine Sloan suffering the same kind of pain as mine, a loss as great as mine. Sloan never knew her mother, so she doesn't wear her grief from that death on her sleeve, but maybe she carries the grief of another.

I rub my fingers across my chin, digesting what she's told me. I can feel her still staring at me, and I look up to find she's doing just that.

"One last question," she says quietly. "Did it bother you when Gareth went up to her at the bar the first night you both worked together?"

Her question throws me off guard. It's a shift from the conversation we've been having, but I've clearly done a poor job at pretending to have a lack of interest in Sloan and who she gets involved with in this city. I also didn't realize Vada had paid that much attention to the man Sloan was talking to that night. I assumed she was too involved with her customers to notice.

But I did notice. It was hard to break my eyes away from her, especially when I saw Gareth sit in front of her, turning on his typical charm. I don't know Gareth well other than the fact that more often than not, he uses my bar and a few others on the same street to pick up different women. Several times I've overheard him bragging about the amount of money he has in the bank and how at least once a month he flies out to his family's vacation home in France. It's all complete, utter bullshit and I never fall for it, but some women do, and I hope Sloan isn't going to be one of them.

Judgment fills Vada's eyes as she stares at me. I know she's thinking we're no different. Yes, we both sleep with women with the intention of knowing it will never go any further, but I know there is no way in hell we are the same.

Gareth uses his lies to pull women in. He manipulates them into thinking he's someone he isn't. On the other hand, I never lie. I never pretend to be someone I'm not.

"You think I care that Gareth was talking to Sloan? That asshole talks to any woman who is willing to sit and listen to the bullshit he spouts off." Again, a thin veil of artificial ignorance. I hope if I play it off enough, my sister will lay off this topic. It bothered the fuck out of me that he was talking to Sloan.

"That's what I thought." She purses her lips, nodding. "Anyway, Sloan's probably done by now. I should head out." She rises from the table. She immediately pivots our conversation, leaving me hanging.

"I'm serious, Vada. I didn't even notice Gareth talked to her that night, or any other one since." I shrug my shoulder, following her down the hallway.

"It's fine," she says over her shoulder. "I believe you."

No, she doesn't. It's clear.

She's still heading toward the front door, but she stops when three knocks sound against my front door, the pounding traveling down the hallway. I move around her to answer it. After all, this is my house, not hers.

When I open the door, Sloan stands on the other side. Her eyes widen slightly, and her bottom lip falls away from her top, making a small opening in the smooth flesh of her mouth. The smell of fresh-cut grass immediately flows in from Sloan's perfectly manicured lawn.

"Hey," she says.

"Hey," I reply, realizing this is the first time she's ever seen past the front door of my house. Her eyes move to my right, finding Vada behind me. She swings her gaze back to me. "Vada said she would be over here."

I'm not entirely sure why she's being so hesitant with me. She clearly sees her standing behind me. Maybe she feels uncomfortable being here. Maybe it's because of the way we left things after the furniture store and how short we've been with each other since.

"Well, she's right here, as you can see." I cross my arms over my chest and turn halfway so she sees her behind me.

"Thanks," she mutters.

I'm giving Sloan the cold shoulder again. It's the only way I know how to keep myself under control when she's around. There's a part of me I've noticed growing weaker the more I'm around her. I haven't quite figured out which part of her it is, the long damp strands of hair resting on her bare shoulders or the way her golden skin is still thick with moisture from her shower.

Sloan mimics me by crossing her arms in the same way. "Hey, Vada." She smirks, her eyes lighting with fire, refusing to break away from mine. "I was wondering if maybe you want to go out for a drink afterward. Didn't you say you have tonight off?"

"I do," Vada replies, standing beside me. She grins. I can already see her mood shifting with Sloan's idea, probably because Colton disappeared on her yesterday.

"Great." Sloan grins. She drags her tongue across her bottom lip and breathes in. Her chest and shoulders rise in satisfaction.

"I'll see you later." Vada rests her hand on my shoulder as she moves past me, following Sloan down the walkway.

I stand in the doorway, unsure of how to process what's happened since Sloan showed up on my doorstep.

It feels as if she's challenging me. Her eyes are daring, shifting to an intense dark blue shade.

Vada is a few feet ahead of her. When she reaches the end of my walkway, she glances over her shoulder with a smirk. "Hope you have a good night, Dallas."

CHAPTER ELEVEN

Sloan

"This place has *THE* best music." Vada spins around, walking backward down the sidewalk of Sixth Street as she talks to me.

The street is busy and unlike anything I've seen before, not even in the largest cities in Minnesota. Neon signs are perched out front of nearly every bar and club, music blasting through the windows and open doors. The concrete beneath my feet pulsates, and it feels as if my chest is bursting open in the best possible way.

Austin is full of life, and I've only begun to touch the surface by being here tonight. Listening to the music and life surrounding me only solidifies my desire to live in the moment. But despite how thrilled I am to be here with Vada, I can't help thinking about Dallas. The expression he had when I walked away this morning has been sitting at the forefront of my mind. I was challenging him, daring him to make a move.

My rules were never meant to be broken and I don't intend on opening myself up to the possibility of dating Dallas, but I can't help the nagging prickle in my chest every time I see him, the one that makes me want to step forward, rise up on my toes, and slam my lips against his.

I already got a few drinks in me at dinner. The pasta and salad I ate acted as a small cushion, absorbing the initial shock of the alcohol hitting my bloodstream. I've been riding a buzz for the last half-hour, certain that if it weren't for the food, I'd be drunk.

I'm following Vada down the street when I pull my phone free from my purse, reading over my texts with Liam from earlier today.

Liam: Ugh, I miss you so much and I wish I could explore the city with you. Call me when you get home and tell me everything.

Me: I will.

Liam: Promise?

Me: …yes, Liam. I promise.

Liam: Listen, I'm just making sure. You never know what can happen. Remember, sis—you're living in a big, exciting city. Live it up, take a few risks. Not too many though.

Me: I'll be fine. Nothing too crazy. I'm having a girl's night with Vada and then I'm going straight home.

Liam: Like I said, don't be afraid to live a little. Rules or no rules, you deserve to have some fun.

I stare at Liam's last text, deciding to follow his advice. He's right. I deserve to loosen up and enjoy myself. I click out of Liam's texts and continue walking down the sidewalk.

When I asked Vada if she wanted to go out tonight, it was more of a way to gauge Dallas' reaction. I wanted to test him and challenge him to offer up any sort of indication as to how he feels about me. He didn't say much when he was standing on the other side of his door, but he didn't need to. I've come to know the changing expression on Dallas' face at the sight of me. His hair hovered above his sharp brow, covering his blue eyes. He no longer looked at me with a vacant, careless gaze. He set me on fire the second he opened the door.

Where Vada and I are now isn't exactly how I'd pictured our girl's night. I figured we would hang out on my couch and snuggle in with a little Netflix while we ordered the unhealthiest food imaginable. I should have known she had other plans in store for us. I've quickly learned that if you plant an idea in her head, she takes it and runs, covering it in glitter and sparkles. I live for her excitement. I need someone like her in my life.

My heels click across the pavement as I try to keep up with her. My bare arms brush against the crowd as I weave through them. The red fabric of my dress stretches with each step I take, pulling against the curves of my thighs. The neckline is a bit deeper than I'm normally comfortable with, plunging down well past the center of my breasts. It's been too long since I've worn a dress like this. I bought it after I found out about Cole's affair. I didn't intend on wearing it when I first bought it, but I knew this was my comeback dress, the kind you wear when you're ready to start living again. Maybe this is what Liam was talking about when he said to live a little.

I raise my arm in the air and quickly snap a picture of myself with the bright neon sign of the bar Vada has brought us to behind me. Vada's in the background, clearly several feet ahead of me already. I grin, staring back at the snapshot of myself. My cheeks are tinted pink, the colors of Austin's nightlife swirling in my eyes. I send it to Liam followed by a few simple words, throwing them back at my brother.

Me: How's this for taking a few risks? Wish you were here. Xoxo

I end my text with a simple heart emoji and quickly hit send before shoving my phone back into my purse and jogging to catch up to Vada. She reaches behind her, grabbing my hand as we weave through a crowd standing outside one of the clubs. I remember passing by this place when I was driving through the city, searching for somewhere to eat lunch then stumbling upon Dallas' bar. We're only a few blocks away from it, and I find myself wondering what Dallas is doing. Is he thinking about what his sister and I are doing? Does he even care?

Probably not.

And neither should I.

There's a bounce to her step, one I am happy to see. She hasn't pulled her phone out since before dinner, but I know there is something going on between her and Colton. He didn't show up yesterday when they were supposed to watch a movie together, and when we were on our way to dinner, I saw his name flash across the screen of her phone before she groaned as she tossed it into her purse without answering it. She hasn't pulled it out since.

"When was the last time you went out like this?" Vada asks. She pulls us past the line outside the club.

"Um, not since college. But to be honest, I've never been to a place like this." I quickly look around, a flood of bright, neon colors clouding my vision. It's all too much to take in at once, but she doesn't allow me to stop long enough to truly appreciate it.

"You're in for a treat then." She quickly pulls us to a stop at the front of the line. "One of the perks of being editor in chief for the city's big newspaper." She tosses me a wink before turning her attention to the man standing outside the front door to the club. He's large with muscles the size of my head. The single word 'Security' is printed in the corner of his black shirt.

"Hey, Joe," she says.

"Vada! It's been a while."

She rolls her eyes. "Too long if you ask me." She grabs my elbow, introducing me to Joe. "This is my friend, Sloan." She grins. "Just us tonight."

"Sure." He holds his hand out toward the door to the club, not even bothering to check our IDs. It truly is a perk to be Vada's friend.

I allow her to take the lead as she takes us deeper inside the club. We pass through a small hallway, and when we reach the end, the room opens up to one of the largest dance floors I've ever seen. The walls are blood red, the loud country music beating between them. The pounding rhythm reverberates through my body as we make our way to the back, toward the bar.

Vada stops in front of it and leans forward, catching the bartender as he passes us. "Two lemon drop shots and two martinis, please."

"Sure thing." The bartender gives her a wink, quickly getting to work on our drinks. Vada spins around and leans back on her elbows. I stand beside her.

"Martinis, huh?" I ask her.

Her shoulders shudder with a small laugh. "Too classy?"

We're both yelling over the loud music. I shake my head, glad I decided to do this with her. "Not at all."

"Good," she yells back. The bartender places our shots on the counter in front of us followed by two martini glasses filled to the brim with clear liquid.

Vada hands me one of the shot glasses and holds hers up. I grab mine and hold it up to hers. "To us."

"To us." I clink my glass against hers and swiftly bring the edge to my lips. The deliciously sweet and sour mix immediately hits my mouth, coating my tongue as I tip my head back. It burns slightly on the way down, warming me from the inside out. I slam it on the counter then wrap my fingers around the stem of my martini glass.

The dance floor is packed, every booth filled. Even if we were to move, I'm not entirely sure where we'd go.

Vada takes a large sip of her martini, observing the crowd in front of her. "Men fucking suck."

I laugh, caught off guard by her choice in subject. "You're telling this to the woman who made up rules on dating. I've sworn off men for the foreseeable future."

Her eyes sparkle under the flashing lights above us. "I think I might just adopt a few."

I scoff, not believing her. "Let me guess—does this have to do with Colton?"

She keeps her focus on the dance floor but gently smiles against the rim of her glass. She arches one eyebrow. "Maybe." She inhales a deep breath then turns to me. "Tell me, Sloan. How long are you exactly sticking to these rules of yours?"

"Not sure." I shrug. "I didn't put a time limit on it. I think I'll know when I'm ready."

She quirks an eyebrow. "You're stronger than I am."

"I don't know about that." It's true. Most of the time I feel weak, and there have been many moments over the course of the past few months when I've considered the possibility that it was my fault Cole turned to Brenna. I worry I was the reason he turned to my best friend. It's one thing to have an affair; it's a whole other ball game when it's with your best friend.

"You are," she says. "I'll ask you this."

The lemon drop shot hits me, followed by the martini I've been sipping on. Suddenly, the shield of pasta sitting in the bottom of my stomach grows weak. "Ask away," I tell her, grinning.

"Now, I know you have your rules and all, but I have to ask—do you have a thing for my brother?"

I laugh, maybe a little too hard. I try to play off her question as absurd, acting as if I haven't imagined him every time I've touched myself this week, shamelessly imagining my hand was his mouth and my fingers was his tongue.

I raise my glass, using it to block my mouth and hoping it will hide the redness in my cheeks. "What makes you think I have a thing for him?"

I tip back the rest of my drink and place it on the counter. I wave down the bartender, pointing to my empty one.

"Oh, I've just seen the way the two of you are around each other. At first, I thought you hated one another. I mean, that's what you told me before you found out he was my brother. You said he was being an ass to you. But then..." She trails off, spinning around to the bar. She's finished her drink as well. "I've seen the way you two watch each other, the way you look at each other."

"I don't look at him in any way." I shake my head. I don't know why I'm trying to convince her I haven't been looking at her brother any differently. Not only am I already a poor liar, but my inhibitions are also weaker due to the drinks I've had.

"It's okay, Sloan. I don't care if you like my brother. To be honest, I like seeing this part of him come out. Even if he doesn't realize it himself."

The bartender places a full drink in front of me. I stare at the clear liquid, wondering how deep I'm in with Dallas if it's enough for Vada to notice. Not only that, she noticed a change in him too. I know it's hard for Dallas to show his feelings, and for a moment, I consider that his sister might be an exception to that rule. Then again, she seems surprised to see the change, happy even.

I don't know what to make of this conversation. The prospect of there being anything between me and Dallas is conflicting. I don't want a relationship, but I can't deny the attraction I have to him.

My chest begins to swell, my heart rate pounding against my ribs to the beat of the music. The warmth of the alcohol falls over me like a warm blanket, covering all the exposed parts of my body.

I twist the stem of my glass between my fingers then turn to Vada. "I have to go to the bathroom. I'll be right back."

I snatch my purse from the counter and push through the crowd surrounding us. I don't know where the bathroom is. All I know is that I need a second to breathe. I need to get away from Vada's interrogation and the overwhelming need for air. I don't know where to even begin to sort my feelings when it comes to Dallas.

I have my rules, and if I'm going to stick to them, I know I need to leave Dallas alone. It doesn't matter if I've touched myself a thousand times, imagining his mouth as the one to give me the orgasms instead of my hand. What matters is that I don't allow my fantasy to turn into reality.

Looking up from my feet, I finally find a break in the crowd. There's a long, narrow hallway in the back corner of the club, a bright neon restroom sign hanging above the entrance. "Oh, thank God."

I step into the hall and groan, noticing the men's room is the first door I see. It's always first. I keep edging my way toward the back, keeping my eye on the door to the women's. The light dims more the farther back I go, and suddenly I'm covered in shadows. A few women exit the bathroom, laughing with one another. Thinking back on my conversation with Liam earlier, I pull on the zipper of my purse to grab my phone to see if he's responded to my picture. Even if our conversation did take a serious turn, I hope he's happy I decided to loosen up and enjoy my night out with Vada. I am enjoying myself, but I can't help how our conversation took a sharp turn to the right. I never stopped to think that others might have noticed the way Dallas and I have been interacting. Since Vada can see it, it makes me wonder if maybe Colton does too.

I brush away the thoughts stirring inside me and hope that by the time I get back to her, we'll be able to move on.

I'm reaching inside my purse when a large hand wraps around my arm, pulling me deeper into the hallway toward the back. My heart leaps into my throat and chills prickle their way along my spine. I open my mouth to scream, but my voice catches in my throat when I'm pulled around a corner into a smaller area near the back door. I'm then pushed against the wall. A firm body presses against me, towering over me. The pressure of his body is familiar, the peaks and valleys of his muscles melding into me. He presses his finger against my lips, keeping them hushed.

It takes my mind a few seconds to recognize the two ice blue eyes staring back at me. "Dallas?" My mouth moves along his finger still held against me. He doesn't attempt to move it, his gaze focusing in on the point where our touch is connected. My heart thrashes inside my chest at the sight of him, or maybe it's the way he nearly scared the shit out of me just now. Either way, I know his body is pressed against mine, and this time it isn't because I tripped and fell on top of him.

"What the fuck do you think you are doing?" he asks. His eyes are narrowed, both fire and ice at war. His hot breath dances across my skin as he slowly drags the pad of his finger across my bottom lip.

"Excuse me?" I ask him. Heat swallows me whole. I'm angry with him. Angry he grabbed me in the shadows of the hallway, scaring the living fuck out of me. Angry he has the audacity to show up here and ask me such a question.

"What," he repeats, this time slower, bringing his face closer to mine, "the fuck...do you think you're doing?" He drags the tip of his nose along my cheek, inhaling as he moves along my skin. My body prickles at his touch, sending shivers down my legs.

His mouth stops at the hollow of my ear, and I bite down on my bottom lip, convinced I'm going to have an orgasm just from how close he is to me. His hardened cock presses between my legs. His subtle movements push the bottom of my dress higher up my thighs.

"What were you thinking going out in a dress like this then having the audacity to send me a fucking picture of you in it?" I bite down on my bottom lip. His thick velvety voice hits my ear. "I wasn't sure if I should be mad at you or fucking thankful."

He pulls away from my ear but still keeps his face close to mine. The tip of his nose glides across my cheek before stopping on the side of mine. His intoxicating smell of pecan wood from the restaurant and motor oil immediately surrounds me when I inhale.

"I didn't send you a picture." I swallow, thinking back to when I sent the picture of myself to Liam. I had closed out of our thread of texts before deciding to go back in and must have clicked on Dallas' name instead. Earlier today, he sent me my work schedule for the week, so his name was at the top of my list. Alcohol truly lowers your inhibitions and skews your judgment. "Shit."

"That's not exactly the kind of picture you send to your boss now, is it, Sloan?" His smirks, clearly amused. He lifts his hand and traces the tip of his finger down my cheek and along my jawline. His other hand grips my hip, keeping me pressed against the wall.

"I sent it to you by accident."

"Bullshit." He's quick to answer, flashes of light sparking in his eyes.

I consider him, thinking about his reaction to me sending

him the photo. This clearly was his breaking point. He took my text as a form of permission slip for him to make a move.

"I knew you were testing me back at my house before you left," he continues. "Seeing what I would do." He's cocky, the arrogance dripping from his irresistible smile. I'm instantly wet for him, the skin between my thighs heating more the longer he's pushed against me.

I figure this could go one of two ways. I could break right now and give us what we both truly want. Or I can push him off a little while longer to find out what Dallas' goals were in coming here. If he wants a relationship, there's no way I will bother giving him the attention we both crave.

"I don't know what you're talking about." I tip my chin up, challenging him. "Why would I send you a picture like that? I told you I wasn't interested in dating anyone."

At least I was telling the truth then.

"Is that one of your rules? To not date anyone?" His eyes search my face, following my expression. My heart is still pounding in my chest, yet somehow his stare grounds me.

He continues dragging the tip of his finger from where he left off. His entire body is pressed against mine, his hips slowly moving back and forth against me. The hallway is nearly empty. We're all the way in the back where it's darkest, and those exiting the bathroom don't bother glancing in our direction. They're too eager to get back to the dance floor.

"What do you think?" I can't help it. My body flutters every time I play this game with Dallas, answering a question with a question.

His finger is now tracing the curve of my breast, dipping into the delicate space between them. His cock grows harder, and his hips push impossibly closer.

"I think there's more than what you're telling me. It's odd." He smirks as he glances down, watching how his own hand moves along my stomach down to the bottom hem of my dress. He slides his fingers under, stopping them for only a second. He traces small circles on my skin. I lift my leg, halfway wrapping it around his calf.

"What's odd?" I ask him.

"You seem to be proud of your rules, but you aren't very good at following them."

"You don't know that."

A humorless laugh spills from his mouth as he drags his fingers the rest of the way between my legs, finding my clit.

"Oh," he says, bringing his mouth in front of mine. "I think I do."

I gasp as his fingers make slow circles between my folds. I rock against his hand as his palm cups me. This man knows exactly what he's doing.

"I, um..." I clear my throat, attempting to gather my thoughts. He keeps his hand moving as I talk. "I told you I'm not interested in a relationship."

My breath catches in my throat, and if he keeps up with his pace, I know it won't be long before I fall apart against his hand.

"Lucky for you, neither am I." With his free hand, he releases my wrist and brings it to my chin, gripping it with his long, strong fingers. He dips his head far enough to slam his lips against mine. I immediately open my mouth when he coaxes it open with his tongue. He tastes like peppermint and bad decisions. I don't know if this is a mistake or not, but I honestly don't care.

Bad decisions are always the ones that taste the sweetest, and Dallas is most likely going to leave me with a toothache.

I lift my hand and wrap it around the back of his neck. My fingers dig into his deep brown hair. We're both a tangled mess of limbs, hot breaths, and rushed touches.

My thighs tighten around his arm, keeping his hand on me.

He moves his fingers from my clit, digging them inside before moving them back. He pulls his mouth away from mine, tilting his head forward, pressing our foreheads together.

I wrap my arm around his back, clutching his black t-shirt. My legs writhe against his, eager to reach my orgasm. I'm close to finishing, but at the same time I don't want this to end. It has been too long since I've been with a man this way, and touching myself with my own hand this week while imagining Dallas was nothing compared to the real thing. This is completely different.

"Come for me," Dallas says before placing his mouth on mine again.

My body ignites, tiny fireworks bursting across every inch of my skin. I rock my hips against him, riding his hand as I finish out my orgasm. Dallas' mouth against mine mutes my scream, and I'm left moaning against him. I grab at his back, digging my nails into him.

After I finish, he moves his hand out from between my legs. We stare at each other while I attempt to catch my breath, wrapping my mind around what just happened. Dallas doesn't speak, only staring at me with his laser-focused blue eyes. They're nearly black with the shadows we're covered in.

I think back to our conversation and how Dallas has now found out one of my rules. I don't intend on being in a relationship, but neither does he. His admission fell from his smooth mouth before he used it to claim mine.

Under the dim lights of the hallway, he lifts his hand and places the tip of one of his fingers in his mouth. The gesture alone brings heat to my cheeks. I'd never had a man taste me afterward, and a part of my heart flutters at his motion.

After he puts his finger in his mouth, he pulls it back out and drags it across my lips. "Before I told you I didn't know if I should be angry or thankful you sent me that picture." He smirks, backing away from me.

I rest my head against the wall behind me and stare at him with hooded eyes. "And were you able to decide?"

"I think you already know the answer to that question." Dallas moves to the exit door in the little corner of the hallway we've been standing in. He doesn't offer me another glance before he pushes against the door and steps outside, leaving me alone in the hallway to catch my breath.

RULE #3

If you decide to sleep with someone, keep it strictly under the sheets.

CHAPTER TWELVE

Sloan

I'M NERVOUS TO GO TO WORK. TO BE HONEST, IT'S THE MOST nervous I've been since landing this job at the bar.

After the heated moment between me and Dallas in the hallway at the club, I found Vada still seated at the bar waiting for me. She asked what had taken me so long, and I used the excuse that I got caught up talking with a woman who'd had a little too much to drink in the stall next to mine. It was a bald-faced lie and it stung as it fell from my mouth, but there was also no way I could tell Vada the person who just gave me the most mind-blowing orgasm in the back of the hallway was her brother. I didn't stay long after, telling her I was too tired.

It's been well over twelve hours since my encounter with Dallas last night, and I still haven't been able to stop thinking about it. The memory of the way it felt to have his mouth move across my throat...the way his hand cupped me, his finger sliding across my clit...it was as if his caresses were phantom touches, refusing to disappear and forcing me to remember. The memories are on a never-ending reel, and if I'm being honest, I don't want them to stop.

The thought of Dallas' hand between my legs immediately

causes my thighs to react, clenching as I walk into the bar. The dining room and bar are empty since this is one of the few days of the week where we're only open for dinner.

I breathe out a sigh of relief when I don't see Vada, and an even bigger one when I don't see Dallas. I'm still not sure she wouldn't be able to see that I was hiding something from her. I also don't know how to act around Dallas.

I'm not entirely sure what last night meant or how it changes things between us. I know in some way it did, but I don't know how much. He vaguely mentioned him not being interested in a relationship either, and that gave me a small amount of reprieve.

Ordinarily, I'd find Dallas or Vada in the dining area of the bar. Instead, I don't see anyone. It's completely empty. The chairs are still resting upside down on top of the tables. The music is still turned down low, barely audible over the noise coming from the kitchen. I drop my purse off behind the bar before making my way into the back, unsure of who I will find today. A few days out of the week, another chef named Brandon fills in for Colton, helping with more of the prep work than the actual cooking of the meats. I'm just not sure which one of them I'll find today.

"Hello?" I ask once I step through the swinging double doors.

"Back here, Sloan." Colton peeks his head out from the exit door leading to the back of the building where all the smokers are located. Large plumes of smoke billow out from three capped smokers built into brick bases standing four feet tall.

When I reach Colton, he's still standing near the door. As I get a full view of him, I notice he's holding a binder in his right hand.

"Hey, Colton."

"Hey." He grins, his eyes brightening behind his thick-rimmed glasses. It's strange, but I don't feel like I've spent much time with Colton. In fact, this might be the first time we've had a conversation with just us two.

He looks down at the binder in his hand then lifts it to show me. "I was just looking through this binder full of cover songs to see which ones you could play for your first performance."

Oh, shit. I'd completely forgotten.

"Cover songs?" I ask him. My throat swells with nervousness. I've been too wrapped up in the back and forth between me and Dallas to remember I still have to practice with Colton's classmate and learn new songs—and perform them on stage.

"Yeah." He shrugs. "I didn't think you had any original ones, so I figured this might be the best bet. I borrowed this from one of the bar owners down the street who also plays in a cover band. It was just an idea."

"I can look it over." I give him a reassuring smile and reach for the binder. He hands it to me, a hopeful expression filling his face.

"Thanks. I'll set you up with my friend to practice sometime next week. I want to get a little promotion behind this thing before we start it."

"Sounds good."

"Great." His voice falls away, and it's then I notice the shift in his mood. His expression changes and his shoulders fall forward, almost as if he's relieved. As a matter of fact, he looks exhausted, maybe even worn out.

"Is everything okay?" I'm certain Colton and I are not at the stage in our friendship where he is going to divulge any piece of personal life, but as a fellow human being, it feels like it's the natural thing to do.

He sighs, removes his glasses, and rubs one of his eyes with his knuckle. He quickly places his glasses back on his nose and walks toward the center smoker. I follow him, wrapping my arms around the binder and holding it to my chest.

"I'm fine." He waves me off, opening the lid. He picks up one of the large metal pokers. "I've just been super busy with school and work."

"I've heard."

"You've heard?" he asks me. I can practically hear his eyes roll with his question. "Let me guess, Vada said something to you."

"Not really." In a way, she did, but I'm hoping if I don't let Colton in on how much I know, he'll share with me. It feels good to have this kind of talk with him, one that doesn't involve smoked meats or me singing up on stage.

Colton hesitates, poking at a few chunks of meat as they slowly rotate on the carousel. "I know Vada wants more than what I'm able to give her."

"Oh," I say. "Do you not feel the same way she does?"

"No, I do, and she knows that." He sighs, moving one last piece of meat before closing the lid. "I just mean she wants more than I can give her *right now*."

I open my mouth, ready to answer him. I can tell his feelings for Vada are buried deep. He's conflicted, and it's clearly wearing on him as much as it is her.

Before I'm able to speak, he stops me. "It's complicated and I wish I could say more, but I can't. I wouldn't even know where to begin. There's just too much..." He inhales a deep breath and blinks several times as if he's brushing away his thoughts. He starts to walk back into the kitchen. "I'll see you inside."

"Okay."

IT'S BEEN three hours since I talked to Colton outside and he gave me the binder of cover songs to go over. For the most part, I haven't thought too much about it since. It's not that I'm not excited about the prospect of singing to a large group of people; it's a combination of two other reasons that has my mind floating off elsewhere. The first is that we are in full business mode tonight. The restaurant is packed wall to wall, and it seems as if my to-make drink list will never end. Just when I think I've made it to the end of my stack of orders, Vada brings up another twenty.

The second and most nerve-racking distraction is the thought of Dallas. I am pathetic when it comes to trying to shut off my thoughts. I can't stop thinking about the way I felt under his hands, the way he molded me, easily bending me to his will. My cheeks enflame as I dig my scoop into the ice bin and fill three glasses before pouring the mixture I just spent the past thirty seconds shaking in a tall silver canister. I lift the cup and evenly distribute the bright green liquid.

"Hey, girl. Sorry to ask, but are those almost ready?" Vada sidles up beside me, her heavy breaths spurting out of her chest in quick succession.

"Yep," I tell her, popping my lips. I grab three cherries and drop one into each glass. "Just had to add these."

"Thank you." She sighs. "You're a lifesaver."

"Not really." I attempt to laugh her off, knowing she's only being dramatic because the restaurant is dramatically busy for a Sunday. Her mood tends to shift in the direction of the restaurant. If it's loud and chaotic, so is she.

My mind shifts back to my second distraction of the night. I try not to be too obvious by shifting my gaze to the front door, waiting to see if Dallas walks in, but I fail. Miserably.

He hasn't shown up yet.

Vada is too busy to notice her brother hasn't arrived, and

since I haven't spoken to Colton, I assume he hasn't noticed either. Maybe she assumes he's working in the back with Colton, but I know he isn't. He's supposed to be out here with us tonight, hence why she's racking up her step count for the day and my drink list never seems to end.

"Where's Dallas?" I ask her. She still doesn't know about what happened between us last night, and I'm hoping my question comes off more business related than personal. "I thought he was working tonight."

She shrugs, pushing her bottom lip. "He's not in the back with Colton? That's strange. He must have gotten caught up doing something. He never misses work unless it's something that's absolutely worth it." Vada doesn't break her concentration away from what she's working on, loads the three drinks onto her small tray, and walks off without another word.

I'm filling a draft beer when I see a familiar face sit in the vacant barstool across from me.

"Long time no see." He displays his pearly white teeth. "Sloan, right?" He points to me across the counter then crosses his arms over the wood like he did the first night we met.

"Oh, yeah." I nod, grinning. "Whiskey sour, right?"

"Right." He laughs over the music. "Name's Gareth, but I'll take the drink as well."

"Okay, Gareth." I lift the glass and start to move a few seats down the row from where he's sitting. "I'll be right back to make that for you."

"Sure thing, darlin'."

Gareth's use of the word slithers down the back of my neck, leaving me to remember how it was the first night I met him. He was charming but also forward, a little too forward. But I'm also the new person in a new city, and this is Texas after all. Maybe Gareth is just being extra kind, like when I go to the grocery store and the cashier calls me 'sweetheart'.

After I quickly drop off the beer, I dive right into making Gareth's drink. I can feel his eyes on me the entire time I'm mixing it, all the way down to the last pour of liquor into the small glass.

"Here you go." I slide it to him as he hands me his credit card.

"Do you mind keeping a tab open for me?" He grins, lifting his glass to his mouth.

"No problem."

"Thanks, sweetheart."

I resist the urge to roll my eyes. Cashier or customer, it doesn't matter. It seems to be a common term of endearment around here.

"I didn't get the chance to find out the last time I talked to you," he starts. "Where are you from?"

"Minnesota." My eyes shift to the front door, finally catching Dallas walking in.

Suddenly, I'm nervous. My mouth runs dry at the sight of his hands reaching up to his hair and adjusting the sleeves of his shirt. His expression is tense and dark under the warm lights of the restaurant. He weaves his way through the tables, only stopping occasionally to greet a customer. I watch as he disappears into the back without noticing me behind the bar.

"Minnesota, huh? I've been up there a few times to go skiing with some friends of mine."

"What?" I turn back to Gareth, realizing I didn't pay much attention to what he was saying, something about skiing in Minnesota.

His mouth curls and his eyebrows dip in confusion. "I was telling you I've been to Minnesota before. To go skiing."

"Right." I attempt to give Gareth a grin. "It's a great place to visit in the winter, but only if you can hack the frigid weather."

"Don't let this Texan fool you." Gareth laughs. "I'm pretty

sure I can handle it. Maybe you can tell me some of the best places to check out the next time I'm up there."

"Sure." I give Gareth a smile. He's being kind, and the more I think about it, the more I realize I have no reason to not return his kindness.

"Hey, Gareth. I can't say I'm surprised to see you here."

My bottom lip falls away from my top when I turn to my right to find Dallas standing beside me. I'm unsure of how long he's been behind the bar or how much of our conversation he's heard.

"Oh, hi Dallas."

He smirks, his eyes shimmering under the golden lights of the bar. The restaurant is dim aside from the lights overhead and the city lights out on the street pouring into the windows. The small amount of light is enough to highlight all of Dallas' shadows, forcing them to show themselves even if just a fraction.

"Isn't this the fifth time I've seen you in here this week?" Dallas asks Gareth. "Tell me, which is it that keeps you coming back—the service or the food?"

Gareth's eyes shift between me and Dallas. A part of me deflates on the inside knowing Dallas has just put him on the spot. I try hard not to turn to Dallas and ask him why he feels the need to ask Gareth why he comes here so often. Obviously, Dallas knows Gareth enough to be on a first-name basis. There is clear tension between the two men.

"Oh, well I think it's both." Gareth's eyes shift back over to me, and another part of me slightly cringes with the way he's looking at me.

It's not to say I'm not flattered, but there is no interest in Gareth whatsoever. Possibly as friends, definitely not in the way he wants with how he's looking at me right now.

I glance over at Dallas long enough to see him mulling over

Gareth's answer. The storm is brewing behind his eyes, and the corner of his smooth lips curves up as it always does when he's deep in thought. I try not to think about how those lips were all over my neck less than twenty-four hours ago.

The tension between the three of us is palpable. I can't quite figure out Dallas' expression, but the feeling it gives me is enough for me to walk away. I am far too busy to try to discern Dallas' relationship with Gareth.

"I'll be right back." I'm a coward. I don't know where I intend on going. After making Gareth's whiskey sour, I took a quick inventory of all the customers sitting at the bar that needed a refill. They're all set. No one needs a drink, and Vada is too busy to notice me walking away. If anyone needs anything, they can ask Dallas.

I walk through the kitchen and push my way through the back door. The warm, sticky summer air slams against my skin. I breathe in and tip my head up to the sky. The city lights are too bright for me to make out the stars against the black backdrop, but it's still a beautiful night.

"What are you doing?"

Dallas steps out of the back door and moves to stand in front of me.

"I just needed a minute. I've been working non-stop for the past three hours."

"You can't just walk out in the middle of a rush."

"Are you kidding me?" I rest my hands on my hips and stare daggers into Dallas. It isn't because he is accusing me of walking out in the middle of a rush. It's because he's a hypocrite. "You're the one who didn't show up until fifteen minutes ago."

He quickly moves closer to me, closing the space between us. His boots hit the pavement. "Not that it's any of your business, but I had something important to take care of."

"You're right. It isn't any of my business, and I honestly

don't care where you were—but it does bother me when Vada and I are struggling to keep our heads above water."

His blue eyes are a deep shade of black since we're standing outside. The way the colors swirl and the intensity behind them is enough to take my breath away. I try not to let Dallas know how he's affected me, but I fail miserably.

"I'm sorry if you felt like you and Vada were drowning without my help, but I do have to ask you one thing." His hand touches the bottom of my stomach, inching its way under the hem of my tank top. I'm wearing an open flannel shirt over a black tank, Dallas' logo printed in the top corner. His eyes fall to it, but his fingers keep moving.

I can already feel myself start to become wet from his touch. My attraction to Dallas is a contradiction. Part of me wants to give in, but the other part of me wants to push him away. If I know anything about Dallas, it's that he hates when he can't get what he wants. But when it becomes a battle between my head and my vagina, I know my head doesn't stand a chance around him, especially not after last night.

I'd been touched by Dallas, and I have a feeling he doesn't intend on letting me forget it.

"Ask away," I say, challenging him.

He smirks as if he knows he's already won. His eyes shift to my mouth and watch as I slide my tongue out and swipe it across my bottom lip.

"How long after I left did it take you to stop thinking about the way my fingers touched you here?" His fingers hook onto the edge of my shorts, pulling me toward him. My body presses against him and I gasp as he leans down, bringing his mouth close to mine. "Or maybe you didn't forget. Maybe you haven't stopped thinking about it since."

"What makes you so sure I enjoyed it that much?" I've brought my mouth closer to his, standing on the tips of my toes.

My calf muscles ache as I attempt to stand taller against his large, towering frame.

Chills prickle down the back of my neck when he brings his mouth to the hollow of my ear the same way he did last night. "Because in all the time I've spent with you, I've never heard you make that sound before or seen your body move the way it did against my hand."

My chest flutters against the words spilling out of him. Dallas definitely knows how to push my buttons. He infuriates me. He is secretive, arrogant, and, for the most part, doesn't care if I'm struggling to keep up at work.

But his lack of care is also what keeps me wanting more. I like that Dallas doesn't care whether he pushes me over the edge or not. As he said last night, he isn't looking for a relationship, and this only confirms his confession.

My heart beats against my ribs, thrashing as it tries to decide what feeling to focus on more, the way Dallas' hand continues to move farther south or the way his lips ghost across mine. I lean forward, hoping he'll press his mouth to mine, but he doesn't. Heat spreads across my legs, and my body nearly begs for him to keep going. The truth is, I did enjoy last night. Even if it was brief and we were practically hiding in the shadows in the back of the hallway, I wanted it. I imagine what it would feel like to have more than Dallas' hands on mine.

I tip my chin up higher, ready to take whatever he's willing to give me, but I'm left highly disappointed when he quickly steps backward. I immediately feel the absence of him. I've quickly learned he has a knack for teasing me right up until the point where I'm about to completely give in, only for him to pull away.

"You should get back to work." His words are stiff, full of resignation to the situation we're in.

I immediately cross my arms over my chest, shame pricking

its way into my chest. I've let Dallas reel me in again, the same way he did last night, only tonight was worse.

I'm ready to walk back into the restaurant and lose myself in work. I know Vada is most likely pissed that Dallas and I disappeared on her, especially during the busiest part of the shift.

Dallas stays ahead of me as he heads toward the door leading back into the kitchen.

I'm ready for this to be the last time I hear from him for the rest of the night. I'm also ready to give myself more time to get over the way it felt to have his hands on me and his mouth claiming mine.

But I stop when his voice cuts through the warm, midsummer night air. He turns his head only long enough to deliver me an order over his shoulder. "Meet me at my house tonight after work."

CHAPTER THIRTEEN

DALLAS

By the time I pull into my driveway, Sloan is already waiting outside my house.

She's standing against the wall near my front door, scrolling through her phone. The bright blue light shines onto her face, highlighting it in the darkness. Her ankles are crossed, leaving her perfectly smooth long legs on display. My dick almost hardens at the sight of them, remembering what it felt like to have my hand between them.

Last night was completely unexpected. I knew showing up at the club where Sloan and Vada were at was taking a risk. I didn't want Vada to see me and wonder why I had shown up there in the first place, but I was in luck when I walked in at the exact moment Sloan was headed toward the restrooms.

Whether or not she sent me the picture of herself on accident doesn't really matter to me. I only took it as a challenge considering the way she had looked at me the last time I had seen her leaving my house with my sister. The way the neon lights on the street reflected off her brown hair popped against the bright red color of her dress. Fucking hell, I'd never seen a woman look the way she did standing there on Sixth Street. She was even more gorgeous as she stood in front of me in the shadows of the hallway we were in. The picture truly didn't do her justice.

I step off my motorcycle and set my helmet on my seat. When Sloan notices me walking toward her, she pushes off the wall and tucks her phone into her pocket. She's still wearing the same clothes she had on when she left work: cutoff shorts and her black tank top covered by a flannel shirt, rolled at the sleeves.

I dig my keys out of the pocket of my jeans and pass by her to unlock the front door. I don't say a word, and neither does she. It isn't an awkward silence. Up until tonight, I've obviously never invited Sloan to my house before. She knows something between us has shifted. How could she not?

Both of us stay silent until we step through the front door and make our way deeper into the living room.

"This is beautiful." She points to the piano I have set up in the corner of the room. The moonlight pouring in through the windows surrounding us reflects off the shiny coating.

She taps her fingers along the edge before she presses a few keys. None of the notes she plays go together or make a tune, but she doesn't care. Neither do I.

"I've had that piano for a while now," I explain. "Since I was in college."

"I didn't know you could play. I thought you only knew how to play guitar."

I shake my head and walk closer to her. She turns to where her back is to the piano and tips her chin higher to look up at me. This is quickly becoming my favorite view of her. Her eyes always shift in a way that causes my heart to beat against my chest a little harder, and my thoughts seem to go cloudy. Her bright blue eyes flicker with green, and her mouth subtly twists as if she's trying to read me. She's attempting to figure me out. It only makes me want her more.

When I take another step closer, her chest deflates with an audible gasp. She both relaxes and tenses at the same time, and my dick twitches with excitement.

She leans back against the piano, pressing her round ass into the keys. The chord she strikes sounds awful, but it doesn't matter. It bounces off the walls around us, mixing in with our bated breaths.

"There's only one regret I have from last night." I decide to start tonight with a small confession. Seeing Sloan here in my living room only resolidifies the arrangement I have in mind for us.

She holds her breath as her eyes search mine, unsure of where our conversation is headed. Then again, I'm not sure what she thought it meant when I invited her here tonight. She lifts her hand and grasps the front of my shirt with her slender fingers, clutching the fabric in her fist.

"What regret would that be?"

I lean forward, gripping the piano at her sides. My mouth is dangerously close to hers.

She opens her legs, allowing me to stand between them. She clenches her thighs around me when my hardened cock presses into her center. There's entirely too much fabric between us. I hope it isn't long before we can rectify this small inconvenience. She keeps me close by wrapping her legs around mine with her calves pressing into the back of my knees.

I take a deep breath and tilt my head, lowering my face closer to hers. "I regret that my hand was the only thing to have the privilege of touching you."

She gasps.

I slide my hand down to the button of her shorts, popping it open with a quick turn of my fingers. "It's a shame we were in a public place." After undoing her button, I open the small zipper before sliding my hand inside the opening.

She gasps again. The fabric of my shirt twists between her fingers as she pulls me even closer, but I can't let her go any further until I've told her my intentions. I need to make it clear that we can't be any more than we are now.

"I need to ask you something." She surprises me when her voice cuts through our heavy breaths, delaying me from being able to tell her what's been on my mind. I narrow my eyes as I stare at her, waiting to hear her question.

"Go ahead," I tell her. "But make it quick." I curl the corner of my mouth and press my hips into her center, letting her know exactly how I'm feeling. My hardened cock presses into her, and I can't help but notice how her mouth slightly twitches the second I push against her.

She swallows as she evidently struggles to keep with her train of thought. At this rate, she might not make it to the end of her sentence without coming first. "Last night you mentioned something about not wanting a relationship, and I need to make sure that's what you want."

"I did," I tell her, ghosting my lips along hers. "Are you sure this is what you want?" I'm fucking thankful she's thinking the exact same thing I am right now. I slide my fingers farther into her shorts and tease them along the front of her underwear. Her hips start to move against me like they did last night. I'm hoping we can finish this little deal of ours quickly so we can move on to what we both truly want.

"Nothing's changed in the past twenty-four hours, Dallas. My rules are still my rules."

"Good." I swallow the excitement coursing through me, knowing there are only two more points I need to confirm with Sloan before we can keep going. "You have your rules, and I have mine."

She immediately shifts her eyes up to mine, gazing at me with hooded eyes. She keeps a fistful of my shirt in one hand but starts to slide the other around the waist of my jeans. She scrapes her long nails across my skin, causing a tingling sensation to shoot down my spine.

I don't know Sloan's past as far as relationships or love are concerned, or what brought her to the decision to handle sex the same way I have. I can sense it in her urgency. I can feel it in the way her body moves against me, begging to be touched. Although the curiosity of why Sloan is the way she is lingers in the back of my brain, I push the thought aside, burying it behind my desire to be inside her. My hand simply won't do tonight as it did last night. We need to take this one step further.

A part of me wants to say fuck it and forget the rules I want to put between us. I know I don't want anything more than sex right now, but shit, Sloan is making it increasingly difficult to stick to the plan I have laid out for tonight.

"What rules would those be?" she asks.

I move my fingers down the front of her underwear until I've reached her center. She's already soaked through the thin mesh fabric.

I smirk. "You're already fucking wet for me, so I'll only say them once."

Her eyelids flutter before closing. She tips her head back and slowly swipes her tongue across her lips.

"Open your eyes," I command. "Keep them on me."

Her eyes slowly open with my order. At first, they open wide, as if she's challenging me again, but as I move my fingers faster along her wet center, she relaxes into me. Her eyes soften as her hips rock against me, moving in rhythm with my fingers.

"Rule number one," I tell her. "We keep this strictly about sex. Nothing more, nothing less. And we don't talk about it at work."

She bites down on her bottom lip then pops it out from under her teeth. "Agreed." The word is spoken on a heavy sigh as she tilts her head into my other hand resting on her cheek.

"Rule number two." I stop moving my fingers and remove my hand from between her legs. Disappointment immediately takes over her expression. I grip her jaw with my fingertips, being sure not to be too rough with her but strong enough to let her know this is the most important rule. Her eyes are laser focused on mine as I press the pad of my thumb into her bottom lip. "You don't ask me about my past. Ever."

Her eyes shift between mine as she understands what I mean. Her neck dips as she swallows, digesting my words. In a way, I guess my rule could come across as selfish. I know more about Sloan than I realize, and considering the game we played when we went to the furniture store, it seems contradictory to be telling her this. It's a game I willingly played, even sharing the details of how my mother ran away with me and Vada before it was even legal for her to drink.

I still haven't moved my hand, returning it to her warm center. Instead, we're both frozen, allowing my unwritten rules to toss around between us. She considers me for a moment, and every thought is clearly written in her expression. She's wondering how tragic my past must be for me to give a rule such as this one, but some things are better left unsaid. Sloan doesn't need to know, just as much as I don't need to know hers. I know there's more to her past than her lack of relationship with Ellie. Sloan's scars aren't well hidden. Instead, she attempts to hide her pain behind her urge to change the interior of her house and busying herself at my restaurant.

As tempting as it might be to ask her, I won't. I may want to keep whatever this is between us strictly down to sex, but I'm not a hypocrite.

"Do you agree?" I ask her, returning my fingers between her legs.

"Yes."

I take her one-word answer, not wasting another minute. The corner of her mouth curls just before I claim it. I slam my lips against hers, immediately coaxing them open with my tongue. The piano emits an obnoxious tune once again as Sloan shifts her body under mine. Her legs tighten around me, keeping me pressed against her. My hardened cock presses up against her hot, wet center, and I'm wishing I had completely removed her shorts and underwear before reaching our agreement to my rules.

Her mouth tastes sweet and I breathe in, taking all of Sloan in. Her scent is a mixture of the smoke from our barbecue and her vanilla lip balm. Her soft, supple lips mold to mine as I slide my hands along her thighs, reaching under the ends of her shorts. Her back arches up and her swollen breasts peek out of the top of her tank top. One of her hands reaches up behind my neck. She grabs a fistful of my hair and tugs on the ends, urging me to move downward.

I try not to waste any more time. I want to savor this feeling, the feeling of Sloan beneath me, her want for me clearly soaking into her underwear, showing me just how ready she is—but I decide not to.

I bite down on Sloan's bottom lip before pulling away from her. I lean back far enough for her to get a clear view of my face. She relaxes her legs around mine as I stand, straightening my back. Her ankles still rest on the back of my calves.

"Don't move off the piano." I point to the keys on either side of her. "Put your hands at your sides and lift your ass off the keys."

She doesn't question me and places her hands against the keys beside her. She pushes herself up high enough to where her ass is no longer resting on them. I bend down and slide my hands around her waist to her back. I grab the hem of her shorts and pull them down, making sure to grab her panties as well. Once I've gotten her shorts past her full round cheeks, she lowers herself back down onto the piano.

"Open your legs," I tell her, sliding each of my hands along her thighs, pulling them apart. She follows each of my commands without hesitation. I fucking love it.

I step between her legs and drag a finger down her middle, starting with her chest. I trace over the top of each of her swollen breasts before moving farther down. When I reach her hot center, she moans, tipping her head back.

"Dallas." My name escapes from her mouth as she keeps her hands at her sides.

I only circle my fingers across her clit a few more times before kneeling in front of her. Once I'm perfectly centered, I lift one of her legs, resting it over my shoulder. Looking up at her, I find her staring straight back at me. Her chest dramatically rises and falls as if she's anticipating my next move. She knows exactly what I'm about to do, and I can practically feel her body humming against mine.

I lean forward without breaking my eyes away from hers. My mouth meets her warm, wet skin. She tastes sweet, like the lip balm she was wearing on her lips.

"Oh, fuck."

Once Sloan's words fall from her mouth, she tries to pull back slightly, lifting her hips off the keys of the piano. I hold her, wrapping my arms around her legs and resting my hands on her thighs. I slide my tongue up and down her center, circling her clit. Her legs start to vibrate around my shoulders. She reaches down and threads her fingers through my hair, tugging on the ends.

In truth, it's been a while since I've been with a woman this way. Usually, we get straight to the point, not bothering to waste any time in between, and if we do, usually it's the other way around, with her mouth on me instead of mine on her. It's not that the thought of having Sloan's mouth wrapped around my cock doesn't thrill me, but there is something in the way Sloan's body reacts to my touch. I want to know how far I can push her, how far she's willing to go. There is also a part of me that is even more excited by what it looked like to see her coming undone with me being the cause of it.

Her hips rock against me, pressing my face harder into her clit. The faster I move my mouth, the faster she moves against me, and the closer she gets to falling apart around me. As much as I'm willing to see that now, I pull away from Sloan before she completely unravels.

She immediately looks down when I pull away. I pull myself to a stand in front of her. I drag my tongue across my lips, tasting what's left behind of her on my mouth.

"What are you doing?" Her breath is ragged, and her hair is cascading down her shoulders, resting on top of her swollen breasts. Her eyebrows dip, both confused and angered by my sudden absence.

But we're far too clothed to be having this conversation, and there is no fucking way I can keep this going without seeing all of her.

I swipe my thumb across my wet lip then reach out to touch Sloan's.

"Do you trust me?" I ask her.

"Yes." She nods and tilts her head. She slides one of her own hands down her chest until she reaches her center, sliding her fingers between her legs. Her fingers start to move in slow circles.

Holy shit. I've never seen a woman as confident, bold, and

fucking sexy as Sloan is right now. My cock strains against the constriction my jeans are putting on it.

"Do you trust me?" she asks with a heavy breath. Fuck, she's about to rob me of what I've been wanting to give her, what I held back from her only seconds ago. Her fingers start to move faster.

I give her a small chuckle and smirk. "Yes."

"Good," she says, narrowing her eyes and pulling her hand away. "Then I need your hands on me. Now."

Her thumb rises to her mouth, and she bites down. She's tasting herself, and that one single gesture alone is enough to make me nearly explode.

Her legs are still spread open, and I step forward, filling the space between them. Leaning down, I crash my mouth against hers, claiming it with every excited nerve pulsating through me.

Her back hits the piano with me towering over her. Both of my arms are at her sides, and I'm standing right above her. Her head is tilted back as she looks up to keep our mouths connected. She moans against me, her mouth vibrating on mine.

I wrap my hand around her back, pulling her off the piano. I truly don't care either way if it's ruined with the way she's sitting on it. There is no sentimental value in it, and although I got it in college, it only cost me fifty dollars. Nonetheless, I know it probably isn't comfortable for her to be sitting on the multiple keys, and we don't need the constant sounds echoing off the walls. I spin us around and walk Sloan backward until her back presses up against the wall beside the piano.

My hips press into hers as she lifts her arms above her head. I grab the hem of her tank top and remove it, tossing it behind me. Sloan's breasts are on perfect display under the thin lace fabric of her bra. It's a simple one that doesn't shy away from allowing me to see nearly all of the two smooth, round peaks.

Her nipples are clearly visible through the mesh fabric, cresting to two hard pebbles against my touch. I bend my head down far enough to press my lips to her nipple. I drag my teeth across the small, tight pebble. She gasps, gripping the back of my head, keeping my mouth pressed against her chest. I pull her nipple into my mouth and circle my tongue around it a few times before letting it go. The mesh grates across my tongue, but Sloan's reaction to my move is evident when she moans once again.

I reach behind her and unhook it. She allows the straps to fall away from her shoulders and slide away from her body without effort. She's now completely undressed, and she reaches forward and unbuttons my jeans, removing the rest of my clothes as well. My cock sticks straight out once it's free from my constrictive clothes.

I drag my finger along the top of her breast before pinching her nipple between two fingers. My cock presses against her lower belly as she gasps, tilting her head back against the wall. She lifts one leg up, wrapping it around the back of mine. I lift her up, holding her body against the wall with my torso.

"Dallas." She threads her fingers through my hair again, pulling on the ends long enough to bring my gaze up to hers. She stares directly into my eyes, her eyes sparking with the same energy I feel inside me. "I know I said I need your hands on me, but I lied."

I almost stop and pull away from Sloan. The deal between us might just be sex and there's no possibility of us being in a relationship, but there is no way I will go into this deal with Sloan if it isn't what she wants. I am only in it if she is. We both need to be on the same page, and if she were to ever want to back out, I wouldn't stop her.

I open my mouth to ask her how she lied, but she stops me, pressing her hand to my cheek, pinning my stare to hers. "I need you to fuck me."

Oh, shit. Her order catches me off guard.

Match fucking lit; fire fully sparked and raging.

Pulling my hips back, I grab my cock and press the tip against her entrance. She's completely soaked, ready for me. I inhale a deep breath and push myself into her, watching as my dick quickly slides into her. The more I fill her, the farther back she tilts her head. She wraps her arms around my neck, digging her nails into my flesh as she moans. My name falls out of her mouth, her lips making the perfect O.

"Fuck, Sloan." Once I've filled her, I pull back out, watching myself as I slide back in. The movement is easy and almost effortless. It also feels amazing. "You're so fucking wet."

"Harder," she says, biting down on her bottom lip. She brings her mouth back to mine, parting my lips with her tongue. My heart thrashes against my chest and tingles prickle their way down my spine, the sensation shooting to my toes. I feel Sloan everywhere. Her smooth skin surrounds me as I slide my hand along her side and push into her harder and faster.

I pick up my pace just as Sloan picks up her breathing. I can tell she's starting to unravel under me. Her legs vibrate and tense around me. I reach up, placing my hand along the smooth plane of her jaw, bringing her eyes to mine.

"Come for me," I tell her. I need her to or else I'll finish before her. I pull out of her then push into her one more time. Her heart thrashes against her chest and I can feel the echo of it beat against mine. With my other hand, I reach under her, gripping firmly. Her full, round cheek fills my palm, and I grasp her flesh, holding her against me.

"Oh my god, Dallas. I'm coming," she yells, tipping her head back. I press my mouth against her neck, tasting her as her body shudders beneath me.

Having Sloan's body vibrate against mine as she rides out the rest of her orgasm sparks mine. Bursts of electricity shoot across me and I start to cum. I pull myself out of her just in time, shooting my cum at her lower stomach, beneath her belly button. The warm liquid drips down her smooth, tan skin. I normally don't like to finish this way, but Sloan and I didn't discuss birth control means, and I didn't bother checking to see if I had any condoms left.

"Shit." I breathe out, burying my face into her shoulder as I finish.

Sloan's hand slides down the back of my neck and across my shoulder. Her legs relax as I pull away from her, her toes landing on the hardwood floor beneath our feet.

"I'm sorry," I tell her as she looks down at her stomach. "We didn't use a condom and I didn't think to ask you about birth control. I didn't know what else to do."

"It's okay," she says, the corner of her mouth curling into a smirk. Her neck is flushed as she comes down from her orgasm. My legs thrum with the echo of the memory of my own.

I look back down at Sloan's entire body. Seeing my cum splashed across her stomach spurs this feeling inside me, but I push it back and leave her to grab a paper towel from the kitchen. I quickly run it under the sink then return to where she's standing. She takes it from me and gently wipes it away.

"It doesn't bother me." She looks up at me once she's finished. "But for future reference, I'm on birth control." She steps onto the tips of her toes and places her lips on mine. It's a quick kiss, more like one of appreciation than the romantic kind. She leaves me standing in the front room before heading back to the kitchen. She's still completely naked. I watch her as her long brown hair sways across her shoulders, the ends dancing across the middle of her back with every step she takes.

My dick hardens again at the sight of her, so I follow her into the kitchen. I round the corner as she tosses the paper towel into the trash. She spins around and leans back onto the counter, resting her elbows on the edge.

Her breasts are on full display. She puffs out her chest, the cool air in my house perking her nipples up. I step forward, admiring how she's standing. She is clearly enjoying this new deal we've made. It's as if we've finally given ourselves permission to do what we've both been wanting to do for weeks, just without all the fluff and mess that comes with normal relationships. What Sloan and I are doing is simple and uncomplicated.

Sloan drags the tips of her fingers across her stomach in the same place where I allowed my orgasm to spill. Her eyes travel along my body, taking me in. It's as if she's imagining me as she touches herself.

She smiles, displaying her perfect white teeth. Although Sloan and I have our unofficial rules set out between us, it doesn't mean I can't appreciate her. She is fucking gorgeous, and from the way her eyes flicker as she looks at me, she knows exactly what I'm thinking.

"So, Dallas," she says. "Are you going to stand there and watch, or are you going to come over here? Please don't tell me you have another rule to lay out." Her full lips curl into a devious smile when I step forward, crossing the kitchen to meet her.

"No." I shake my head, covering her hand with mine. I guide hers down to her center, pressing her fingers over her clit. She hisses, closing her eyes with the sensation. "Those are the only rules. I think we've pretty much covered them all."

I lean forward and claim her mouth with mine as both our hands work her swollen clit. She's already wet again, and the memory of what it feels like to be inside her rushes through me.

Yeah, these rules are perfect. No revisions needed.

CHAPTER FOURTEEN

Sloan

I CRACKED.

I said I wasn't going to take it there, but I did.

Maybe it's because Dallas had his own rules, placing extra boundaries on the ones I already had set between us. That made it easy to give in.

Of course, Dallas made it easy by simply being himself. I'm having an increasingly hard time pushing him away, struggling to keep him at a distance. I'm also not entirely sure I want to.

It's been nearly six months since I've slept with a man. I say 'a' man, but Cole was only the second man I had ever slept with up until tonight when I had sex with Dallas. In high school, I lost my virginity to a guy I hung out with at a party. He was nice, but I knew that was all there was between us. He was my first, but I certainly wasn't his. I never saw him after that. It truly didn't bother me since I ended up meeting Cole that fall anyway.

With Cole, our sex life had become routine and redundant. It was like pulling teeth to even get him to touch me or try new things. In hindsight, looking back on it now, it was only because he was too exhausted from having sex with my best friend to try to put in any extra effort with me.

So, when it came to Dallas' hands on me a few hours ago, it was like I couldn't stop. I didn't want him to stop. I'd had one taste, and I knew it wasn't going to be enough. He touched me in a way that was intentional.

He wanted me just as badly as I wanted him.

Although we aren't romantic in the way a couple would be, there is still a romantic notion in the idea that he wants me purely for me, not out of obligation. It feels nice to be the one desired.

Dallas' rules weren't difficult to agree to. The first is completely understandable since that's how I feel as well. There is no denying I want Dallas; I just need to figure out how deep that want goes. It was buried inside me until Dallas finally released it with his touch. His mouth explored my body, and I suddenly awakened as if it hadn't been touched in years. Even the sex before Cole and I grew apart wasn't as intense as it was with Dallas.

This is an entirely different feeling, or maybe it isn't since I haven't slept with a man in months. That conclusion isn't entirely clear, but I don't care.

My arms and legs are Jell-O. My muscles ache in the best way possible. My breasts are sore from Dallas' mouth tugging, licking, and pulling on them. The memory of his cock inside me echoes from the inside out. Goosebumps prickle down my skin as I remember the multiple orgasms I was given tonight. Every feeling hits me one after the other.

After Dallas and I moved from the piano to the kitchen, we moved again to his room. There was no denying I was thankful we moved to a place a bit more comfortable and one where I was able to relax afterward, but it was a place I didn't think he would want to go to. Dallas has many secrets, and there's a reason his second rule is to never ask about his past. A part of me questions why it's a rule to begin with. No doubt the answer is buried somewhere here in the walls of his house, but I trust Dallas enough not to go snooping or asking questions I'm not sure I want to know the answer to.

When I crack my eyes open, the only source of light is from the moon pouring through the two windows behind me. There are no pictures in Dallas' room, not even a single decoration. The walls are painted a deep dark green. Placed along the far wall are two tall black dressers. It's a very masculine room filled with rich, dark colors, but something feels empty. It's as if his color choice makes up for the lack of furniture and decorations.

I turn my head to find Dallas sleeping beside me. The only fabric covering his body is the bed sheet over his lower half. His hardened, muscular chest rises and falls with his drowsy breaths. His dark eyelashes rest on his all-too-perfectly sculpted cheekbones, and his hair rests across his forehead. It's a gorgeous messy mop on the top of his head.

I move my arm, ready to reach out and wrap it around his waist. But I stop, remembering our rules. Girlfriends cuddle with their boyfriends after sex. Girlfriends also spend the night at their boyfriend's house. Two people who've struck a deal with one another to make this as uncomplicated as possible do not do those things. Dallas and I aren't at that level, and, fighting every instinct in me, I stop myself.

I sit up, holding the sheet to my chest, covering myself. I take it with me as I turn. The sheet slides across Dallas' body, but he doesn't make a sound. He simply turns away from me before I hear his breathing even out again. I pause, making sure I haven't woken him, and attempt to move again.

I inch my way out of the bed, allowing the sheet to fall away behind me. I tiptoe out of Dallas' room and head downstairs to where my clothes are still in a pile in the middle of the floor along with my phone. I quickly slide into my shorts and tank top, not bothering to put on my underwear. Instead, I bundle them inside my plaid shirt. I'm still sore, and a hot shower sounds like the perfect remedy before falling asleep in my own bed.

I successfully and quietly shut Dallas' front door behind me, leaving him to sleep in his bed without waking him.

When I step outside, the night sky is still fully awake. The stars pop against the intense blue-black canvas hanging above me. It's amazing how the farther out from the city you are, the closer you feel to nature. Living out here in the suburbs, I don't get lost in the crowd or the upbeat city lifestyle.

I walk with my clothes bundled inside the bend of my arm, crossing the street barefoot with my shoes in one hand and my phone clutched in my other. Suddenly, my screen lights up and my phone vibrates in my hand. Liam's name flashes across the screen along with the time. It's not even five in the morning—perfect timing to sneak out of Dallas' house, just before his usual morning run. I'm sure he's going to appreciate me dipping out before he wakes up.

I swipe the green button and wedge my phone between my cheek and my shoulder as I quickly tiptoe across the concrete dividing Dallas' house from mine. "Hey, Liam," I whisper into my phone. It's odd for him to be calling me this early in the morning. "Is everything okay?"

"Hey," Liam says. "Why are you whispering?"

His voice startles me even though I'm the one who answered his call. It clashes with the quietness blanketing my neighborhood. When I reach the door, I fumble with my keys, searching for the right one.

I scoff, finding him amusing. "Why are you calling me so early?"

"You don't remember?"

"Remember what?" I'm still whispering even though I'm finally inside my house. I lock the door behind me and quickly bound up the stairs. I immediately regret it. My legs ache, and the space between my thighs burns.

"Mark and I are driving out to see his mom. She's getting surgery this morning."

I smack my palm across my forehead and wince. I'm a shit sister. Guilt eats away at me. "Oh my god, Liam. I'm sorry I forgot." I've met Mark's mother once before. Although I've only met her that one time, I know she's an amazing woman. According to what I've heard from Mark and Liam, her ovarian cancer has spread, and the doctor suggested she get surgery to remove all of it, including her ovaries.

"Yeah, you asked me to call you once I was about to hit the road." He pauses. "So here I am."

"I'm really sorry." I sit on the edge of my bed and lean forward. I press both of my elbows into my thighs and look down at my feet.

"It's okay." Liam sighs into the phone. "You still didn't answer my question though—why were you whispering?"

I sit up and throw myself back on my bed. I badly want to take a shower, soaking my lady bits in some hot water. They are in delicious pain, and with the way Dallas and I spent our night, we're likely to do the same today.

I'm staring at my ceiling fan, deciding whether I want to tell my brother about Dallas or not. Part of me wants to keep him a secret, but another part of me wants to talk to someone about it. I know I can't talk to Vada about it because she's Dallas' sister. I need to tread lightly around that topic with her, but as far as my brother is concerned, he has no stake in the game. No harm, no foul.

"I was over at my neighbor's house."

"Which neighbor?" Liam asks, but then he gasps, quickly realizing I've only ever spoken about one neighbor in particular. "Wait, you mean your extremely hot neighbor across the street? The same one who happens to be your boss?"

I cringe, biting down on my bottom lip. "Yes."

"Wait a minute," he says excitedly. "Normally, this wouldn't be a big deal, but not only did you tell me you thought he was an asshole, you're also sneaking out of his house at four in the morning? Spill."

"Liam..." I sigh, rubbing my forehead with my fingertips. "Can we talk about this later? I really need to get some sleep."

"Why is that, Sloan? What did you do over at his house that kept you up all night?"

I roll my eyes and turn on my side, still unsure whether it's a good idea to tell Liam or not. His reaction is proof enough that maybe now isn't the best time, especially considering the situation his mother-in-law is in.

"Don't worry about it. We can talk about this later after your visit with Mark's mother. I don't want to distract you when you should be with family."

"Stop. Mark's filling the car up with gas and grabbing us a few snacks for the road, so I have some time. Plus, it'll be a nice distraction."

I lay my arm out beside me and turn my head to the side, looking out the window facing Dallas' house. All the lights are still off, his house blanketed by the night sky. A small sliver of orange and purple begins to peek out from behind the tip of his house. Morning is starting to break, and if I don't get sleep now, I'm going to be a zombie the rest of the day.

"I'll try to give you the CliffsNotes version since I haven't slept much and I have work tomorrow. Remember the other night when I went out with Vada?"

"Of course."

"Well..." I sigh. "I took a picture of myself in this super sexy dress I bought after Cole and I broke off our engagement, and since you and I had that conversation earlier in the day, I thought I'd send it to you as proof that I was actually going out and living my life."

"I never got a picture of you."

I grab one of my pillows and pull it against me, thinking back to the other night. "You didn't because I never sent it to you. I sent it to Dallas on accident."

"No shit."

"Yeah. Anyway, since Dallas recognized where I'd taken the picture, he showed up at the club we were at and ran into me in the hallway, asking why I had sent him the picture."

"What did you say?"

"Um..." I rest my head on the pillow and keep my stare out at Dallas' house. It's slowly being swallowed up by the sunlight, but I have yet to see him leave to go on his morning run. "He didn't really give me the chance to explain it to him before he kissed me."

"They didn't have any hazelnut-flavored coffee, so I had to get you vanilla." Mark's voice cuts off our conversation.

"That's okay," Liam says. "I'm just on the phone with Sloan. I should be finished in a couple minutes."

"Actually," I tell him, "I really should go. There are a few things I need to do around the house. Text me when you get there so I know you made it safe."

"Fine." Liam groans. He's slightly upset I'm ending our conversation, but I can tell he knows I don't exactly feel like getting into it right now. I'm still trying to make sense of it myself. "Wait, I meant to ask you—Mark got a promotion at work and we are wanting to throw a small party together with his family. We're hoping his mom will be well enough by then, and I would love it if you could make it."

I wince, the thought of going back to Minnesota causing my stomach to flip upside down. "I don't know, Liam. I'm not sure I'm ready to handle that and everything that comes with it yet."

"Sloan, please," he begs. "Mark and I would love it if you were here. It just won't be the same without you, and I promise you won't run into anyone. You'll just be here for us."

I reach my arm up and rest the heel of my hand on my forehead. Going back to Minnesota automatically brings the risk of running into Cole and Brenna, even if I try hard to avoid it. Everyone knows everyone in the town we're from, and people like to gossip.

But my love for my brother and brother-in-law mean more to me than the prospect of running into the two people I despise the most.

"Okay." I groan. "I'll go."

"Thank you. Oh my gosh, it'll be so good to see you." Liam gushes. "I have to go, but I'll send you some info on some flights so you can book it."

"Sounds good." I sigh again. "I love you, Liam. Let Mark know I'll be thinking of him and his mom."

"Love you, too."

Liam ends the call before I even have the chance to pull my phone away from my face.

I toss it beside me and roll to my side. I can still see Dallas' house now that the sun has risen more in the past ten minutes. There's no sign of movement, and I start to wonder if leaving so soon was the right thing to do. I know the rules of our arrangement, but I don't know the specifics, like how long I'm supposed to stay afterward or if I'm allowed to wrap my body around his when we fall asleep. Instinct wanted me to; rules kept me from testing the stability of that line.

My head fills with too many thoughts for my sleep-deprived brain to keep up with. My eyes start to feel like two heavy weights, fighting to stay open. Then, the sun rising behind Dallas' house is the last thing I see before they finally give up on their fight.

CHAPTER FIFTEEN

Sloan

Bright flashes of yellow and orange wake me a few hours later. I crack my eyes open, afraid if I open them too wide, I might suffer permanent damage. That's the thing about the sun—it feels as if it's suddenly ten times bigger than in the north.

I groan as I sit up, rubbing the sleep from my eyes. Before I can think of anything else to do, I head toward my bathroom and warm the shower.

I take my time, allowing the water to wash over me. Each drop that hits my skin soothes every inch of the places Dallas touched. I stand under the stream, remembering all the places he touched as if they're permanently etched into my skin. I start to imagine what it would feel like to have him in the shower with me, how the peaks and valleys of his abs would feel under the scorching hot water, how my fingers would trace the lines of his hip bones and how they dip into a perfect V.

Imagining him here heats my center, and I know I'm already wet between my legs—and not from the shower. If a simple thought of Dallas does this to me, I'm not sure how long I can go without seeing him again.

For now, I'll have to make do. I keep thinking about his hands as I slide my fingers across my lower belly, touching the same place where he orgasmed on me. Then I trail them farther down until I slide them between my folds, finding my center. I circle my fingers under the hot water, remembering Dallas' tongue lapping against me. My legs were wrapped around his neck, his large hands gripping my soft flesh to keep me pressed against his mouth. Small bursts break out across my legs as I rock against my own hand. I rest my head against the shower wall, wishing his mouth were on me right now, his lips pressed against my hot skin. I move my fingers faster in smaller, more concentrated circles until my legs begin to quiver. I keep my hand moving as I ride out my orgasm.

It isn't nearly as satisfying as the ones Dallas gave me last night.

Once I step out of the shower, I wrap a towel around my chest and walk past the window facing Dallas' house. His motorcycle is no longer sitting in the driveway. He must have left after I hopped into the shower.

I sit on the edge of my bed and run my hand over my blanket, fishing for where I tossed my phone earlier after I hung up with Liam. When I find it, I swipe the screen to unlock it, finding two text messages in my inbox. Neither are from Dallas.

One is from Liam. The other is from Colton.

I quickly read Liam's text, knowing it's probably just an update on where he is on his trip out to his mother-in-law's. After sending him a short reply, I open my text from Colton. I have yet to receive one from him since most of my work-related conversations are either through Dallas or Vada.

Colton: Hey, I know your schedule says you aren't supposed to come in today, but would you mind coming in for a bit before we open? Maybe

around 2? I'd like to talk to you more about our live music night.

A few minutes later, he sent a second one.

Colton: Oh, and I'm having my friend come by too so you guys can meet. He's the one that'll be playing the guitar.

I tap my finger on the side of my phone and stare at Colton's text while I think of how to respond. I'd nearly forgotten about my deal to sing up on stage, and now I'm wondering if this will complicate things with Dallas.

Dallas doesn't yet know that I'm the one who Colton hired to perform on stage, filling the position he still refuses to fill. I don't know how he's going to take it when he finds out, but I figure I'll leave that part to Colton.

Then again, according to both our rules, it doesn't matter what we do in our personal lives. Maybe Dallas won't care at all.

After taking care of a few more things around the house, I get dressed and head out to meet Colton at the bar. When I pull up, I already see his car parked out front. Beside it is a large lime green truck. The fucking thing is obnoxious, clearly screaming for attention. I thought Dallas' truck was bad enough, but his doesn't hold a candle to this one. It's true what Dallas said that day—nearly everyone in Texas owns a truck. I've never seen it parked here before, and I assume it must belong to the guitar player Colton is having me meet.

The bar is quiet when I walk inside except for the two voices I hear coming from the far end of the bar. Each of the metal chairs is still turned upside down on the tables scattered throughout the dining room. Music is subtly playing overhead in the background.

"Oh, Sloan. There you are." Colton stands and walks

toward me with a large grin. It's probably the largest grin I've ever seen on him.

"Sorry if I'm a little late." I'm not late at all. The lie falls from my mouth faster than I realize why I've said it. I'm unexpectedly nervous. Regret ebbs its way into my chest, tugging and pulling its way up my throat.

"You're not late," he assures me, nodding his head behind him to the man still sitting at the bar.

He's resting his head in the palm of his hand as he looks down at the open binder in front of him. He looks vaguely familiar as I get closer to him, and when he looks up, I know exactly who he is. His dark hair dips across his tan skin, and the fabric of his baby blue button-down shirt is pressed to near perfection. His brown eyes spark when he sees me.

Shit.

"Sloan, this is my classmate, Gareth." Colton introduces him with a grin.

I narrow my eyes and attempt a small grin. "I've seen you in here a few times."

It's not that I don't like Gareth. He seems nice enough, but his multiple attempts at asking me out haven't gone unnoticed. The man is relentless, and now I find myself questioning his true motives for being here today.

"It's true." He laughs me off. There is no denying this man drips with arrogance. "I do enjoy coming in here from time to time."

"I didn't know you and Colton went to school together."

"We were in a few graduate classes together last semester," Colton explains. He sits back in his chair and turns toward me.

"Oh. Nice." I sit down in the stool beside him, using him as a buffer between me and Gareth.

"Yeah." Gareth nods. "I'm working on my master's in statistics."

"Studying statistics, huh?" I say. "I never would have pegged you as a guitar-playing kind of guy."

He shrugs. "Well, you never can tell, can you?"

"I guess not." My eyes move to the open binder sitting in front of him. "Is that the binder you talked about before? The one with the cover songs?"

He nods once. "It is."

"I'm sorry I haven't had a chance to look yet."

"It's okay. I get it." Colton sighs, leaning forward to pick up the binder. He places it in front of me and flips through a few pages. "I was looking through them to see if there were any good ones. I wasn't entirely sure what you felt comfortable singing, so it's up to you whether you want to look at them or not."

I give Colton a reassuring smile. His tired eyes are visible behind his thick-rimmed glasses, but I can tell he's relieved we're finally getting this started.

Apparently with Gareth playing guitar.

"I'll take a look," I tell him, sliding the binder across the counter, pulling it in front of me.

"Cool," Colton says. "Do you guys want to try one out right now?"

I trade glances between Gareth and Colton. I can't explain it. Something feels off, but I take it as a sign that it's just been a while since the last time I sang.

Singing is a small part of me, a talent I never envisioned using. If I did, it was only to sing to my students, but this is on an entirely different level.

I swallow back the nerves, Liam's words playing in the back of my mind. I've been building a new life here in Austin, and the pieces are starting to come together. The house my mother left me. Working here at Dallas' bar for the summer. My arrangement with Dallas. And now, singing on stage to hundreds of people.

"Count me in." Gareth's voice pulls my attention toward him. "I'll go grab my guitar." He pops out of his chair and jogs to his obnoxious truck parked out front, moving so quickly he's back within a few seconds.

When Gareth comes back, Colton stands up. "I'll be back in the kitchen working on some prep for tonight."

"Great." Gareth beams beside me.

Yep, this is going to be great.

WE HAVEN'T PLAYED a single song from the binder like Colton suggested.

That said, Gareth is way more talented than I initially gave him credit for. As they say, you shouldn't judge a book by its cover, and as far as Gareth is concerned, I absolutely did judge him.

But along with Gareth's talent comes his arrogance. For the past thirty minutes, all he's done is play a few songs with no lyrics, never once cracking open the binder to see what we could work on. I feel like I'm sitting in the audience, watching someone perform at an open mic night.

Every time I've attempted to open the binder, Gareth cuts me off by changing the subject. His fingers strum across the strings, serving as background noise to his endless talking.

"I started playing when I was five," he says. He strums another chord. "My mom insisted I take as many extracurricular activities as I could, said they would look great on my college resume. Can you believe it?" He scoffs, strumming another chord. "As if a five-year-old is thinking about their college resume. Am I right?"

"Right." I nod, trying as hard as I can not to roll my eyes.

His phone rings inside his pocket. Finally, he stops long

enough to reach inside his khaki shorts to answer it. He reads the screen then looks up at me with apologetic eyes. "I'm sorry. I have to take this. I'll be right back."

"Okay."

He sets his guitar on the stand then heads toward the back hallway near the restrooms.

I sigh then turn my attention back to the binder in front of me. In truth, none of the songs look too appealing. Unless Gareth has actual songs written and prepared, I don't know what we're going to do.

I shut the binder and think about Colton. I don't want to disappoint him.

I look up when I hear a loud rumble coming from outside the bar.

Dallas' motorcycle pulls into the spot beside my car. After he steps off his bike, he removes his helmet, and his gaze immediately shifts to the glass between us. He's a considerable distance away, but our view of each other is perfectly clear.

The sky outside is bright blue, and the afternoon sun shines down on Dallas. His torn jeans are tucked into his heavy black boots, paired with his black bar shirt. I shake my head. The man is crazy to be wearing that outfit when the cement is hot enough to cook an egg.

I stop shaking my head when he opens the door. He's carrying his helmet in one of his hands, and he sets it down on the counter when he reaches me.

Despite all the hours, minutes, and seconds since the last time I saw Dallas early this morning, nothing has prepared me for how I'm feeling in this moment. I haven't thought about how it would feel, knowing I snuck out this morning. All I've been able to think about is how incredible last night was.

Every memory of it comes flooding back, heating my skin like the unforgiving sun outside.

"Hey." There's a slight tilt to the corner of his mouth, but then his expression shifts as his eyebrows knit together.

"Hey." Seeing Dallas for the first time since this morning feels different, at least it does for me. My heart thrashes in my chest, bouncing around like one of those old alarm clocks, rocking back and forth.

"I was surprised you left so early this morning." He plays his statement off as indifferent, not caring whether I did or not, more of an observation than any form of concern.

"I thought this was part of rule number one, to not let this interfere with our work."

"We aren't working right now," Dallas says, his eyes moving around the empty bar. The dining room is empty aside from the both of us, and Gareth is still tucked away in the back on his phone call.

"Whatever." I roll my eyes and give him a small smile. "I wasn't entirely sure where we stood on that topic. I thought you would rather have me leave. Isn't that what you do in arrangements such as ours?"

His sculpted jaw twists in thought, considering my answer. "You have a point. But I can't deny that I was slightly disappointed to find you had snuck out." He takes a step closer to me and leans on the counter beside him, using his elbow to prop him up.

"Really?" I ask, surprised by his confession.

"Let's just say in the future, sleeping over is optional." He smirks, and fuck if it doesn't make me want to lunge forward, claiming his mouth with mine. But I bite back the feeling, thinking back to our first rule.

"Okay." I swallow.

"Glad we cleared that up." Dallas steps even closer to me as his eyes shift down to the binder I'm still holding in my hand. He points to it.

"What's that?"

"Oh." I shift my gaze down then swing it back to his. "It's nothing, really. Just a bunch of cover songs."

"For what?"

"For me…" I pinch my bottom lip between my teeth, unsure of how to answer him. "For me to look over." It's the only answer I'm able to come up with.

From the looks of it, he doesn't know I'm the one Colton has suggested takes the position, but I can't see a reason why he wouldn't want him to know either.

He steps closer to me, eliminating the remaining space between us. His heated breath mingles with mine as he pinches a chunk of my hair between his fingers, tucking the strands behind my ear.

"Look over for what?" His forehead creases in thought. He's poking and prodding, coaxing an answer out of me.

I sigh, reveling in the way it feels to have Dallas' body pushed against mine. I blink, shaking my head and swiping my tongue across my mouth. "It's on a trial basis, but Colton asked if I could perform on stage one of these nights this summer. I nonchalantly blurted out that I can sing when he hired me, and I offered to do it just to see."

"You can sing?" Dallas lowers his arm and steps back a couple inches, breaking our touch. I can't explain what caused him to suddenly back away from me, but I try not to think too much about it. We still haven't put a name to what this is between us, but I know I shouldn't care what he thinks about me singing.

"Yeah." I step away from the wall. "I wouldn't say I'm record-worthy, but I've sung a few times here and there."

"Colton didn't mention you were the one he hired."

"Well, I am." I twist the corner of my mouth. "In a way. Like

I said, it's just on a trial basis to see if I'm even comfortable with it."

"You're kidding." His dark eyebrows arch across his forehead in surprise.

"No," I tell him. "Is it really that bad of an idea? You've never even heard me sing." Anger simmers under my chest at his reaction. I admit I haven't been my own best cheerleader, but Dallas' lack of enthusiasm digs deeper than I expected. I'm confused to say the least.

"It's not a bad idea," he says, scratching at the stubble on his chin. "So, what kind of music are you singing to? A pre-recorded track, or are you singing acapella?"

"No." I pick at the plastic cover on the binder, not sure how Dallas will take the news that someone else will be playing the guitar, on his stage in his bar. "Colton hired someone to play guitar."

"Who?" he asks. There's no denying that his dark blue eyes have somehow grown a few shades darker than normal. Anger ebbs its way into his body language, and his jaw clenches tighter as his body tenses.

"Me."

Dallas' eyes move past my shoulder, and I spin halfway around in my stool to find Gareth standing behind me.

"What the fuck?" Dallas says. "Colton hired you?"

Gareth sidles up beside me, and Dallas' eyes shift to the guitar resting on his stand.

"He did." Gareth gives Dallas a sly grin, and the same feeling I felt when I saw the two of them before washes over me now. There's something between these two men, and now, knowing Gareth will be the one to play with me on our live entertainment night has set Dallas off.

CHAPTER SIXTEEN

DALLAS

AFTER WAKING UP LATER THAN USUAL AND FINDING SLOAN was no longer at my house, I decide to run through the park near campus. It's been well over two years since I've been there. The last time was with Hailey, just after we played a full night of shows, hopping from one bar to the next across the city. Even though we were both exhausted, we sat down on one of the benches. We sat together as people passed us. Hailey sang. I played my guitar.

I pass by that same bench today, forcing myself to acknowledge that it still exists. The trees surrounding it are still there. Their branches are swaying in the early morning breeze, not yet touched by the sun. Everything is exactly the same as the last time I was here, yet everything in my life is completely different.

After my run, I go home to shower then head over to the bar. Colton told me he was going to be there, working on his plans for the next month to drive up business. I have a few ideas up my sleeve, first starting with a new signature drink menu. It's my way of making up to Colton for my lack of attention to the restaurant these past few months.

The outline of Sloan's and my rules for each other were damn near perfect.

Rule number one: Keep it simple.

Rule number two: Don't ask about my past.

But everyone knows there's no such thing as perfection.

Our rules are almost like an undocumented contract. There are clauses in the contract, the fine print no one ever mentions and almost everyone ignores.

Like how I'm supposed to deal with the fact that Sloan snuck out of my house before the sun even came up. Her escape shouldn't bother me. In fact, it doesn't, but that doesn't change the fact that I was completely caught off guard to find she had left without a single word, especially after the night we spent together. Sloan doesn't come across as the type of woman who disappears after a night like we had.

I can't deny I was disappointed.

I imagined her straddling me in the middle of a deep sleep, lowering herself down onto my hardened cock. Instead, I woke up with my cock as hard as a rock and the space beside me empty.

Though Sloan and I have now ironed out the fine print for rule number one, it doesn't prepare me for the person standing in front of me now, or the guitar resting on my stand.

The unfamiliar instrument belongs to the familiar man standing beside Sloan, staring back at me. He's wearing khaki shorts that are a few inches too high above his knee, and his hair has a bit too much gel keeping it pulled back off his forehead.

"I didn't know you play guitar," I tell him. Honestly, I'm surprised he knows how to do anything other than drink and hit on women in my bar.

"Yeah." He waves me off. "I've played since I was a kid. I've never played on stage before, but I can't wait to try it out, especially with a beautiful woman singing beside me."

Sloan turns her head to the side, caught off guard by Gareth's comment. Then her smooth cheeks blush pink when she shifts back to me.

She shrugs one shoulder then rolls her eyes. Her elbow is propped on the counter as she rests her head in her hand. She looks bored with this conversation. I am too, but I can't see past the fact that Colton somehow thought this was a good idea.

"When are you guys supposed to perform?" I ask them.

Sloan sits up and her lips part as if she's about to answer, but Gareth cuts her off. "Colton said he's shooting for two weeks."

I cross my arms over my chest. "Two weeks?"

"Yeah. I figured Colton mentioned it to you." Gareth nods then turns to grab his guitar from my stand. He places it into his case, snapping the clasps shut. "I should head out though. When did you want to meet up again, Sloan? Would tomorrow be okay?"

"Um..." She reaches behind her, rubbing her palm against the back of her neck. "Sure."

"Great, we can meet here again tomorrow. Same time." He reaches out and places the tips of his fingers on Sloan's arm. I curl my fingers into a near fist then stretch them back out. Seeing him touching Sloan stirs something inside me.

His hand falls away and he grabs his guitar before he starts heading to the front door.

"Later, Dallas," he yells, not bothering to look over his shoulder as he pushes through the front door.

When he's gone, I turn back to Sloan, but she's already standing, placing the strap of her purse on her shoulder. She looks just as annoyed as I am, but I can't understand why. I don't know her true feelings toward Gareth. Was she just as caught off guard as I was when she found out he's the one she'll be playing with? Does she dislike him as much as I do? Or maybe she does like him, and she is too embarrassed to admit it.

"Why did you agree to play with him?"

"What?" she asks, stunned by my sudden shift in mood. I can't help it. I hate Gareth for reasons I don't want Sloan to know. All I know is the man can't be trusted.

I step closer to her. "Why did you agree to this?"

"Colton asked me to help out." She scoffs. "He needed someone who could sing, and believe it or not, Dallas...I can sing."

"I never said you couldn't."

Her eyes turn to two small slits as she tips her chin up. "You haven't done a very good job hiding your skepticism."

I pause, not knowing what to do. I do know I want to talk to Colton and figure this out. I can hear him moving around in the kitchen, talking to one of our prep chefs.

"I have to go," Sloan says, bringing my attention back to her. She's ready to walk out the door, but I stop her before she's able to pass me.

"Are you sure this is a good idea working with him?" I wave to the front door where Gareth is hopping into his truck. It's entirely too big, and the color is the shade of cat vomit.

"I don't know." She shrugs. "I don't know too much about him and not enough for me to make a proper assumption. It isn't fair if I immediately write him off. Colton thinks he's a great fit to play, so I have to give him a chance, right?"

"You really don't," I tell her. I leave out the part where the thought of him playing guitar to her singing makes my head pound and my arms tense. Gareth isn't as great of a person as everyone makes him out to be.

"What does it matter, Dallas?" She crosses her arms and narrows her eyes. "I don't have to, but I want to. I want to do this for Colton and Vada, and for your business. What's the big deal?"

I stare at her, thinking of the best way to answer her. A

battle rages inside me. My first instinct is to tell her not to get involved with Gareth and explain that this is a bad idea. The man only wants to sleep with her, that much is clear. But the other part of me knows I shouldn't care.

"I just think you should be careful."

"I can handle it, Dallas. Seriously, it isn't that big of a deal."

"Okay. Forget it then."

"Are you sure? Because that's the second time I've seen you with Gareth, and both times it looked like you wanted to connect your fist to his face. You obviously don't agree with this arrangement."

"Don't worry about it." I hate leaving Sloan this way, but I also can't get the image of his fingers touching her skin out of my head. My thoughts are all fucked up, and the only thing I can think to do is talk to Colton.

"Fine, but I'm just letting you know you have no right to be upset. Colton was only doing what he thought was best for the business."

I let silence fall between me and Sloan. I'm too angry to even fight with her on this. She doesn't understand how far back Gareth and I go.

The silence swells, becoming too much for either of us to handle.

Sloan sighs, and her shoulders fall in retreat. "I'll see you later."

I leave the dining room, but not before I watch Sloan storm out the front door, the binder resting in the crook of her arm.

I push through the kitchen doors and make my way toward one of the prep stations. Colton's standing over a large metal pot, adding several cups of brown sugar. He's making barbecue sauce.

"Why in the hell did you think it would be a good idea to hire Gareth to play with Sloan on stage?"

"Hello to you too, Dallas." Colton's eyebrows arch across his forehead above his glasses. He pours the last of the brown sugar in then grabs the whisk, stirring the mixture in circles.

"I don't understand." I brush off his sarcasm; I'm too angry to deal with it. "You know he's a shitty person."

"He's not that bad, Dallas. I didn't see I had much choice." He shrugs as he continues whisking.

"How so?" I ask him, leaning on the counter with closed fists. My knuckles dig into the cold metal, but I don't care. I need Colton to reconsider letting Gareth perform with Sloan.

"Let me see." His back is now turned toward me as he lifts the pot and moves it to the stove behind him. He clicks on the burner, and the flames underneath spark to life. "Other than working out front and taking inventory of the liquor, you haven't been around much to discuss business. You refused to talk about some sort of live entertainment night or the possibility of you playing again. Other than you, Gareth is the only one I know who knows how to play guitar and plays it well."

He doesn't look angry, and he doesn't seem defensive. He looks defeated, as if he's too exhausted for this conversation. I can't understand why he's acting as if hiring Gareth isn't a poor decision. I may have been absent from the restaurant this past year, but at least I had a legitimate excuse. Colton is running on fumes. Part of me feels guilty, knowing a part of it most likely is because of me. I don't want Colton to feel as if the burden of this business solely falls on him.

"I can't believe this." I push off the table and run my palm down the side of my face. I feel betrayed by my best friend. He not only went behind my back by hiring Gareth, but also didn't come to me to let me know. "How come you didn't talk to me about this before you had him come over here?"

"I did. Remember when I told you I had the live entertainment night figured out? You literally said 'Great' and then walked away. As I said before, you haven't exactly been interested in making any serious business decisions or coming up with new ideas. What's the big deal?" Colton's still whisking the sauce, not bothering to face me. "I've seen him in here talking to Sloan, so it's not like he's a complete stranger to her. They've talked before."

"Yeah, that's because he comes in here almost every night of the week and hits on all our female customers. Does Vada know you hired him?"

"No. Why would I tell her? This is a business decision and has nothing to do with her."

Anger stings across the back of my neck and heat swells in my chest. "Right, Colton. This was a business decision, and you didn't even tell me, and my name is on the fucking sign." I wave to the far wall in the kitchen where our logo is painted, similar to the one out in the dining room.

"Exactly." He raises his voice. "You're an owner."

Silence settles between us, and he sighs and stops whisking. He turns around and leans forward on the counter.

"I've been patient and I've been understanding, but even that has its limits, Dallas. You can't expect me to sit by and let this place slip away when you aren't willing to make any of the decisions or even be present. We're supposed to be partners in this. And as far as Gareth is concerned..." He nudges his glasses up his nose and crosses his arms. "I know he comes here almost every night, but I also know he brings in a lot of business. Despite what you think about him, he's fairly popular in this town. What I don't understand is why you're so concerned who Sloan performs with. I thought you would be happy that I figured out a way for us to have live entertainment nights and you don't have to play."

"I don't care who Sloan performs with."

He raises his eyebrows, unconvinced. "Sounds to me like you do."

"I don't," I insist.

"I mean, the offer still stands for you to play. Don't you have some original songs? I bet Sloan could learn them easily."

"No." I shake my head. "No fucking way. You know I can't."

Colton holds up his hands. "Then that's it. Find me a better solution. Otherwise, Gareth is all I've got."

I step back, massaging my forehead with my fingertips, and put a hand on my hip. Colton's sympathy is staring straight back at me from the other side of the counter. I think back to the last time I played my guitar, and my stomach twists upside down.

"I can't do it. I can't play."

I can't stand here anymore, staring at my best friend. There are too many contradictions floating around the room, threatening to swallow both of us. Colton doesn't feel like he has a choice in hiring Gareth. I refuse to play, leaving Sloan to sing with him. And Colton and I can't seem to stay on the same page as far as our business is concerned.

"I'm sorry you feel like I went behind your back, Dallas, but I did what I had to do. Your name may be the face of this bar, but both our lives are in this place. I'm just trying to make it as successful as we thought it would be."

"You're right." I nod, stepping backward. "And I'm sorry I haven't been as present as I should be, but this thing with Gareth is fucked up and you know it." I spin around and push through the kitchen door leading to the dining room. "I'll see you tomorrow."

RULE #4

Rules aren't meant to be broken. So, try not to break them.

CHAPTER SEVENTEEN

Sloan

THE LONGER I STAY IN TEXAS, THE EASIER IT'S BECOMING to go through my mother's things. It's as if the time I knew her as a stranger, even when I believed her to be dead, somehow pushed me further away from getting to know who she was.

The mystery made it easier for me to dislike her. She could have been the worst human being on the planet, and I was better off not knowing her. Maybe she was selfish and didn't do one single good thing in her life. Maybe she betrayed those who cared for her and stole from those who trusted her.

Believing my mother was a horrible person justified her absence in my life, but living in her house has forced me to get to know the real Ellie. It's forced me to see the sides of her I refused to face for so long.

Since moving here, I've slowly made my way through each room, sifting through the belongings my mother left behind. I started with the front entrance, changing out the curtains and the paint. I then moved to the kitchen, cleaning all the tools and appliances she left behind. Then I dealt with her bedroom, donating nearly all her clothes. I kept a few pieces I recognized from some of the pictures hanging throughout the house. Keeping those made her even more real, and a small part of me feels like it's something she would have wanted me to do.

The only room left in the house is the attic. Three boxes. There are only three boxes sitting in the middle of the narrow space. I pulled one down twenty minutes ago and placed it on the coffee table in my living room. I sit back on the couch and rest my legs on the edge of the table, crossing them at the ankle.

The box doesn't look old. The cardboard isn't faded, and the top flaps aren't bent to the point of near destruction. There's a single strip of tape stretched across the top, keeping the nearly perfect flaps shut. The cardboard is blank, no sign of any kind indicating what's inside.

I tilt my head and study the box, thinking of all the possibilities of what could be inside. I swallow down my nerves and sit up. I should treat it like a Band-Aid, just rip the whole thing off at once.

I start to pick at the edge of the tape with my fingernail then there are three knocks on my front door. I leave the box on the table and head that way. When I open it, I find Dallas standing on the other side.

It's late afternoon, and the large orange sun paints the sky behind him. His smooth hair is slicked back off his forehead. One single drop of sweat slides down his cheek, rolling over the curve of his sharp jaw. His blue eyes move across my body as if he wasn't expecting me to actually answer.

It's been two hours since I left him at the bar after my meeting with Gareth. I still don't know if I want to work with Gareth. I didn't hear him play any songs, and I wasn't afforded the opportunity to even sing.

But what bothered me the most was Dallas' reaction. He couldn't offer any reasonable explanation as to why he thinks it isn't a good idea for me to perform with Gareth, leaving me only with a warning to be careful. I don't even know what that meant.

The prospect of me working with Gareth bothers him, that I know for sure. He tried not to show it, but I could see it in the way his arms tightened and his eyes shifted to Gareth's hand as he was saying goodbye.

Even if I didn't already suspect Dallas' hatred for him, I certainly did in that moment.

"Hey," I say to him, unsure of where we stand after this afternoon. Nonetheless, I hold the door open for him.

He walks inside, and I shut it behind him. "Hey." He clenches his fist at his side but spins around to face me. "I wanted to come over here and talk to you about Gareth."

"Shit, Dallas." I roll my eyes and sigh. This is getting ridiculous. "Isn't this why we have rule number one? So we don't involve work in with this?" I wave my hand between us and move to walk past him.

He grabs my hand, pulling me to a stop. He spins me around and tugs my body against his. "Actually, no. I think you misunderstood the rule. We don't talk about sex at work, not the other way around." He reaches up and places his hand against my cheek. His long fingers thread through my hair, pressing against the space behind my ear.

"What?" I ask him.

He studies my face, taking his time before speaking. "I never said we couldn't talk about work." He clears his throat. "I told you I didn't think it was a good idea to perform with Gareth."

"Duly noted." I raise one of my eyebrows, confused as to why he's so insistent. "If it bothers you so much, what do you suggest I do?"

He considers me for a moment. Then his mouth curls into a devious smirk. It's enough to make me wet between my thighs. "Sing acapella."

I roll my eyes. "Trust me, that is not a better plan." I laugh for the first time in what feels like forever. It's a real laugh, the kind I feel blooming in my chest, the kind that makes me realize I'm actually laughing.

His smirk fades. My breath is taken away when he leans forward, claiming my mouth with his. His kiss is hard and rushed, everything I didn't know I needed in this moment. Every thought of my mother and singing on stage evaporates the second he coaxes my mouth open with his tongue.

His tongue slides across mine as he places his hand on the small of my back. Tiny bursts tingle down my spine as his hands explore my body. He slides his fingers underneath the bottom edge of my tank top and pulls up. I break away long enough for him to remove both my shirt and my shorts. He moves quickly, not wasting another moment. He leads me over to the far wall. He pushes me against it, lifting my arms above my head. My fingers slide between his when he grabs my hand, holding it against the wall. His mouth moves from my lips down to my chest. He hooks his fingers into the collar of my tank top, pulling it down to expose my breast.

He cups it in the palm of his hand, massaging it under his fingertips. He pinches my nipple and twists. The sting causes me to release a hiss between my teeth and heat to spread across my skin.

Being with Dallas is unlike anything I've ever felt. His touch is commanding yet attentive. His fingers ghost along my skin as if it's the last thing they'll ever touch. My heart skips a beat as I get lost in him. It's hard to admit, but I am slowly becoming more invested in this arrangement. The more I get my daily dose of Dallas, the more I want another hit, and another. Then another. I hate that he is changing the way I feel about cutting men off completely, but I also revel in it.

My body easily and willingly bends to his touch. I arch my

back when he replaces his fingertips with his mouth. His tongue circles around my nipple before he pulls it in, wrapping his lips around it. He tugs on the tip of my pebbled bud with his teeth.

He continues working me with his mouth, reaching down between my legs with his hand. His finger immediately finds my clit. I nearly sigh with relief because he didn't keep me waiting like the last few times his hands were on me.

"Thank you." The words spill out of me on weighted breaths.

"Is this what you've been waiting for?" Dallas asks me, breaking his mouth away from my chest. He continues his circles on my clit, slowly increasing his speed. He adds another finger, increasing the pressure, and I push my shorts down the rest of the way, spreading my legs a bit farther than before, allowing him more access.

"Yes." I lick my lips, doubting I'll be able to keep up with a conversation. My thoughts are already starting to float away, disappearing with every stroke of Dallas' touch.

"Tell me something, Sloan."

Oh no. My legs burst with warmth, and I start bucking my hips against his hand. He rests his palm against me. He's still holding my arms against the wall.

"Please, Dallas." I start moving my legs around his hand and point my toes to the floor, digging into the hardwood.

"Please, Dallas, what?" he says.

"I want you inside me. I need to feel you." I gasp, rocking harder against his hand. "I'm going to come."

"I want you to tell me something first." His fingers slow. "When you left me this morning, did you think about me? Do you remember how it felt to have my dick inside you?"

My cheeks blush as he pins me with his sinful stare. At first, I almost decide to lie and tell him I don't, but a feeling in my chest pulls me to tell the truth. "Yes."

He loosens his grip on my hands. I lower them and begin to unbuckle his jeans. Once I've lowered the zipper, I tug them and his boxer briefs down his waist and thighs. His erection pops free, the tip grazing across my stomach. I grab his length, sliding my hand up and down. His eyes flutter shut, and he groans, his chest trembling with the sound.

"In the shower...I touched myself and imagined my hand was yours. I imagined you with me under the steaming water. And I thought about the way you fucked me yesterday, wishing it was you in there with me."

"Fuck," he says, opening his eyes. They've transformed. His ice blue stare sparks like the blue part of a raging flame. "I've never wanted someone as bad as I want you right now."

"Show me," I tell him.

His gaze snaps back to mine and my heart skips a beat again, only this time it takes longer to restart again. It's clear something has shifted with Dallas through the course of the day. Perhaps it was me sneaking out this morning, or maybe it's the fact that I haven't agreed to not perform with Gareth yet.

What I think about the most is if he's so against Gareth playing with me, why wouldn't he just play himself? He has the power to change it.

Without hesitating, he lifts me up, and I wrap my legs around him as he starts carrying me toward the stairs. "Where's this shower you're talking about?"

My wet center presses against him. I lay my arms over his shoulders and run my fingers through his hair. "Second door on the right, through my bedroom."

He leads us down the hallway, placing his mouth along my jaw and neck the whole time. Every now and then he pauses, glancing over my shoulder to make sure we don't hit anything along the way.

Once we're inside the bathroom, Dallas walks straight into

the shower. It's a large square space surrounded by three walls of glass. The back wall is covered in tile, where the knob is to turn on the water. Dallas presses me against the tile wall beside it and turns it completely around, setting it as high as it will go. Water shoots out from the head above us. He pulls me back far enough to get us both wet before placing me back against the wall. Steam billows around us, coating the walls of glass.

"Show me." He repeats my words from downstairs. For a second, I'm unsure of his meaning, but then I realize when his hand wraps around mine. "I want to watch you."

Heat blooms in my cheeks, and it isn't just from the hot water spraying against us.

I hesitate. I've never touched myself in front of a man before. Not Cole, not anyone.

But Dallas is different. His confidence in what we're doing is enough to make me knock down every wall I've built around myself. The blue flames in his eyes flicker when he takes a step back. Water soaks his hair. It turns a shade darker, his blue gaze popping below the dark strands resting on his forehead.

I reach out my hand and swipe my thumb across his bottom lip. "I started by thinking about your mouth..." Water collects on my hand from his lip as I move it down to my center. I slide it between my folds, letting the water mix with my arousal. "...here."

Dallas grabs his length and starts stroking himself as he watches me. I bite down on my bottom lip as I increase my movements. I slide my hand forward, pushing one of my fingers inside myself. My palm presses against my clit and I lean back, tilting my head up. I close my eyes, using my other hand to pinch my own nipple.

"Then I thought about you pushing into me, sliding down until your whole length was inside me." I move my hand faster, plunging my fingers in and out. I think about Dallas and how our relationship has transformed over the past several weeks. It's gone from embarrassment to hate to co-workers, and now we're sleeping together with our own rules tucked into our metaphorical back pockets.

Dallas' breath starts to mix with my own heavy breaths. Small groans escape his chest every few seconds, and I know he's likely to lose himself as quickly as I will.

"I can't watch you like this and not feel you." A warm hand wraps around mine, causing me to open my eyes. My attention is pulled back to Dallas as he steps forward. He dips low enough to wrap his arm around the back of my thigh, lifting it over his hip. I keep my other leg down, pressing my toes into the smooth tile beneath my feet. Hot, steaming water pours down on us, blanketing every inch of our skin.

Dallas reaches down and grasps his length, centering himself in front of me. He quickly pushes into me, slamming his hips into mine. The feeling overwhelms me, hitting every sensitive part of my body. I wrap my arms around his neck, pulling him closer to me. He buries his face in the crook of my neck, letting the hot water pound against his back as he pulls out of me before pushing back in.

I gasp and tilt my chin up, closing my eyes. I wrap my hands around the back of his head. His hair is smooth under the water, and I can't help dragging my nails through it.

"Come for me, Sloan." He moves faster, plunging himself into me even deeper. My legs start to quake against him, and there's a trickle down my spine.

"Dallas!" I yell his name as I feel my orgasm vibrate through me.

He rocks his hips a few more times before he finishes. This time he doesn't pull out of me, now that I've told him I'm on birth control. I wrap my arms around him tighter, surprised by how different it feels with him coming inside me. Not only does it enhance the orgasm I'm still coming down from, but it feels more intimate. The feeling catches me off guard. We aren't supposed to feel intimate. This is strictly sex, but I can't deny that having Dallas orgasm inside me sends my stomach flipping upside down.

His face is still buried into my neck, but once his body stops moving against mine, he places his lips to my collarbone before pulling away.

I lower my leg and rest against the wall. My hair is stuck to my cheeks from the water and Dallas reaches up, tucking the strands behind my ear. He reaches behind me with a grin and grabs my bottle of body wash from the shelf built into the wall. He squirts some in his hand then starts rubbing it across my chest.

He's both confusing and intriguing at the same time.

"What are you doing?" I ask with a smirk.

"Washing you," he responds matter-of-factly. He glides his whole hand across one breast before moving to the next.

"Fine," I tell him. I reach behind me to grab the same bottle of body wash and squeeze some into my hand. With a grin, I copy the movements he's using on me. I start with his chest then move down his stomach. His dick is still partially erect. I wrap my hand around it, sliding my palm up and down his length. It slowly starts to fully harden again, and his lips part as he releases a small gasp of air. The soap makes it easier for me to stroke his length, and it doesn't take long before he's as hard as he was before.

"Sloan."

My name falling from his mouth pulls at the part of me I've kept buried in the shadows.

"I—" He starts to speak, but his words fall away and he never finishes. His eyes are closed, and his body is leaning into mine. I stare at him, watching how he reacts to my touch. In the time I've known Dallas, I've noticed two versions of the man he's shown himself to be. There's the hardened one who's built a solid wall around himself, and then there's the one who shows slivers of the person I assume he used to be. He's vulnerable, allowing himself to open up to me long enough to give me a tiny bit.

But Dallas' second rule prevents me from learning about the man he was before. I'm not sure he will ever share, no matter how much I might be wishing the circumstances were different.

Dallas' hand falls away from my chest and his eyes open. He catches my gaze, pinning me with a stare. There's a sadness to his pale blue eyes. He's looking at me as if I've somehow wounded him. The expression on his face is somewhat surprising considering the orgasm I just gave him. The longer he stares at me, the more I can read the thoughts going on inside him. His eyes transform under the stream of water. At first, they're soft, but then they quickly harden.

Silence falls between us. The only sound that can be heard is the steady stream of water splashing on the tile beneath our feet. I stop stroking him the moment I realize this is it for now. He wants to stop.

He takes a half step back then reaches beside me, turning off the water. All the soap has rinsed off our bodies. When the water stops, Dallas steps out of the shower. I'm still standing under the shower head, wondering how we went from washing each other with soap to whatever this is now.

"We should order some food," he says over his shoulder.

With that, he grabs a towel from my shelf in the corner of the bathroom and steps out into my bedroom, leaving me standing by myself.

CHAPTER EIGHTEEN

Sloan

By the time I dry myself off and get dressed, Dallas is already downstairs waiting for me.

He's sitting in my living room on my large couch, scrolling through Netflix. His eyes shift to me the second I step into the room. After getting out of the shower, I decided to switch into my favorite pajamas, a silk tank top paired with matching lace-trimmed silk shorts. Sure, I haven't worn them in months, but a feeling tugged in my gut, telling me to put them on. Maybe it's my form of sweet punishment to Dallas for the way he acted about me performing with Gareth.

His gaze catches me walking toward him, and he clears his throat and adjusts himself on the couch. I sit beside him. The collar of my tank dips, and my shorts ride up my thighs as I cross my legs.

"Um, I ordered a pizza," he says. "It should be here in a little bit."

"Oh," I tell him, unsure of what's happening. This morning Dallas clarified the rule on sleeping over, but he never said anything about hanging out. Seeing him this way is strange.

This is the first time I'm seeing him inside my house, sitting on my furniture.

"Do you like pizza?" he asks.

I want to laugh, though not because I think it's a silly question. There are plenty of people in the world who hate pizza. I want to laugh because compared to our typical conversations, this one seems trivial. Conversations with Dallas are always intense to the point where I feel like my heart might explode out of my chest.

"Yes, I like pizza."

"Good." He looks down at the remote in his hands, picking at the power button. He's changed back into his clothes, aside from his boots. They're placed neatly near the front door. His feet are flat on the floor as he leans forward, resting his elbows on his knees.

I look up at the TV to see what show he's picked, but he hasn't chosen one yet. The white box is still set over my profile name.

"What's in the box?"

I look away from the TV to see Dallas pointing to the box still sitting on top of my coffee table.

I tilt my head to the side and curl my mouth into a curious smirk. "I don't know yet. I found it in the attic. It's the only room I haven't gone through yet."

Dallas straightens his back and looks around the room. His smooth lips turn down into a small frown before he turns his attention back to me. "So, basically it's a mystery box."

"It is." I scoot closer to him on the couch and lean forward, pulling the box to the edge of the table. I run the tip of my finger along the tape, feeling the smooth plastic. "When I moved in here, there were so many pieces of my mother scattered around." I swallow my words, digesting the confession I'm about to make to Dallas. "But I knew nothing about her."

"We don't have to talk about this," Dallas says, clearing his throat again. I look over my shoulder, resting my chin on the exposed skin as I look up at him. My skin smells like the soap he smeared all over me earlier.

"I want to," I say, lifting one of my shoulders. "You told me about your parents."

Dallas doesn't speak another word, and I take his silence as an agreement for me to continue.

"My father told me she died when I was a baby. I used to ask him about her when I was younger because everyone I ever knew had a mother, and if their mother didn't live with them, they at least got to see her every summer. They would come to school on the first day, bragging about all the things they did on their summer vacations, how their moms took them to all these amusement parks and road trips across the country. Anyway, after a few years of disappointment and unanswered questions, I just stopped asking." I push the box away and sit back on the couch, tucking my legs underneath me as I play with the drawstring on my shorts. "My father died several years ago in a car accident. He never did tell me about my mother, and until her lawyer showed up at my doorstep with the deed to her house, I thought she was long dead."

"Oh." Dallas scratches at his jaw. The short hairs on his chin scrape across his fingers. "I'm sorry your father passed away without ever telling you the truth. That's kind of fucked up. Does it bother you that he lied to you for so long?"

I scoff and follow it up with a smirk. "I'm still working on that."

It's true. I haven't quite been able to forgive my father for his twenty-year lie.

I haven't thought about my father's death in a long time. It left me with a slow sort of grief. It didn't feel real for a few weeks, and then I learned to live around the grief.

"In a way, I'm thankful my mother left me this house. I still don't know what happened for us to be separated or if she ever had any interest in getting to know me, but I was more focused on building a new life after what Cole did than worrying about why my father chose to lie to me about my mother. Honestly, I couldn't be more grateful for the timing of this house."

My throat swells at the thought of what I'm about to tell Dallas. I'm still not sure why I feel the sudden need to explain my situation to him, but the relationship between us has shifted. I know it isn't deeper than the sex we've been having. That isn't what Dallas wants. It isn't what I want. Or at least, I don't think it is, but I can feel the wound of Cole and Brenna's betrayal dissolving with each day that passes. The pain has faded to near non-existence, but it doesn't change the fact that it's still a part of me, a small bump in the road that is my life that has forever changed it.

"Several months ago, I was engaged." I look up at Dallas and bite down on my bottom lip in nervousness. I don't know how he'll react to knowing I was once engaged, and at such a young age. I'm only twenty-two. Dallas is twenty-six and lives a full bachelor lifestyle.

His reaction isn't what I expect. "What happened?"

"I, um…" I clear my throat, the day I found Cole and Brenna still a vivid memory. "Cole and I weren't engaged for very long, but we had been dating for years before that. He started to grow distant from me those last few months. He'd make excuses as to why he couldn't have dinner or come home after classes. Then one day I came home from one of my student teaching days at the elementary school near our apartment." I inhale a shaky breath, holding back the tears welling behind my eyes. I look up at Dallas. "I found him fucking my best friend, Brenna, on our dining room table."

Dallas releases a heavy sigh as he processes my confession. "Are you fucking kidding me?"

"No." I close my eyes and inhale a deep breath, allowing it to fill my chest like a balloon. "Her back was flat on the silver table runner I had picked out myself. He was standing between her legs, completely naked. I didn't know what to do when I first saw them. My mind went blank, and then I just left. They heard me come through the door and stopped when they saw me, but I didn't say a word. I stood there like a deer caught in headlights. And then...and then I just left. It's one thing to catch your fiancé having an affair. It's another to realize it's with your best friend."

"Shit," Dallas says. A tear slides down my cheek when he shifts on the couch, pulling me toward him. He wraps his long arms around me, holding me to his chest. I bury my face in the crook of his neck, breathing him in. He smells the same as me, the scent of my soap still lingering on his skin, but mixed in with the soap, he still smells like he usually does. His hold on me is warm, and a tear slides down my cheek again, soaking and disappearing into the fabric of his shirt.

I sit up and swipe at my cheeks. "I'm sorry."

"Don't be," he says. He clenches his jaw and stretches out his fingers. He flexes them a few times before he relaxes them. "It was fucked up what they did, and I'm so sorry. If Cole was the kind of person to fuck his fiancée's best friend, you're better off finding out when you did than if you had gone through with marrying him."

"You're right." I nod, swipe my fingers across my cheek again, and sniff. "I never talked to Brenna after I found her at my apartment that day. I did see Cole since we shared the apartment together. He didn't even bother trying to convince me to forgive him or take him back. He said he loved her and had been in love with her since I'd introduced them the first year we were together. He had no excuse to give. He acted as if it wasn't a big deal and that he hadn't been fucking my best friend behind my back. I moved most of my things out that week, and I was staying with Liam until I could figure out where I was going to go or what I was going to do. That was when my mother's lawyer showed up, telling me she had left me her house."

I look at the box sitting on my coffee table, unopened. Dallas' focus turns on it as well. His eyes sadden and a small frown appears on his all-too-perfect mouth. I can't figure it out, but it seems as if every time I talk about my mother, a piece of his hard exterior cracks.

He doesn't say another word about my mother or Cole's affair.

"Do you ever think about performing on stage again?" I ask him, thinking back on his issue with me performing with Gareth. His irritation with the performance goes beyond just his problem with my singing partner.

"Sloan..." My name rolls off his tongue, vibrating from his chest. "We agreed not to talk about this kind of stuff."

"No," I say pointedly. "You said not to ask about your past, not that we couldn't talk about our hobbies."

"Right," he murmurs reluctantly. He sighs and runs his hand down the side of his face. "I haven't really thought about it, but no, I probably won't. It's been a long time since I've picked up my guitar, and I'm probably not that great anymore."

I release a small laugh. "Somehow I don't believe that."

"Yeah, well..." Dallas looks down and traces the lines of his palm with his index finger.

"Yeah." I press my lips together and shift my focus back to the box sitting in front of us. I can tell I'm not going to get much more information from him.

Maybe letting Dallas see the broken pieces inside me will help him to better understand me.

"Do you have any ideas of what could be in there?" I ask

him, trying to lighten the mood. His silence weighs on my shoulders as he lets it linger and stretch.

"No." He shakes his head.

I turn back to look at the box. I'm still staring at it when Dallas' hand slides over mine. He tugs on it, pulling me toward him. I slide myself between his legs as he lies back and rests his head on the arm of the couch. I lie on top of him and rest my head on his chest, listening to the sound of his heart beating against his ribs.

The steady rhythm pulsates against the side of my face as Dallas reaches up, threading his fingers through my damp hair.

I don't know if telling him about my past will have him reconsidering his second rule on not asking him about his, but I'd be lying if I said a small part of me isn't hoping it will.

CHAPTER NINETEEN

DALLAS

Secrets and lies co-exist. One simply can't live without the other.

The fact that I lied to Sloan about knowing her mother when I first met her is still staring me in the face. Quite literally.

I truly don't know what's inside the box that sits on Sloan's coffee table. There's no label, no sign of any kind that would give a tell as to what's inside.

But that's the type of person Ellie was. She always left you guessing.

The secret I've kept from Sloan about knowing her mother starts to eat away at me. For a while, I've been able to push it aside and shove it under the rug. It wasn't a big deal when we first met. I never thought I would be this close to Sloan—well, in a co-worker's who sleep together sense.

That's the thing with secrets and lies. Once you're in them, it's hard to imagine a way to get yourself out.

I hate the idea that I'm keeping a secret from Sloan the same way her father and Cole did. Her father lied to her all her life about the fact that Ellie wasn't dead. With the passing of her father years ago, she'll never be able to know the truth of why he lied to her in the first place.

And then there's Cole. Knowing what he did to Sloan sparks a new kind of anger inside me that I haven't felt in a long time. There have been multiple times since she told me about his affair when I've imagined how it would feel to have my fist connect with his face. Cole's secret affair uprooted her life. What made it worse was he was having an affair with her best friend. Now Sloan's rules on relationships make sense.

All those times she ignored the attention she got from men, she truly had no interest, but there's something different in the way she is with me. She's willing to open up in a way she hasn't been able to for a long time.

Sloan is asleep beside me. She feels like silk with her legs tangled up with mine. Her hand is resting on my chest.

I slept over at her house last night. When I woke up nearly thirty minutes ago, my stomach flipped as my mind caught up with the fact that I had woken up in her bed. In truth, I was the one who clarified the rule of sleeping over, giving both of us permission to stay. So, it shouldn't have been shocking to me. But it was.

I don't actually sleep with women. Ever. Sloan is the first since Hailey, and I'm not sure how I feel about it.

"Good morning." Sloan stirs on top of me, tilting her head up to look at me. She grins as she sighs. Her naked body is glowing under the orange morning sun. She's fucking gorgeous. There's no denying that.

"Hey," I say back. The guilt from our conversation last night is still eating away at me. I can't help it, but the longer I keep seeing Sloan, the harder it is to keep my secrets. Which is why I created rule number two. It was the only way I could think of to keep a line drawn between us.

If Sloan knew the man I used to be and how I knew her

mother, she wouldn't be lying with me now, her warm body wrapped around mine.

"Did you sleep good?" I ask her. I run my fingers through her long hair. It's fanned out behind her, the strands resting on the inside of my bicep.

"Mhmm. What time is it?" she asks in a sleepy voice.

"Um…" I quickly glance at my phone on the nightstand. "It's nine in the morning."

Fuck.

Not only have I missed my morning run, I've stayed at Sloan's longer than I intended.

"Oh." She rubs her eye with the heel of her palm. Her cheek is still pressed against my chest. "I didn't mean to sleep this late."

"Neither did I." I chuckle. It's the truth. I haven't slept this late in forever.

"Are you working today? I can't remember if you were on the schedule or not."

"Yeah. I have a few things to do at my house, but I should be there later. What about you? Colton made the schedule this week so I'm not sure what he put you on."

"He put me on for tonight, but I also have to practice with Gareth at some point." She groans against me. "We only have two weeks to prepare."

The idea of Gareth playing guitar while Sloan sings still bothers me. "Are you sure?" I ask her. I don't want to come across as the jealous boyfriend because I sure as fuck am not, but I know the kind of man Gareth is.

"What's your deal with him?" She rests her chin on her hand that's pressed against my chest. She's looking down at me with hooded eyes. All I can think about is claiming her mouth with mine, but I can see the curiosity in her eyes, so I resist.

"Colton and I have known him for a long time. He's been

coming into the bar since we opened, and I've caught him flirting with a lot of the female customers. There were a few times I had to usher him out because he got too drunk and tried to hit on Vada when she was working." I clench my hands into fists. "He didn't do anything awful to her, but she definitely wasn't interested, and he wasn't getting the hint. So, I kicked him out."

"You kicked him out, huh?" She grins, giggling against me. "I bet he loved that."

"You're terrible, you know that?" I grin, pretending to push her off me. I catch her before she rolls too far.

She places her hand on my chest again. "If it'll make you feel any better, I'll make sure to be careful around him. I don't think Colton would have set us up to play together if he thought we couldn't make this work."

"You're right." Fuck if I know if I'm right. My agreement is wavering at best. I do feel better knowing Sloan will be more cautious around Gareth.

But it isn't simply Gareth's past that has me cautious of his performing with Sloan. It's the fact that he was so quick to agree to playing. It's that he gets to sit beside Sloan and play. I know technically this situation is the result of my refusal to play, but it still doesn't change the fact that I fucking can't stand Gareth.

"Do you want some breakfast?" She pauses, realizing how her question comes across. She clenches her teeth in a wince. Her sharp breath in, causes her to hiss. "Shit. That's probably not in our arrangement. Forget I said anything."

She starts to push away from me, but I grab her. Her long brown hair is curtained around her face, creating a perfect frame around her smooth cheeks. Her breasts are dipping into two supple mounds. My dick twitches then hardens.

It's that goddamn orange sun pouring out over her tan skin. "No, wait." I place my hand against the side of her face and pull her forward. She inches up my body until her face is close enough to mine for me to kiss her. I place my lips on hers and pull back just enough to keep them barely touching. My fingers thread through her hair as I slide my hand down her back, down to the curve of her hips. "In fact, I think I would like some breakfast."

AFTER LEAVING SLOAN'S, I head back home to change my clothes, and Sloan leaves to go to the bar. I don't plan on showing up there until a bit later. I haven't seemed to be able to get my mind off my situation with Sloan. It's difficult to sort my thoughts when no one knows about us. We still haven't told Vada and Colton what's going on between us, and I'm not entirely sure they would understand.

Colton already told me how he felt about the way I handled things with Kylie. Even though I know it's somewhat different between me and Sloan than it was with her, a part of me still doesn't think he'd get it.

But I also need someone to talk to. Normally, I don't go out of my way to talk to others about what's going on in my life. Hailey used to be the one person I could go to about anything, but ever since she's been gone, I keep most everything to myself, even with Vada. I never told her about Ellie to begin with.

I can't sort between what's right and what's wrong when it comes to telling Sloan I knew her mother. One day I will have to tell her, that much I know. It's only a matter of when and if I have the guts to.

Before meeting Sloan at the bar, I decide to stop by Colton's apartment. It's been a while since I talked to my best friend, and I owe it to him. I've been a terrible friend lately and an even worse business partner.

I bound up the stairs to Colton's second-floor apartment. When I reach his door, I knock a few times before he answers.

"Dallas." He's surprised to see me. "I didn't expect to see you until later."

"I should have texted you, but I figured I'd just stop by. Do you mind if we talk for a minute?"

"Sure." He holds the door open for me. My boots hit the tiled entrance as I step into his living room.

Colton walks into the kitchen and opens his fridge. He pulls out two water bottles and hands me one. If it wasn't so early in the morning, he'd hand me a beer. It's been a while since I've come over, but that's always the first thing Colton does when anyone walks in the door. He always offers them a drink.

"What did you want to talk about?" he asks, sitting in the large brown chair in the corner. I sit down on the couch and look up at the TV. He's paused it in the middle of a soccer game.

The coffee table is covered in sheets of lined paper and thick books all about statistics. I move one of the papers aside, clearing a space to set my bottle down. I lean back on the couch and run my fingers through my hair, pushing it off my forehead. A heavy, long-winded breath releases from my chest.

"Do you remember when we couldn't decide whose name should be on the bar and we were arguing about it outside my house with Hailey?"

"Of course I do." Colton nods, his eyebrows knitting as he tries to understand where I'm going.

"Ellie was outside checking her mail when she saw the three of us standing at the end of my driveway. She walked over, pulled a penny from her pocket, and told us to flip for it."

"Yeah." Colton laughs. "She couldn't catch it after she tossed it, so it landed on the ground. You're the asshole who lied and said it counted even though it bounced off the concrete. Which it doesn't, by the way."

He's eyeing me over his glasses. Hard to believe he's still bitter after all this time.

"Whatever, man." I wave him off.

Colton pauses and sits back in his chair. He takes a sip of his water. "Why are we talking about this?"

I sit back the same way Colton is, but I close my eyes with a sigh. "I lied to Sloan." I open my eyes after my confession and roll my head on the back of the couch to face Colton.

"Um, okay. Must be a big lie if you're coming over here to talk to me about it. Plus, you kind of look like shit over it."

"Thanks," I deadpan, unamused. "I can't really talk to Vada about this because she never knew Ellie, and she's Sloan's best friend."

"Makes sense." Colton shrugs in agreement.

"I lied to Sloan about knowing Ellie," I confess. "When we first met, she asked if I knew her, and I said I didn't. At first, I didn't give a shit whether I lied about it or not. I didn't expect to ever really talk to her again, maybe in passing outside of our houses, but never more than that."

"Why did you lie about knowing her?"

"Because I figured Sloan only showed up after Ellie's death because she chose not to be in her life when she was alive. I knew if I told her about Ellie, she wouldn't stop asking questions about her."

"What does that have to do with you now? For the record, I don't see why you lied in the first place. We were pretty close to Ellie, especially you." Colton stands from his chair and heads back into the kitchen. He tosses his water bottle into the trash. He doesn't come back into the living room, instead leaning his back on the counter dividing the kitchen and the living room. He crosses his arms over his chest. "I'm sure having Sloan work at the bar doesn't help with the guilt, but it shouldn't be that big of a deal. Did something happen that made you reconsider telling her the truth?"

"Well, Sloan and I are kind of…" I allow my words to trail off, hoping Colton will get where I'm going with this. I'm validated when his eyes spring open and he pushes himself off the counter.

"Shit, Dallas. Please don't tell me she's your next Kylie." He takes a step forward, and I can see the sliver of anger starting to simmer. He's worried for Sloan. "That's fucked up for so many reasons."

"It isn't like that." I sigh, hating that he brought her into this conversation. Sloan is not Kylie, and I've never thought of her in that same way.

"Oh." His body relaxes and his interest is piqued. "So, you guys are dating?"

"Not exactly." I lean forward and rest my elbows on my knees. I don't plan on telling Colton about the rules I set between me and Sloan, or about Sloan's own personal rules against relationships. He doesn't need to know the details. "Don't worry. We're both on the same page about what we want out of this."

"Now I get why you came in here looking the way you did."

"I honestly forgot I told her I didn't know Ellie until I was at her place yesterday. She found a box in her attic, and I'm afraid it might lead her to find out about me, and Hailey. I just wanted to come over here and talk to you about it because I'm so confused on what to do. I don't know if I should tell her now before she opens the box or leave it."

"Do you know what's in there?"

"I'm not sure." I frown, thinking of a few possibilities. "I have a few ideas, but it could be anything really."

"Honestly, I would just tell her, man. Better to tell her than her find out some other way."

I nod, standing from the chair. Colton is probably right. I know telling Sloan is probably for the best, but I can't help the way my stomach twists. My second rule was that Sloan was to never ask about my past, and Ellie was definitely part of my past. If I tell Sloan about knowing her the way I did, I'll be breaking my own rule.

Rules can be bent, not broken.

And I'm not about to start now.

CHAPTER TWENTY

Sloan

"It's absolutely awful, Vada." I look down into my margarita glass and stir the large chunk of ice sitting in the bottom. My squished lime is sitting on top of the green slush. I poke at it with my straw. "Listening to Gareth play is torture."

"Why are you still bothering?" She lifts the pitcher off the blender and pours the slushy mixture into her glass. It's her third one since she showed up at my doorstep with all the supplies in hand. "Didn't Colton say it was on a trial basis anyway? I'm sure he'd understand if you wanted to back out."

"I don't want to do that to him." I frown, standing up from my couch. I grab my empty glass and head into the kitchen to make another margarita the same way she did. I'm only on my second. "Do you remember how thrilled he was when I told him I would do it? Plus, he really went out of his way to ask Gareth to play."

Vada dramatically rolls her eyes over the rim of her margarita glass. "Don't get me started on what I think about that."

I leave my glass on the counter and stare at her, holding back my laughter. I don't know the depth of her dislike for

Gareth, but he must not have done anything too serious to her considering the bit of humor hidden behind her cynical stare.

She blows out a heavy breath between her lips. "He started flirting with me one night when I was working with Dallas. It didn't bother me really since I was more focused on serving than listening to him ramble on about these amazing dates he could take me on."

As she continues telling me her story, it reminds me of the nights Gareth would come and talk to me, asking if he could take me out or if I could give him advice on what ski resorts to hit up the next time he was in Minnesota.

"Anyway, he was talking about taking me back to his place and how he had this hot tub we could hang out in. He said bathing suits were optional then asked if I could bring any of my friends." She shrugs, scrunching her nose. "I don't know. It wasn't a huge deal to me since I wasn't really interested. It was only awkward because Dallas was standing next to me the whole time. Gareth claimed he didn't know Dallas was my brother at the time or else he wouldn't have talked like that."

I pick up my now full margarita glass and head for the hallway closet upstairs. I invited Vada to come over and sift through the pieces of clothing and furniture I didn't want to keep. After letting her pick through, I was hoping Dallas would let me borrow his truck so I could make a trip down to the donation center. She's been here for the past two hours, and up to this point, I've been content sipping on my margarita and spending time with my new best friend. As much as I've been hesitant to put a label on us, I know Vada has become my best friend. Without her, I wouldn't have a summer job, and without her, I wouldn't feel as at home as I do now.

"Gareth did the same to me when we met." I glance over my shoulder as we walk upstairs. Once we reach the closet, she leans against the wall and takes another sip of her drink. I lean against the wall opposite her and do the same. "But that's not what bothers me about him."

"You mentioned something about the way he played, your first day of practice. Has it not changed?"

"No." I step into the closet and place my glass on one of the shelves. I pull on the string hanging down in the middle of the room. A subtle yellow light fills the large space as Vada steps inside. She starts absentmindedly scanning the room for anything that catches her eye.

"We've been practicing for over a week now and we still haven't played through a whole song. He only wants to play certain ones from the binder Colton gave us, and I'm having trouble with those. They just aren't me. We're supposed to play several songs over the course of our set, but none of them stand out to me. It feels like something is missing. You know what I mean?"

"Yeah." She nods and bends down to pick up a red sweater. She places it against her chest, looking down to see how it looks on her. She frowns and tilts her head to the side then tosses it back into the box. "Makes sense to me. I'm not a singer, but I feel like it's one of those things where you have to sing the right song in order for it to show in your performance. It should be in your heart, and it sounds like it's not."

"Exactly." I point to her with a sly smile. The tequila in my margarita is starting to settle in. My heart flutters and my movements are more relaxed. I sit on the floor of the closet and continue sipping on my margarita.

My phone vibrates in my back pocket. I pull it out to find a text from Dallas.

Dallas: Let me know if you're free later and I can come over. Or you can come over here. Doesn't matter to me.

I smile. Since we set up our arrangement, I've learned he's horrible when it comes to messaging me. I'm smiling due to the fact that for the past six days, I've gone over to his house. I figured it would be the same today.

Me: I'll head over later after Vada leaves.

I shove my phone back into my pocket before Dallas responds. It doesn't really matter what he says in response. I'm enjoying my time with my best friend, but I can't help the way my chest flutters at the thought of seeing Dallas. My chest aches to be with him, and I crave his touch.

When I look up from my phone, I catch Vada staring at me with a smile on her face.

"What?" I ask her.

"Nothing." She shrugs. "I'm just wondering who you're talking to that has you smiling the way you are right now."

"No one," I lie. We have yet to tell her about us. I'm not entirely sure what Dallas' reason is other than the fact that she is the closest person I have since moving here. Maybe he's worried she won't take it well, or maybe it has to do with his past. I wonder if Dallas has a reputation for jumping from one woman to the next and never committing. If that's the case, it doesn't bother me since commitment is the furthest thing from my mind. Or at least I think it still is.

The thought of hurting Vada tugs at my chest. The thought of Dallas deciding to break off our arrangement tugs even harder. Each day I am finding it harder to leave his bed. I like the way I feel wrapped up in his sheets with his mouth pressed against me. I've been enjoying our arrangement, but everyday it's getting more and more difficult to stick to my own rules. I've been wondering if Dallas feels the same way about his.

I swallow down the thought with my margarita and pretend it never occurred to me in the first place.

"You're lying," she says, pointing a stiff finger at me. She's still standing near the front of the closet, flipping through a box of CDs. "But it's okay. I figure you'll tell me at some point, when you're ready to share your secret with me."

I sigh with relief. "Thanks."

"Did I tell you I talked to Colton about going back to the newspaper full time at the end of the summer?"

"No, you didn't."

"He wasn't too thrilled with the idea at first. I think he forgot I only started working there because they needed the help after the bar opened."

"I mean, I can't blame him. I'm sad to think about you leaving too."

"Well, you aren't going to be there much longer either, right? Doesn't school start in a few weeks?"

I pick up a small notebook from one of the boxes beside me and flip through the pages. They're all blank. It hasn't even been used. "The first day isn't for another month and a half."

I can't explain it. I should be excited for school to start. It's my career.

"You'll be great. I've always admired teachers. I could never do it." She gives me a tight-lipped smile.

"It's like any job really. You love it if it's your passion."

"Do you love singing?" she asks.

I consider her question, having never thought of it myself before. It's always been a hobby, something I play around with in my free time. I've never taken it seriously, but now that I'm working with Gareth, it's all I've been able to think about. Truthfully, I haven't even started thinking about my class or the supplies I'll need to start setting up my classroom.

"I'll get back to you with an answer once Gareth and I can figure out what we're going to play this weekend."

"I love my job at the newspaper. I can't wait to get back to it. I just have to talk to Dallas about it first. I don't think he's thought about the prospect of me going back to work full time. I mean, he knew it wasn't permanent to begin with, but still..." Vada's words trail off as she sits down across from me and crosses her legs.

"How does Colton feel about it?" I ask her.

She sighs and swirls her drink around in her glass. The ice has partially melted and most of the liquid sits in the bottom. "I'm not sure. We haven't talked in a few days—not because we had a fight or anything. We've just both been super busy and haven't really had the chance."

"Were you guys ever really dating?" I ask her, tilting my head to the side. "I never really understood whether you two were or weren't."

She scrunches her nose. "That makes two of us." Her shoulders fall as she blows out a heavy breath and frowns. "I don't really know where we are sometimes. It's like there are times when he's fully invested in trying with me. Then there are other times when he acts as if he barely knows me. Like I said before, he's working on his degree, which I totally get, but sometimes I don't need an excuse, and I get tired of waiting for him to put in one hundred percent. You know what I mean?"

"Yeah, I do." I swallow, rubbing my finger along the rim of my glass. "I'm sorry it's so confusing."

"That's okay. I'm sure we'll figure it out." Vada plays off her feelings about Colton and changes the subject. She leans forward and taps me on the knee. "Hey, remember when I was talking about checking out a few festivals this summer?"

"Yeah." I nod, taking another sip of my drink.

"Well..." Her mood has changed substantially since our talk of Colton. She grins. "There's one next Saturday I thought we could all check out."

I frown.

Vada glances over and reaches for the glass bowl I placed on one of the lower shelves a few weeks ago. "What are these?" She sticks her hand inside and sifts through the sheets of paper. Most are folded, some are torn.

I lean back on my hands, watching her as she reads through a few of them. "Those are the poems I was telling you about, the ones my mother wrote."

"Really?" She reads through another one then stares up at me with widened eyes. Her curly brown hair frames her face, her big blue eyes standing out. "She was an incredible writer."

"I haven't read all of them, but I think they're pretty good," I say. "I put them in this bowl because I wasn't entirely sure what I wanted to do with them. I've thought about organizing them in a pretty binder or something. I know they were haphazardly shoved into a drawer, but it isn't exactly surprising. She wasn't the most organized person. I may be wrong, but it feels like even though they were stuffed into the desk, they meant something to her."

"I think they must have." She's still sifting through them, reading a few lines before moving on to the next one. "I mean, look at the wording she uses in some of these. I have an idea." She holds one of the pieces of paper in her hand and lunges forward. She rocks onto her knees and stabs my knee with her finger. "You know what you should do?" She falls back onto her ass and grabs a handful of the papers.

"No." I take another sip of my drink. I'm near the end of it.

"You should use one of these for a song," she suggests.

The last bit of margarita slides down the side of my glass into my mouth. I set the glass down beside me and swallow. "What?"

"Yeah!" She beams. "You can definitely use some of these in a song, Sloan. These poems are basically the same as song lyrics. Not all of them, but most of them. Add it to your set list for the night. You'll still have to play those awful songs, but at least with these as an option, you can play one you love."

"Really?" I scoot closer to her, stopping when the bowl is the only thing between us.

"I mean, it's better than torturing yourself another day with only cover songs from that book Colton gave you."

"I guess I could. Do you think my mom would have approved if she were here?"

She drops the paper back into the bowl and rests her wrists on the edge of it. Her eyes sadden. "Yeah," she says, a small smile growing on her mouth. "I think she would have."

"Well..." I point to the bowl, shifting my gaze between it and Vada. "I'll take your advice, *editor in chief.* Tell me which one you think would be the best to try."

Her smile grows even wider, spreading from one ear to the other. She quickly rubs her hands together in excitement and digs in, picking up the first one her fingers touch.

While she's excited about my mother's poems, all I can think about is Dallas and how long it'll be before I can head over there.

CHAPTER TWENTY-ONE

DALLAS

"What took you so long?" I run my finger down the side of Sloan's face, tracing her jawline all the way down to her collarbone. It's only been eighteen hours since the last time I saw her, but it feels entirely too long. I know the decisions I've been making with her lately are walking a fine line of breaking our rules. Well, not entirely breaking them. More like bending.

My hardened erection presses into her thigh as she reaches around me, pressing her hand to my bare lower back. She already removed my shirt the second she saw me. I waited for her inside, in case Vada was still at Sloan's or, for some reason, decided to stop over before heading back to her own apartment. Vada has a knack for popping up unannounced, especially since she has her own key.

I was relieved to find Sloan was the only woman standing on the other side of the door. I slam my mouth to hers, parting her lips with my tongue. Her mouth is sweet against mine and the taste of sour limes lingers. We quickly make our way upstairs to my bedroom, not wasting any time.

She pulls me against her, sliding her fingers along the sides of my hips, trailing them down and across the top of my pants.

My dick twitches. "I don't think checking in with you falls under one of our rules. Does it?"

She bites on her bottom lip as she opens the button of my jeans. They're covered in grease stains and motor oil from me working on my truck earlier in the day.

"Were you working on your motorcycle today?"

"My truck." I dip my head, pressing my mouth to her neck. I thread my fingers through her hair, holding the back of her head. She moves with my grip, tilting her head enough for me to gain access. Goosebumps prickle across her tan skin and her hot breath dances across the hollow of my ear. "And no, it doesn't fall under the rules."

"I didn't know you worked on your truck too."

"I don't trust anyone other than myself when it comes to my vehicles." I smirk.

"Why does that not surprise me?" She giggles, her words a mere whisper. She's breathless as she works the button of my jeans. She can't remove them fast enough.

She slides my jeans down my waist. I step out of them and my boxer briefs before walking her backward toward my bed. The back of her knees hit the mattress and I gently lay her back onto the forest green blanket. Her dark hair fans out around her and her legs move back and forth. She reaches down to slide her shorts off, but I stop her. I take over for her, moving them down her smooth legs. Once I have them removed, she parts her legs, allowing me access between them. I hover above her and place my arms beside her head. My hardened dick presses against her warm center. She's soaking wet for me.

She lifts her hand and swipes her index finger across my cheek. The pad of her finger is smudged with black as she pulls it away and drags it down through the space between her breasts. She must have swiped at a smear of grease I got when I was out changing my oil.

I watch her as she continues touching herself, using the same finger she used to wipe across my face. She drags her finger along each curve of her breast, circling her pebbled nipple.

I lean down and place my mouth on her nipple, lapping the hardened pebble with my tongue. I pull back just enough to blow on it. The cool air dances across her skin and she gasps, arching her back off the mattress. I place my lips on the smooth skin of her stomach, feeling her curvy body writhe against me with every touch.

She rakes her fingers through my hair and looks down at me with hooded eyes. "I need you now, Dallas. I need your hands on me."

My chest twists at her use of the same words she said to me on the day we agreed on the rules I laid out for us.

I place my hand between her thighs, sliding my fingers between her warm folds. I circle my fingers across her clit as she breathes in. Watching Sloan react to my touch has become one of my favorite things. Her tan skin glows in the warm afternoon sun, glistening like a sheer shade of gold. She watches me as I slide my fingers down her center, pushing them inside her.

She moans, tilting her head back again. I plunge two fingers into her, pumping them in and out a few times before sliding my other hand along her stomach, wrapping my hand around her breast. I pinch her nipple between my fingers. She gasps again, this time releasing a small yelp from her chest.

"Fuck, Dallas. I'm going to come." She moves her hands to reach the bottom of my chin. She tugs me forward, pulling me up to her face. I remove my fingers and place both of my hands at her sides again. She bends her legs, wrapping them around my waist. Her wet center presses against me. "I want you inside me."

I reach behind me and wrap my hand around the back of

her knee, lifting her leg higher to give me more access. I pull my hips back and center myself in front of her before sliding into her. I groan once I've fully pushed my length into her. "Shit, Sloan. You feel amazing."

I bend down to place my lips on hers, tasting her mouth as I move my hips faster and harder. She places her hands on my back, digging her nails into my skin.

I reach down and circle my fingers around her clit like I was before. Sloan's body starts to quiver underneath me, her body thrumming with the orgasm building inside her.

"Come for me," I tell her.

"I'm—Dallas...I'm..." As if on cue, she does just that. She grips my back and wraps her legs tighter around me. I lean back and push myself into her harder, letting her ride out her orgasm. Heat spreads across my legs, making its way up my back. Sloan pulls me down to rest against her chest as I continue moving above her. She brings her mouth to my ear, blowing against it, and it's enough to bring me over the edge. I rock my hips into Sloan a few times, riding out my orgasm. After a few seconds, I roll to the side and fall back onto the bed in exhaustion.

Sloan readjusts herself and wraps her arm over my chest. I place my hand on the back of her head, smoothing the strands of her hair under my fingertips.

"By the way," she says. "It took a bit longer because I was picking out a new song for me to sing."

I can't help but smile. I still hate that she's playing with Gareth this weekend, but despite my anger, I can't bring myself to break out my guitar and attempt to play it.

I realize I'm grinning because she's sharing more with me than I expect. Our rules don't cover sharing the ins and outs of our lives. We're supposed to keep it strictly down to sex. These are the pieces Sloan is leaving without realizing it, and I'm not doing anything to stop her. The rules are bending more and more with each day. I just don't know how to stop it at this point.

"I thought you had a few picked out already, in that book Colton gave you."

"Yeah." She shakes her head and giggles. "Those songs are okay, but I didn't feel them in my soul. I didn't connect with them, if that makes any sense."

"That makes perfect sense." I tip my chin up, adjusting my head against the pillow.

"Right," she says quietly. "You understand."

"I do." I smile, glad to know she feels a bit better about singing with Gareth. I hate that he is playing, but I love the joy Sloan gets when she talks about singing. I still have yet to hear her voice. Every time I've asked her to sing, she's refused. "I'm sure you'll blow them away."

"Oh, I know I will." She laughs against me, lifting her chin up so she can get a better view of my face. She tucks her bottom lip under her teeth as her eyes search mine. The deep shade of blue nearly swallows me whole. The feeling in my chest only gets stronger, and I don't know how to make it stop.

I shouldn't be feeling this way about Sloan. I don't want to feel this way. How can you possibly consider a relationship with someone when you've experienced the kind of pain I have?

I turn my head and look up at the ceiling. "Do you miss the life you had before? I mean, not specifically Cole, just the life you had in Minnesota."

She shifts beside me, burying her face deeper into my chest. Her palm rests on the center of my chest, and I hold my breath. My question is already too personal, and that's one place I swore I would never go. I swore I would never get too personal with Sloan.

"Sometimes I do." She breathes in deeply, pausing before elaborating. "I miss Liam the most, and his husband, Mark.

Sometimes I think about how I used to go up to the mountains to ski when I was a kid. But..." She pauses, swallowing her thoughts. "At the same time, I don't. I don't miss it at all. I'm actually supposed to be going up there next weekend."

"Really?"

"My brother-in-law got a huge promotion at work so I promised Liam I'd go for the weekend. It's supposed to be just the two days, but I'm still nervous as hell." She breathes in deeply. "It's a really small town and I would hate to run into Cole or Brenna. I just don't want to deal with that by myself and then come home feeling like shit." She turns her head far enough for me to see her face. There's hope in her saddened gaze. Even she doesn't believe her own words.

Something comes over me, causing me to say the next words that fall from my mouth. "You know, I've never been to Minnesota. I could go with you if you wanted, if it'll make you feel better."

"What?" Her bottom lip pops out, surprised by my offer.

Fuck. Even I'm surprised by it.

I hold my breath and wait for her response. I immediately realize this is a risky decision, one that pushes the boundaries on what we've put between us.

"Are you sure?" she asks.

"Yeah." I nod, looking up at the ceiling. The truth is, I want to go with Sloan to Minnesota. It will give us the chance to escape our lives here in Austin, even if only for two days. I try to clear the lump from my throat, nervous that I've crossed the line, and then Sloan gives me her answer.

"Okay," she whispers, resting her cheek on my chest once again. I swear I feel her smile against me.

MY EYES SNAP open to the sound of my phone vibrating across my nightstand. I sit up and swing my legs to sit on the edge of my bed. I glance over my shoulder and see that Sloan is no longer in the bed beside me. She's gone.

I'm surprised to see she left so late in the night. I'm sure there's a reason. For the past week, she's always stayed until the next morning, only going home to either change or go to work. It's an odd feeling to not have her here. I try to remind myself that we aren't a couple, and this is the kind of dynamic I wanted from her.

I rub the sleep from my eyes with the heel of my hand. The sky is pitch black, save for a few bright stars. I check the time on my phone and see it's after nine at night. Not as late as I thought.

There's an unread text from Sloan sitting in my inbox. I quickly slide on a pair of sweatpants before reading her message. My stomach grumbles since I haven't eaten since lunch. I click on her text and read it as I bound down the stairs to raid my fridge.

Sloan: Sorry I had to head out early. You looked so peaceful sleeping, so I didn't want to wake you. I forgot I had practice with Gareth tonight. I'll talk to you tomorrow.

I blow out a heavy breath between my lips, Sloan's text reading loud and clear. She's sticking to my rules, keeping our relationship strictly about sex. Annoyance makes its way down my spine, and I clench my jaw thinking of Gareth strumming his stupid fucking guitar, using it as an excuse to get closer to Sloan. I know that's the only reason he agreed to perform in my bar.

I drop my phone into the front pocket of my sweatpants as I round the corner to my kitchen. My bare feet stop abruptly on the hardwood floor when I see a bright blue light flash across the wall in my living room. I pass the refrigerator despite my aching stomach to see where the light is coming from.

When I step into the living room, I see Vada curled up on my couch. A blanket is resting over her legs and her hands are resting in her lap, holding the remote to my TV. She turns her head when she sees me.

"Seriously, Vada. You have to stop coming over unannounced. You keep scaring the shit out of me." I turn back around to head to the kitchen. "The least you could do is send me a text ahead of time."

"Sorry," she mutters.

"When did you get here?" My heart drops into my stomach thinking she might have come in when Sloan was still here. Maybe they ran into each other when she was leaving.

"Not too long ago." She frowns, looking at the large clock above my TV. "Maybe ten minutes."

Thank god.

My stomach settles with relief. "What are you doing here?"

"I didn't want to stay at my apartment by myself." She stays on the couch, curling further into herself.

"What, your roommate isn't there to keep you company?"

"No." She looks down at the remote in her hands and absentmindedly picks at one of the buttons. "She moved out last week."

"What happened?" I smear peanut butter onto a slice of toast and cut it in half.

"I don't know." She sighs. "Something about her falling in love with this guy she met through one of her online games. She said they were getting married, and she was moving in with him that week. No notice, nothing. On the bright side, she paid me rent in advance for the rest of my lease."

"Wow," I say around a mouthful of peanut butter toast. I

walk into the living room and sit in the chair opposite the couch. "I guess there's a bright side to everything, isn't there?"

"I guess so." She scrunches her nose and shakes her shoulders as if she's shaking off a chill. "I just hate staying there by myself."

"You watch too many of these investigative shows. That's why you get like this." I point to the TV where she has a murder show still playing on mute.

"Sure." She turns her attention back to the TV but keeps it on mute.

We sit together in silence for a few minutes, and I pull my phone out to respond to Sloan's text.

I type out a simple 'Okay' then shove it back into my pocket.

"So, are you ready to hear Sloan and Gareth perform this weekend?"

I look up as Vada adjusts the blanket over her lap. She settles in as if she's fluffing it, preparing to sleep there for the night.

"I guess."

"I'm only asking since the stage hasn't been used yet since you and Hailey were supposed to play together."

"I'm well aware, Vada." I surprise myself by not immediately cutting her off. Before, any mention of Hailey usually sparked a fire in me enough to not want to talk about Hailey at all. I didn't want to ever think about her because there was no point in inflicting that kind of unnecessary pain on myself. Now though, the sharp pain that once accompanied the mere mention of her name has nearly disappeared. It's only a hollow ache in my chest.

I catch Vada's stare. "Sorry," I mutter.

Her green eyes widen slightly, clearly surprised by how calm I'm being. "Oh. It's okay."

"I guess I'm interested to see how it fares for the bar and to see if it brings in more customers." I shrug, switching back to answering her original question.

She smiles. "Me too. Sloan seems happy to do it even though she isn't that fond of Gareth. That girl has got some commitment. I'll give her that."

"I know. I tried talking her out of it, but she insisted. Hate that fucking guy."

Vada rolls her eyes. "Let it go, Dallas. I have." She laughs, and it's enough to make me laugh in return. She sounds just like our mother. "You talked to Sloan about her performing?" Her eyebrows knit in curiosity.

"Um, yeah." I play it off as if it's no big deal. "She's mentioned it to me a few times in the past week."

"Huh." She nods, tilting her head to the side.

"I guess we'll see how she does this weekend," I say.

"I guess so."

My eyes shift to the clock above the TV, the same one Vada looked at when I came down here. Even though I've finished my piece of toast, my stomach still grumbles. An ache in my chest tells me it isn't because I'm still hungry. I take a deep breath and release it.

"Do you think there's an appropriate amount of time to get over someone before you're given permission to move on?"

"What?" Vada's gaze catches mine and she stares at me from across the room. It's still glowing with a bright blue, the color mixing in with the darkness surrounding us.

I look back at the clock, and Vada does the same.

She breathes out an audible sigh, one that nearly sucks all the air out of the room. "No one gives you permission, Dallas. I don't think you ever truly get over someone. Grief never really disappears. It just gets easier to deal with as time goes on."

"I don't know." I shake my head, ready to tell her she's full of shit. How could she ever understand? Vada isn't the one who lost Hailey. I was. But then I think about how my life has changed over the past year. Parts of me have healed. Other parts have been stuck, frozen in time at the moment Hailey left.

It's hard to navigate something you've never experienced before. Most days I feel like I'm wandering down a long, never-ending road blindfolded. Then when I'm with Sloan, I feel like the blindfold is removed, if only for a little while. She lifts it a fraction and then when she's gone, I'm reminded of the rules laid out before us and why they're there in the first place.

"Maybe you're right." I shake my head and lean back in my chair. "Or not."

I stay relaxed in the chair but look at Vada. Tears line the edges of her eyes, the blue light reflecting in the pools of liquid.

"Hailey's your wife, Dallas. That'll never change."

CHAPTER TWENTY-TWO

Sloan

Nothing prepared me for this.

No matter how many times Colton begged me to do this, I should have said no. I could have backed out and given him a simple *No, I'm not interested.*

That scenario would have been exponentially easier than standing near the small stage in Dallas' bar, getting ready to play in front of the massive crowd spread out before me.

I've never seen as many people packed into the dining area as I do tonight. Wall to wall, the customers are crowded in with drinks in their hands. Most of them are facing the stage, waiting to see who is playing tonight.

Gareth stands beside me with the neck of his guitar held in the grip of his hand. "Holy shit. I didn't think there would be this many people here." His eyes are wide and he seems frightened.

"Me either." We both stare at the crowd wondering what the fuck we've gotten ourselves into. Over the past week, Gareth and I have practiced non-stop preparing for this one night. After I showed him my mother's poem, he finally kicked his ass into gear when it came to actually practicing the songs all the way through, every single one of them. The idea of a new song sparked a change in him. Since then, all he's done is focus on the music, and I was finally able to breathe a sigh of relief.

Gareth's usually tan cheeks have paled. Despite all the times I've seen him confident, this moment is not one of them.

"Don't tell me you're backing out now." I nudge him with my elbow and giggle. It's interesting seeing him anything but arrogant. Vulnerability suits him better.

"I'm not." He swallows. "Like I said, I just wasn't expecting this many people."

I grin and pat him on the back. "Well, there's no turning back now. I'm just going to go to the restroom real quick before we start."

"Okay." He takes a deep breath and reaches for his beer resting on the small table beside the stage.

My heels click across the smooth concrete floor of the restaurant as I make my way through the back toward the bathroom. Colton is busy working the kitchen and popped out earlier to thank us for playing. Vada and Dallas are manning the bar along with two new bartenders Dallas hired last week to prepare for the end of summer. With Vada heading back to the newspaper to finally start her new promotion and me starting school, Dallas and Colton are in need of permanent bartenders.

I'm almost to the end of the hallway when a hand wraps around my wrist, tugging me farther back and against the wall. The breath is nearly knocked out of me when his tall, firm body presses against me.

I giggle, catching those ice blue eyes staring into mine. "What is it with you cornering me in dark hallways when I'm on my way to the bathroom?"

The corner of his mouth twists upward as he looks down. I

lift my chin, trying to match my gaze with his even as I stand on the balls of my feet.

"I can't help it. You make it too easy."

"You think I'm easy?" I ask, pretending to be hurt.

"I said *it's* too easy, not that you are."

"I know." I grin and rise higher up on my toes, bringing my mouth to his.

He glances around the corner, checking to make sure neither Colton nor Vada are walking this way. From where I'm standing, I can still see Vada working frantically behind the bar. Part of me feels guilty that she's stuck back there all night without me, but it only lasts for a moment before my attention is pulled back to the man standing in front of me.

Dallas wraps one hand around the back of my head, pulling me against him. He slams his mouth against mine, stealing my breath away. His mouth is warm, and his smooth lips glide across mine easily as if they were meant to be pressed against them forever. He keeps his hand wrapped around the back of my neck as he moves the other along my back. I decided to wear a simple black dress. The back is exposed, dipping far enough for Dallas' hand to slide across my skin. It isn't nearly as daring as my bright red comeback dress, but it still gets the job done.

"Dallas." I say his name against his lips. I don't want him to stop, but I know if we get too carried away, I won't ever go up on that stage. His erection is already pressed firmly against my thigh, and the space between my legs is soaking wet. "I should get back."

"I can be quick." He pulls back enough for me to see his eyes spark as he starts to move his hand down under the hem of my dress. "I can't watch you up there all night wearing this dress while you sing with that asshole."

"What's wrong with this dress?" I smirk, tilting my head back to give him easier access.

"Absolutely nothing." His mouth moves along my neck with his words and chills prickle down my back. "That's the fucking problem."

My eyes flutter as he continues moving his lips and tongue across my skin. I wrap my hands around his biceps, fighting with myself on what to do.

"Fuck." I tilt my head back against the wall then roll it to the side, checking to make sure no one sees us. There's no one there, but I still need to stop us before this goes too far, unfortunately. "I want to, but I can't. We're about to go on any second, and they'll start wondering where I am if I'm late."

Dallas uses his mouth to gently bite down on the skin of my neck. Heat shoots through me, radiating across my body. He kisses the same spot then pulls back, groaning. "Fine."

I reach forward and place my hand on his erection, rubbing my palm along his length. We're still pressed up one against each other, so my movement is hidden between us. A grunt rumbles in Dallas' chest, and a smirk creeps up across his smooth mouth.

"Wish me luck?" I ask him, grinning.

"No," he says quickly, pushing his hips into my hand. "You don't need luck. You're going to kill it."

"Thanks." I rise back up on my toes and place my lips against his. I linger longer than I usually do. I can't explain the shift between us. We haven't exactly made ourselves official. Claiming each other would go against every rule, both mine and his, but I can't help getting this overwhelming feeling that Dallas might possibly mean just a bit more than I intended. He isn't a man I happen to be sleeping with. He's more than that. I just don't know if Dallas feels the same.

Either way, I savor this kiss he's allowing me to steal. When I pull away from him, I take the feeling with me, wrapping it up and sealing it away to deal with another time.

I leave Dallas in the hallway as I make my way back out to the dining room and stage. He doesn't immediately follow behind me, so it doesn't seem too obvious we were back there alone together.

Once I start weaving through the first group of people, I glance over my shoulder and catch Dallas emerging from the hallway. He heads back behind the bar to get back to work. After making it through the crowd, I meet Gareth up by the stage. He's still waiting for me.

"I thought you ditched me there for a moment." He runs his hand through his hair then straightens out his light blue button-down shirt.

"Sorry, Gareth." I inhale a deep, nervous breath. "I got caught up in the crowd getting there and back. I wouldn't do that to you."

"Thanks." He grins in appreciation.

"Are you ready?" I ask him.

He gives me a single nod before stepping up on stage. He sits on the farthest barstool and wraps the strap of his guitar around his neck to rest on his shoulder. I step up onto the stage and sit in the stool beside him, bringing the microphone closer to me.

Holy shit, there are even more people in here than I thought.

I clear the nervousness building in my throat, swallowing the lump. My gaze shifts to the bar where I find Vada and Dallas watching me. He fills a glass of beer, never taking his eyes away from me. She leans on the counter and gives me a small nod of encouragement. Colton is standing in the door to the kitchen, a large grin spread across his face.

I take a deep breath and lower the microphone to sit in front of my mouth. I glance at Gareth, and we exchange a silent agreement that we're ready.

I lean into the microphone. "Hello, everyone! How are we doing tonight?"

The crowd cheers, some people yelling over each other.

I laugh, their energy pouring into me. I point to Gareth and then myself. "This is Gareth. I'm Sloan, and we'll be playing a few songs for you tonight. Some you'll recognize, some you might not." I wink. "Either way, we hope you'll enjoy it. Now grab yourself a pulled pork sandwich and a large beer and settle in."

Gareth starts to pick at his acoustic guitar, his fingers slowly strumming across the strings.

"Here we go," I say softly.

As soon as Gareth plays the first chord to start off the song, I open my mouth and sing. I sing for the first time on stage in front of a group of people that doesn't include my brother. The buzz from the crowd expands and reaches out to me, filling me from the inside out. With every word I sing, my body reacts more to the crowd. It feels as if my heart is about to explode out of my chest. I've never experienced anything like this before in my life.

Gareth and I play through the first several cover songs. The crowd somehow grows even bigger. Most of them sing along with me, some even grabbing the person beside them and slow-dancing. I glance over at Gareth during the last cover song, surprised by how well he's been playing. He's never played this well in all the times we've practiced over the last several weeks.

When we've played through all the cover songs, the only one left is the song Gareth and I wrote using my mother's poem. We pause long enough for the crowd to applaud. Once it dies down, I chance a look over behind the bar. Vada and Dallas are still behind it. Vada is still hard at work with the other two new bartenders. Dallas is leaning against the wall beside the kitchen door with his arms crossed over his chest, watching me. No one notices his stare except for me. His ice blue eyes reach across the room to me on the stage. I start to wonder what he might be feeling in this moment, watching me up here on the stage that was initially built for him.

The corner of his mouth turns up in the same way it did when we were hidden back in the hallway. The memory of his last kiss is still on my mouth as I turn my attention back to the crowd and the song I'm about to sing. I silently tell myself to relax, hoping my mother would be proud of me for turning one of her poems into a song.

"Thank you." I clear my throat and scoot myself closer to the edge of the barstool. I nod at Gareth before speaking into the microphone. "Alright, this is the last song of the night, and it's a special one." I grin, finding Vada staring back at me as she claps her hands in excitement. "This is a poem my mother wrote before she passed away, and we decided to turn it into a song. It's called *Torn Together*. We hope you enjoy it."

Gareth starts to strum the guitar, and I tap my fingers on my knee as we settle into the beat. The music fills the entire space, the sound of Gareth's fingers hitting the strings perfectly echoing off the brick walls. Inhaling a deep breath, I open my mouth to sing the words my mother wrote.

I'VE ALWAYS LOVED *you*
>   *It started with the blue*
>   *There you were under the neon hue*

YOUR SMILE WAS *both a blessing and a curse*
>   *Forever scored in this verse*

The pain of what the future held
Would forever meld

I ALWAYS THOUGHT *love could*
  I always thought love could
  Tear you apart, tear you apart
  But somewhere along the way
  We've been torn together, torn together

I STOP SINGING long enough for Gareth to play his solo. I keep tapping my fingers across my knee to the beat. Before my lines start up again, I swing my gaze to the bar. Vada's standing behind it the same way as before, only this time she's swaying along with the rest of the crowd, enjoying the song. Dallas is no longer standing along the wall, but I figure he must be intermingled with the audience, serving them drinks or taking orders, or maybe he's in the back, helping Colton in the kitchen. I try not to think about where Dallas might have gone in the middle of my performance and shift in my stool to face Gareth.

He nears the end of his solo, and I sing once again.

YOUR PAIN IS *mine*
  It always will be
  Because we're not torn apart
  We're torn together

WHEN THE SONG is finished and Gareth has played the last note, I sit on the barstool and stare at the crowd. I'm left breathless, reminding myself to inhale. My body is still vibrating with the same adrenaline I had from playing the earlier songs, but this was a different kind of rush. Somehow, I feel closer to my mom, hearing her words being sung to an audience, using my voice.

The crowd erupts into applause, and I gasp, caught off guard by their reaction. Gareth steps off his stool and grabs me by the wrist, pulling me to a stand. He slides his guitar around to his back, using the strap to hold it up, and wraps me in a tight hug. His strong arms tighten around my shoulders as he whispers in my ear.

"You were fucking incredible."

I laugh, the shock of this moment still jolting through me. "You were amazing, too." I release my hold on Gareth and turn my attention back to the audience. "Thank you everyone," I say into the microphone. "We hope you enjoyed it, and we can't thank you enough. Good night, Austin!"

I step down off the stage and am immediately wrapped up in Vada's arms. She squeals and releases her hug, holding me at arm's length. Her brown curls bounce with her excitement. "I can't even tell you how amazing that was. You guys were incredible."

"Thank you," I tell her. "You made a great choice in picking that poem."

"Are you kidding me?" She steps back and crosses her arms as she trades glances between me and Gareth. "I didn't do anything. You two are the geniuses who turned it into a song."

"Great," I say to Vada, nodding my head toward Gareth. "Now you're only inflating his ego even more by calling him a genius."

"Don't worry," he says. "I already knew I was a genius before tonight. This only solidified it."

Vada rolls her eyes at his comment, but our conversation is cut short when his attention shifts across the dining room. A man sticks his arm up out of the crowd, raising his hand and calling out Gareth's name.

He turns to me and gives me a quick hug. "I'll see you later, okay? You killed it."

"You did, too."

It's odd seeing Gareth this way. He isn't flirting with me tonight. He isn't trying to convince me to go on a date with him. He is simply enjoying the high we are clearly still riding. He disappears in the direction of the man who was waving him over, and I rise up on my toes, looking for the only man I care to see.

"Have you seen Dallas?" I fail in my attempt to see over the crowd. I'm certainly not the tallest person in here. I fall back on the heels of my feet and keep looking around the restaurant for him.

"No," Vada says, looking herself. "Not since earlier." Her attention shifts behind me then she smiles and nods her head over my shoulder. "There he is," she says.

I turn around and spot him pushing his way through the crowd in our direction. We're standing near the back of the crowd and the entrance to the hallway leading to the bathrooms and back alley. My heart pounds inside my chest at the sight of him, thrilled to hear what he thinks of my voice. A balloon expands within me, realizing I have feelings for this man that reach far beyond our verbal contract of rules.

But that balloon inside my chest is immediately deflated when I catch Dallas' expression. His hair has fallen against his forehead, the ends swaying against his skin with each measured step. His chiseled jaw is clenched, ticking with every inch he closes between us.

My smile falters and practically disappears when he reaches me. Vada is still standing beside me, and the crowd has started to slowly dissolve. I can feel it in the air around me.

But it's Dallas' anger that hits me the hardest.

"What the fuck were you thinking?" he asks. His hands are at his sides, clenched into fists.

Confusion hits me nearly as hard as his furious stare. His ice blue eyes have frozen over, piercing me with every second they're pinned on me.

"Excuse me?"

"I asked you what the fuck you were thinking playing that song. Where did you get it?"

"Hey, calm down man." Gareth reappears beside me. He must not have made it far before hearing Dallas' words. He takes a step forward, nearly coming between me and Dallas. "It's just a song."

"Gareth." I tell him, pulling him back away from Dallas. "We're fine."

Dallas keeps his stare pinned on me but shakes his fists at his sides. His jaw ticks. "Stay the fuck out of this, Gareth. You have no idea what you're talking about."

"What is your problem?" I stare at Dallas wide-eyed, my stomach flipping.

There's clear anger in his eyes, but there's also pain hiding behind it.

I quickly glance over at Vada. She's just as confused as I am. When I turn back to Dallas, it's as if he hasn't even noticed his sister. He's only pinning his daggers on me, not even paying any more attention to Gareth.

My heart sinks into the bottom of my stomach and the blood drains from my face. "It's a poem my mother wrote. I found hundreds of them in her house and thought it would be nice if I turned one into a song. I thought she would like it."

Tears spring up in my eyes, not only because of Dallas' anger but because I finally felt truly close to my mother tonight, and Dallas just tossed that moment down the drain.

"I, um, I don't understand," I say, stepping closer to him. "I don't understand why you're so upset. What did I do?"

"Those aren't fucking poems, Sloan." His top lip curls and his cheeks redden, seething with anger. "They're songs—songs your mother wrote for me and my *wife*."

CHAPTER TWENTY-THREE

DALLAS

"What?" Sloan raises her hand and holds it against her chest in disbelief as she inhales a deep breath.

The better part of the past year has seemingly come crashing down on me in a matter of the past five minutes. I clench my fists at my sides and grind my teeth as I stare at Sloan. It's been a long time since I've talked about Hailey out loud, much less said the word *wife*.

"You—" Sloan swallows, her lashes already lined with unshed tears. Liquid pools in her eyes. "You have a wife?"

Her dark blue eyes are two large glass orbs, wide and staring at me. She's gorgeous under the golden lights above her, but I can't help looking at her in a different light than before. Her expression shifts from one of confusion to hurt. Gareth is still standing beside her, and I resist the urge to punch him in his fucking smug face.

"Where did you find that song?" I ask Sloan, ignoring Gareth and dodging her question.

She shakes her head, confused by my questioning. I can tell she wants to talk about Hailey, but I need to know where she found the song she played. She hesitates before deciding to answer me. "I found it in my mother's old desk when I cleaned it out before buying my new one. She had a ton of them shoved into her drawer. I thought they were poems. What does it matter?"

"I can't fucking believe this." It's as if a giant hole has been carved out of my chest, leaving me feeling both hollow and heavy at the same time. I glance around the restaurant. People are surrounding us, and some turn their heads in our direction, watching us.

"What is wrong with you, Dallas?" Vada's voice cuts through the endless chatter of the bar. Her arms are crossed over her chest, and she looks nearly as confused as Sloan is right now.

I stare at both women, wondering how in the hell we've gotten to this point. Vada doesn't know about us, and I don't know what kind of label I'd put on me and Sloan anyway. After listening to Sloan playing that particular song, it might not matter anymore.

I bite down on the inside of my cheek and look over Sloan's shoulder at the stage, remembering everything it was supposed to be a year ago.

"I can't." I shake my head and shift my gaze back to Sloan. "We can't do this. We're done."

A tear slips down Sloan's cheek, and the hole in my chest only gets bigger.

I immediately leave the bar through the front door, shoving my way through the crowd. When I push through the large glass door, I breathe in the hot, humid air of summer. A drop of rain lands on my shoulder and I look down the street and up at the sky. There's a storm rolling in. Large, puffy clouds start to cover the few stars that are shining despite the flood of neon lights of the city. The city swallows me whole, dragging me under to a depth I haven't seen since I lost Hailey.

"Dallas." Sloan's hand stops me when I reach the sidewalk, on my way toward my motorcycle parked on the side of the building. Unlike inside, Sloan is now covered in a myriad of colors. Bright greens, pinks, and reds are cast down on her. Tears stream down her cheeks, the clear liquid capturing those colors. "You can't just say something like that to me then walk away."

I breathe out and pinch the bridge of my nose, releasing a hot breath. There's no point in talking about Hailey because it won't bring her back. All tonight did was make me realize why I've sworn off any kind of relationship that involves anything beyond sex. It doesn't matter if Sloan and I used rules to put boundaries around our relationship. There are always going to be reminders of the husband I used to be and the life I used to lead.

"It doesn't really matter," I tell her, taking another step toward my motorcycle.

Sloan's hand reaches out again, stopping me. "Of course it fucking matters. You came up to me after I got off stage demanding to know where I got the song from. So, I think I deserve to know." Her voice quivers and she swipes her tongue across her lips, the same lips I claimed only an hour ago. Her eyebrows knit in confusion as another tear spills from her wounded eyes, and she inhales a sharp breath. "You have a wife?"

"I *had* a wife." The word *had* spilling from my mouth feels like a knife twisting in my gut.

"*Had?*"

"Hailey was my wife." I swallow, realizing this is the first time I've said her name in I can't remember how long. "She died a year ago."

"Um..." Sloan is still standing a considerable distance from me. She takes a step back, wrapping her arm around the middle of her stomach. "You've never mentioned Hailey before. No one has."

"It doesn't matter."

"Quit saying that," she says, raising her voice. "Because it does fucking matter. I'm sure you had your reasons for not telling me about Hailey, but that doesn't change the fact that everything I thought I knew about you has been a complete lie. I feel like I don't know you at all."

Drops of rain start to pick up, falling all around us. The curls in Sloan's hair start to sag as more rain falls, straightening the ends to stick to her shoulders. The street starts to empty out, the surrounding crowd seeking shelter inside the never-ending strip of restaurants and bars along the street. Suddenly, we're standing on the sidewalk by ourselves.

"What do you want to know, Sloan?" I ask her, yelling over the pouring rain. Water drips down my face and soaks into my black shirt. "Hailey and I met our last year of college, and I knew I wanted to spend the rest of my life with her, so much so that I asked her to marry me three weeks after we started dating. We were married within a month." I swallow, trying to remain calm, but any time I talk about Hailey's death, it feels as if I'm reliving it all over again. "Everything was fine that first year. We bought the house. Colton and I started to get to work on building the bar. But then she went in for a routine checkup and they found a lump. They told her all she needed to do was take a test and she was going to be fine. They fucking lied because it came back positive for breast cancer, and she died nine months later. There. Does it make you feel better to know?"

"Look..." She clenches her fists at her sides. She's completely soaked. "I'm so sorry for what happened to Hailey and that you lost her." She looks straight into my eyes, letting me know she means it. "But that doesn't change the fact that you lied. You lied about knowing my mother."

The rain causes my hair to stick to my forehead. I lift my hand and push it back. I let silence fill the air between us. The only sound is the rain splashing onto the sidewalk. I open my mouth, ready to defend myself, but I don't. I come up empty, knowing there's no reasonable excuse, not one that could counteract the salt I've poured into Sloan's wounds.

It's hard to tell if Sloan is still crying. Her tears have gotten lost in the rain streaming down her face.

"You said my mother wrote that song for you and Hailey, so you must have known her well enough for her to do that for you. Tell me how well you knew her."

I swallow, knowing it's time for me to tell her the truth. "Hailey and I used to travel around Austin, playing in bars and clubs. Sometimes we would go to the park or play at small festivals in the area. We weren't famous and we didn't have a record deal or anything like that, but we were well known in the city. Every song we played was written by Ellie. She was our lyricist."

Her mouth pops open as she listens, stunned by my confession. "Wow." She scoffs. "She must have meant a lot to you for you to cover up a relationship like that with a lie. There were hundreds of songs, Dallas. If my mother was so important to you, why did you lie?"

My words have wounded her even more, like a dagger to the heart. It's as if I'm watching Sloan fall apart in front of me. She is a strong woman, but my truths have hurt her where it matters most—a mother she never knew, and me, the man she is seeing. Even if our relationship were strictly physical, there's no way she wouldn't still be hurt.

"I never thought I would see you again after that first day," I admit. "You went on about how you had just moved in and how your mother used to live there, but in the time I knew Ellie, she never mentioned having a daughter."

"That doesn't exactly make me feel better, Dallas. Do you know what it felt like to find out my mother made absolutely no effort to get to know me when she was alive? That still doesn't explain to me why you lied about it."

I release a hot breath through my nose and press my lips together. I don't want to give her an answer, because I know it will only make the situation worse. "Because I knew if I told you the truth, you would start asking questions about her."

"So, you thought it was better to just lie and never say anything at all?" she yells, bringing her hand to her chest. "What about all the times since then? All the times we've slept together and spent the night with each other? You used your rules to keep me at a distance because you couldn't deal with all your lies and secrets. What were you wanting from this?" She waves her hand between us.

My gaze meets hers, and I watch the tears continue to spill down her cheeks. I realize I want more than the physical with Sloan. I'm falling in love with her, but falling in love with Sloan is nearly impossible when you've experienced heartbreak like I have.

"Did I not mean anything to you at all?" she continues. "Was your suggestion to go to Minnesota with me a test that I failed?"

"It wasn't supposed to be like this." I push the words out through gritted teeth. The pressure builds inside my head, and I'm starting to question if I did the right thing by getting involved with Sloan. My chest pounds with a thunderous ache, reminding me of what it feels like when you care for someone, because the truth is, I care for Sloan, no matter how hard I try to avoid it.

"What was it supposed to be then? Because apparently I must be incredibly confused."

I inhale a deep breath and chew on the inside of my cheek.

Everything around me is suddenly falling apart, and I'm too slow to pick up the pieces. My mind reverts back to what I've been doing the past year: pushing away anything that might resemble happiness. I clench my jaw right along with my fists and narrow the remaining distance between us.

"You're upset because I put rules between us," I tell her, "but don't act as though you weren't using yours to keep me away either. If you've forgotten, you were the one who created rules of heartbreak for yourself first, and you never intended this to be more than what it is. Admit it."

"Seriously?" Her eyebrows arch across her forehead and she steps back. "You're fucking unbelievable, Dallas. My rules were not being used as a coverup for how I feel about you. At least I was honest about Cole and why I didn't want to be in a relationship when I first moved here. I may have had rules to prevent being blindsided again, but at least I didn't use mine as an excuse to lie, and at least I was willing to put them aside because I was falling for you."

"You were falling for me?" I ask, stunned by her confession. It seemed to pour out of her without her even realizing it.

Her blue eyes widen, and she closes her mouth, hardening her expression.

"I don't think it matters now anyway." She steals my words from earlier, throwing them back at me. They hit me in the gut, twisting and pulling until it's painful. She's hitting me right where it hurts.

"You show off your rules as if they're something to be proud of," she spits out, "but all you do is hide behind them to keep your lies and secrets. If you didn't want to tell me about Hailey, fine. That I understand, but there was no reason to lie to me about my mother."

"Sloan..." I inhale a deep breath, feeling myself beginning to crack. Sloan's stare breaks me in the worst way imaginable. "I don't—"

"No." She raises her hands, stopping me. The rain continues to pound down on us, soaking us from head to toe. Her eyes size me up, moving from the top of my head down to my black boots. "Actually, I don't think I need to hear any more of your lies, your excuses, or reasons. Nor do I want to. How would I even know if you were telling the truth? How do I know if you ever felt anything for me at all?" Tears continue to fall down her face. "For all I know, ever since we met, this entire time has been one giant, fat lie."

I roll my head and run my hand down the side of my face, exhausted and hurt by this conversation. Every part of me is screaming out to wrap Sloan up in my arms, but my brain holds me back, wondering how we can ever move past this. Maybe our hearts are too broken to be mended. "I haven't lied to you this entire time. Other than not telling you about Hailey and your mother, everything else I told you is the truth."

"I don't know what to believe anymore." She presses her lips together with saddened eyes. I've never seen them this fragile before. She's on the verge of shattering while I'm on the edge of falling. "You're right." She quivers, moving a step back. "We are done. We never should have started this in the first place." She takes another step back toward my restaurant, her eyes never moving from mine. "Consider our rules officially broken, Dallas. You're off the hook."

RULE #5

Whatever you do, under any circumstances, DON'T fall in love again.

CHAPTER TWENTY-FOUR

DALLAS

Dallas' motorcycle roars out of the parking lot as I make my way back into his restaurant. The rumbling sound of the engine fades as the seconds pass. I try not to look back, knowing if I do, I might change my mind about letting Dallas go.

When I step back into the bar, it's just as packed as when Gareth and I were performing, only this time Dallas isn't working behind the bar, and I'm left standing near the front door, soaked from head to toe. The crowds of people surrounding me are lost in their conversations, oblivious to the storm waging outside. Some are dry and some are soaked, having just come inside. They have drinks in their hands as they tip their heads back, smiling and laughing with one another, having a good time. Country music booms overhead as I stare at them.

"Oh, shit, Sloan—you're soaking wet. What the hell was that all about?"

Vada's voice snaps me out of the trance I've caught myself in. She's standing in front of me near the entrance to the bar, holding her hand out to the street. Her long brown curls are pulled back into a high bun sitting on top of her head, displaying her large green eyes. They're open wide, and her eyebrows are arched across her forehead.

"What?" I whisper. My chest is hollow, my beating heart echoing within the empty cage. My lashes are dotted with raindrops. They soak into my skin with every blink.

"Why did you both storm out of here?" She crosses her arms over her chest.

"It's nothing. I didn't want him to think I'd chosen that song on purpose. I didn't know about Hailey."

Vada frowns and steps closer to me. "I'm sorry I didn't tell you about her. Dallas hasn't exactly handled the past year very well after losing her, and—"

"No, I get it. It wasn't your place to tell me."

"Right."

"You didn't know he knew my mother?" I ask, unsure if I want to know the answer. It's hard enough knowing Dallas knew her, but I don't think I can take knowing Vada was in on the secret too. "You didn't know she was the one who wrote all of their songs?"

"No." She quickly shakes her head. "I didn't. I was too busy with school and the newspaper so I never met your mother. Colton was around for them in those days more than I was."

"Okay." I nod, a tiny, minuscule part of me relieved to know Vada didn't lie the same way Dallas did. The relief I feel does nothing to fill the immense emptiness still buried deep inside.

"Um, I was thinking about something." She twists her mouth as she looks down at her feet with her eyebrows drawn together. After a few seconds, she lifts her eyes back to me. "What did Dallas mean when he said you two are done?"

"What?" I play her question off as if I have no idea what she's talking about, but I know exactly what she means.

"When Dallas came up to you and told you about your mom

writing that song for them, he said you two were done. What did he mean by that?"

"Oh." I bite down on my bottom lip, staring at my best friend. I consider the alternative. I could lie to Vada, keeping up with the way I've been since Dallas and I started seeing each other. Or, I could tell her the truth for once.

After my conversation with Dallas outside, the last thing I want to do is lie to my best friend, pushing her away. The secret I've been keeping from her has started to eat away at me, and it leaves me wondering if I can ever let go of the past. I've known from the start of my friendship with Vada that she's different. It was wrong of me to not tell her about her brother and me. Nothing good comes from secrets. I learned that from Brenna, and now Dallas.

My chin quivers and tears spring up behind my eyes again. The pressure of everything around me is enough to allow them to break free. They flow down my face as I struggle to take in a breath. "Um, Dallas and I were sort of seeing each other." I wince, moving to the side, out from the entrance of the bar.

I push my way through until I reach the far brick wall. I lean my shoulder against it and close my eyes, breathing in. Breathing feels like a chore, and when I open my eyes, Vada is standing directly in front of me. Parts of her expressions resemble her brother—the way her bottom lip pops out as she exhales, the way her eyes narrow as she listens to what I'm saying.

"What?" Her narrowed eyes open wide, and they cloud over with an emotion I have yet to see on her. It's one I know is caused by me.

"I'm so sorry I didn't tell you, but it all kind of happened so fast." I struggle with the right words to explain my relationship with Dallas. "We weren't trying to make a big deal of it, and we promised each other we would keep it between us." I sigh and let the tears flow down my cheeks. I leave out the part about the rules and nearly everything else that goes along with the deal Dallas and I made. I look out the front window. The rain is still pounding onto the pavement as thunder growls across the sky.

"I don't know what to think of this," Vada says, taking a step back. "You were sleeping with my brother, and you didn't tell me?"

"I didn't do it to hurt you, Vada."

"Telling me you and Dallas were sleeping together wouldn't have hurt me," she says. "But knowing you kept it from me this whole time..." She pauses, and tears pool in her normally bright eyes. "That's what hurts me."

"Vada." I push myself off the wall and step toward her, reaching my hand out to touch her arm with the ends of my fingers.

"It's fine." She sniffs. "I just...I think I need some time to figure this out." She nods her head toward the front door. "Plus, I should check to make sure my brother made it home safe."

She quickly swipes her hand across her cheek and spins around, heading in the direction of the kitchen. I watch her until she disappears behind the swinging door, and I can't help wondering which situation is worse: finding my fiancé fucking my best friend or discovering I've fallen in love with Dallas the same night I lose him.

THE FLIGHT from Austin to Duluth is long, unbelievably long. I don't know if I should be annoyed or grateful.

Knowing I am going back home to the one place I never thought I'd return to has my stomach in knots the entire flight. I try to use the time to drown my thoughts by reading a book or watching one of those awful in-flight movies, but nothing keeps my attention long enough. A few lines read in my book and my thoughts wander to how Dallas was supposed to be on this trip with me. My overnight bag sits in his empty seat, reminding me of that simple fact. I picture him sitting beside me, criticizing the lines in the book he thinks are the most dramatic. I also picture the way his mouth used to curl into a smile at the sight of me, one side twisting up more than the other.

But then after those thoughts come all the lies and secrets. Hailey and Ellie. Songs that weren't poems. Vada and the last look she gave me when I told her about my relationship with her brother. It's only then that I decide to finally give up.

I slam the book shut and try to sleep the rest of the trip.

Now, with my feet on Minnesota soil, the knots inside my stomach have twisted even tighter, and my thoughts about Dallas haven't quit.

It's been an entire week since the last time I saw him. Every morning, I'd make sure to leave after he'd already left for his morning run. He made it easy to avoid him other times throughout the day. I never saw him outside working on his truck or his motorcycle. I decided to quit Dallas' bar the day after our fight in the parking lot. I sent Colton a text letting him know I didn't think it was in anyone's best interest for me to stay. He agreed. I'd be lying if I said his agreement wasn't another twist of the knife in my gut.

He didn't even bother asking me to stay a little longer to finish out the shifts I had scheduled. Maybe it's because he already hired a few new bartenders, or maybe it's because I was never meant to stay there permanently. The reason I considered the most was that mine and Dallas' relationship had bled out into the workplace.

That meant rule number one was truly broken. Oops.

When I decided to go to Minnesota without Dallas, I thought my biggest worry would be running into Cole or

Brenna. But the truth is, they haven't even crossed my mind until now.

I only feel slightly better when Liam pulls up to the pickup lane at the airport. I'm standing on the sidewalk with my suitcase beside me as his black car pulls directly in front of me. Mark is driving, and he barely has the car in park before Liam jumps out, swallowing me up with a hug.

"Oh my god," he says, wrapping his arms around me. "I didn't realize how much I fucking missed you until right now."

I sniff, tears building in my eyes. "Me either." He smells the same and he feels the same. Everything about being here in Minnesota feels the exact same.

Liam pulls back as he wipes his tears away.

"I told Liam I wanted to take bets on how long it would take him to cry after seeing you. He wasn't having it." Mark walks around the car and steps up onto the curb, pulling me in for a hug. "I would have won by the way." When he pulls back, he grins and places his hand on my cheek, admiring my face. "Look at what the Texas sun has done to you. Your skin is glowing."

"Thanks." I give him a small smile as he pulls my suitcase away, stuffing it into the trunk of his car.

Mark and I have always had a close relationship, and I consider myself lucky to have such an amazing brother-in-law. Not only is he gorgeous, he's also one of the smartest people I know. So even though I feel a heaviness inside me, I don't let him see it. Mark deserves only the best for his promotion celebration.

Mark slides his glasses down from the top of his head and opens the back door for me. I cross my arms and twist my mouth. "I can open my own door, you know."

"Well, of course you can." He laughs. "But why should you when you have me?"

"Oh my god." I roll my eyes. "Please don't tell me you're both spoiling me like this for the entire weekend."

Liam sits down in the passenger seat and looks over his shoulder. "You're only here for two days, sis. Deal with it."

When Mark puts the car into drive and we pull away from the airport, I can already feel my heart starting to lighten.

LIAM DECIDED to host the party at my father's old lake house. The large home sits on the edge of Lake Superior, and when I find myself walking down by the water, I'm remembering every single summer we used to spend here. I arrived in Minnesota yesterday and my flight home is scheduled for tomorrow afternoon. I've only just gotten here, and I am already preparing myself for when I have to go back.

The warm breeze brushes against me, blowing my long summer dress back. My feet hit the sand, and I try to imagine the grains as they slide between my toes. When I left Minnesota months ago, I swore I wouldn't miss a single thing. But now, as the sun shines down on my face and I breathe in the fresh air, I think I might have changed my mind. This is the one thing Texas doesn't have on Minnesota.

"I thought I'd find you out here."

I spin around on the beach to find Liam walking toward me. He's wearing a white button-down shirt, the sleeves rolled up his arms. He's untucked it from his black slacks, and his matching black tie hangs loosely around his neck, undone. The ends dance across his chest as he makes his way down the beach to meet me.

I shrug, squinting my eyes against the late-afternoon sun. "It's been a while since I've felt sand beneath my toes."

Liam grimaces, twisting his mouth as he looks down at the

sand. "I've never been a big fan. It's such a bitch to remove, and you can wash yourself a hundred times and still find the grains somewhere."

I give my brother a tight smile and tip my head toward the lake house. "How's it going up there?"

He glances over his shoulder then swings his gaze back to mine, stuffing his hands into his pockets. "Not bad. Mark is talking to a few of his co-workers about the new research they'll be undertaking now that he's been promoted. I don't understand one bit of it."

"I wouldn't either." I twist my mouth and shake my head. Mark works for a biomedical company as one of their engineers. His work is admirable, but it also confuses the hell out of me.

Liam steps toward me and grabs my hand. He wraps it around his arm and pulls us forward, walking us farther down the beach, away from the house.

I smile and rest my head on his shoulder. We're walking slowly, allowing the gentle waves from the lake to fill the silence growing between us.

I'm enjoying my walk with him until he decides to break that silence. "So when are you going to tell me about what happened with Dallas?"

"What do you mean?" I ask, keeping my head resting on his shoulder. There's a pull in my chest as if someone has tied a piece of string around my heart and is trying to tug it free from my chest.

"Sloan, we've been brother and sister long enough for me to know when you're heartbroken. I would say you looked the same as when you found out about Cole, but I'd be wrong. This time is different."

Tears spring up behind my eyes, and I breathe in a heavy sigh. I don't want to cry—again. I've already done enough of that this past week.

I lift my head and look at Liam. It's amazing that he can still guess what's going on without me having to say a word.

I take in a deep breath, allowing the Minnesota air to give me the strength to get through this conversation with my brother. "Dallas lied to me that first day we talked. He knew Ellie. He knew my mother."

"What?" Liam blinks in disbelief. "How?"

I roll my head along with my eyes, knowing it's going to take even more strength for me to get this next confession out. I also haven't admitted this part out loud since Dallas told me. "Dallas and his wife used to perform duets all across the Austin area, and Ellie would write all their songs."

Liam stops, turning his body toward me. He keeps my arm hooked onto his, but his eyes turn down in confusion. His normally bright green gaze is now clouded with a million thoughts. "Um, did you say wife?"

"Yeah." I sigh. "She died a year ago from cancer." The sadness pounds away at me, thinking about Hailey and the short life she lived. I don't know one thing about her, but I can tell she was a woman who left her mark on the people she left behind. Dallas, Vada, even Colton.

After my argument with Dallas that night, I realized they've all been grieving her for the past year. I was the odd man out, throwing a wrench into their lives just by simply showing up. The death of my mother was the cherry on top. They grieved for her in a way I never could, in a way I never would.

Tears spill over my lashes down my cheeks. They're cool from the breeze blowing over them, but the warm liquid flowing down them warms my face. I release a sob, the vision of my brother growing blurry. "Everything is a mess, Liam. Thinking it was a poem my mother wrote, I turned it into a song and decided to play it the night of my performance at the bar with Gareth. Dallas recognized it as one of Ellie's that she'd written for him, and he got angry with me. As if I was supposed to know that." I'm explaining the story faster than my thoughts are able to catch the words pouring out of me. It's as if Liam's simple interest in my life has broken the dam. "We were supposed to keep our relationship strictly about sex, but somehow I think we both crossed our lines. We both broke the rules."

"First of all," Liam starts, holding my hand firmly. "You should know better than to think it can ever be *just* sex. A one-night stand, maybe, but not when you're constantly sleeping with the same person. Somewhere along the way, the lines get blurred, and confusion starts to set in. Then neither person can tell who crossed the line first and who didn't. It becomes a finger-pointing game."

"Okay, I get it." I sniff, cutting Liam off. He isn't exactly making me feel better, no matter how right he may be.

"Second," he continues. "What rules?"

"Well, you knew about the ones I set up after I found out about Cole and how I didn't want to start a relationship with a man after. I truly wanted to focus on myself when I moved to Austin, but you see how that turned out. When Dallas and I started sleeping together, we laid out a few rules. One was to never let our sex life extend into work or our personal lives. And again, you see how that turned out. He was going to come with me this weekend." Another tear spills over. I only feel slightly better having told Liam about Dallas.

He inhales a weighted sigh then wraps his arms around me in a tight hug. I relax my body into his, allowing his embrace to act as a soothing balm, hoping it will somehow heal the wounds on my heart.

He rests his cheek on the top of my head. "I'm sorry to say it, sis, but you don't look like someone who stuck to the rules without allowing herself to bend them, even just a little bit."

I cry against Liam's chest, breathing in his scent. He smells like a mixture of his woodsy cologne and laundry detergent.

We stand holding each other for a few minutes before I can bring myself to pull away.

"I don't know what to do," I tell him, turning. I look out to the lake, watching as the sun shines down on the surface. It looks like it's covered in crystals. Boats float through the water, and I look up at the sky, watching as a flock of birds flies across the clear blue canvas.

This place is beautiful, and there was a time when this place was home to me. But as I stare out at the seemingly never-ending water, I know it is no longer mine. This place no longer lives inside my heart.

"I think you do," Liam says.

I turn my head, catching him looking out at the water the same way I was.

"How can I go back to him when I don't even know if what we had was real? How can I forgive him even if it was? He may have lied, but I'm the one who ended it. He might not want me back at this point. It's been over a week."

Liam shrugs. "I don't know, but I think you should trust your gut. When that lawyer showed up on your doorstep and said you inherited your mother's house, you didn't know where it would lead you. Accepting her house meant you had to move thousands of miles away from your family and the only home you'd ever known, but you still went despite all that. You took a chance and trusted your gut. Look where it led you."

"Yeah," I scoff. "My heart's been broken all over again."

"No," Liam says. "It led you to falling in love again."

I hold my breath as my heart pounds inside my chest, knowing Liam's never spoken more truthfully than he has now. No matter how nosey he is when it comes to my personal life, I know he's right.

I've fallen in love with Dallas, and I didn't even realize it until I lost him. I think about Dallas' blue eyes and how they looked at me the night he showed up at the club, claiming I'd sent him a picture of myself. His eyes sparked with a fire I'd never seen on him before, and it was then that I felt that same fire burning through me. He'd somehow touched every inch of my body before he even laid one finger on me.

My mind wanders to the day he showed up in my yard, offering to help trim my bushes after I'd fallen off the ladder and then again when I was trying to move my mother's old desk. Dallas went out of his way to help me, and those times were when we ended up spending the most time together. Even so, uncertainty still lingers in the back of my mind as Liam and I continue to stand on the beach.

"How do I even know if Dallas is ready for more than what he was able to give me before?"

"There's only one way to find out, and I can tell you right now, you aren't going to find it standing on the shore of Lake Superior."

I roll my eyes and give him a tight smile while wiping the tears from my cheeks.

Liam grins then drapes his arm across my shoulders, pulling me toward him and away from the beach. We start heading back in the direction of the house. "Come on. Let's get back inside before we both get in trouble with Mark for ditching him."

CHAPTER TWENTY-FIVE

DALLAS

I'M STARING AT THE LARGE BLACK CASE THE WAY SLOAN was staring at the cardboard box she found in her attic a couple weeks ago.

I haven't spoken to her since the night of her performance. The image of her standing in the rain with tears streaming down her face has been ingrained in my mind ever since that night outside my bar. It's an image that is impossible to forget and that left me gutted.

Not only have I not spoken with Sloan since that night, I also haven't seen her.

The day after our argument on the street, she quit her job at my bar. I can't exactly blame her. Keeping the secret of knowing her mother and having had a wife before are two things I don't expect Sloan to quickly forgive me for. After all, she's the one who told me I was off the hook.

All week, I expected to see Sloan in some capacity. After all, we're still neighbors, even if she quit the bar. It could be coincidence, or it's possible Sloan is avoiding me on purpose, and to be honest, I can't blame her. But the deeper part of me, the one that realizes I fell in love with Sloan, hopes it was coincidence.

I check my phone for the hundredth time since I sat down at my dining room table an hour ago. Although I know Sloan is in Minnesota this weekend for her brother-in-law's promotion, I still find myself hoping for a message. It's a naïve notion considering I was supposed to be on the trip with her. I've struggled thinking of her being there without me, picturing the off chance that she'd run into Cole. What would he say to her? What would she say to him?

Is Sloan thinking of me, wishing I were there beside her?

I drop my phone back on the table when I see that my inbox is empty. It lands against the hard wood with a dull thud, the sound echoing off the walls of my empty house, walls that are scarcely decorated. The only decoration left from Hailey is the clock above the TV. Hailey's loss was a pain unlike anything I'd ever felt in my life. She was the rare kind of love you believe you'll only ever find once in a lifetime. When Hailey first passed away, the thought of loving anyone else made me feel like I was crumbling from the inside out. I've used the past year, losing myself in meaningless one-night stands and busying myself with work—that is until work started to feel like work and Colton brought up me playing again.

I reach out my hand and run my fingers along the edge of my guitar case. The stiff stitching on the leather grates against the pad of my index finger. I sit back in my chair and run my fingers through my hair, hesitant to open it. My guitar has been buried in the back of my closet, left untouched and unused. I only decided to bring it out today because I feel like ever since Sloan and I terminated our rules last week, I've been losing myself more than ever before.

Music used to be my escape. It used to heal me from the inside out, bringing out the parts of me I loved the most. Any time I think about when I was the happiest in my life, it always involved my guitar.

I take in a deep breath and flip open the silver clasps. The top of the black case pops up, cracking slightly. I slide my finger through the thin crack but stop when I hear a knock on my door. I head to answer it, leaving my guitar sitting on the table.

When I swing the door open, I find my sister standing on the other side. Two brown paper bags are dangling from her clenched fists. She lifts them up to show me.

"Thought you might be hungry, so I got us a couple burritos for lunch from our favorite place. You look like shit, by the way."

"Thanks." I spin around and leave the door open for her to follow me. I head back to the dining room. "I'm surprised you knocked and didn't just see yourself in like you usually do."

The door shuts, and the sound of Vada's steps tapping against the floor follows me. "I'm trying to be a bit better about that."

"Oh." I raise my eyebrows, shocked.

"That's what you wanted, right?" She sets the bags down on the dining room table. Her eyes shift to my guitar, but she doesn't immediately bring it up. "Besides, since I'm going back to the newspaper full time, I won't be coming over as much."

There's a hint of sadness to her eyes, and once I catch it, I stand up and cross the room. I lean forward and wrap my hands around the top of the chair in front of me, stretching them out. I dip my head, willing Vada to look up at me. She's sorting through the bag, arranging the items. She stops and finally lifts her eyes to mine.

"It's dumb," she says, sitting in her chair.

I remove my hands from the back of the chair and cross my arms over my chest. "What's dumb?"

She lifts one shoulder into a shrug as she unwraps her burrito. She folds the corners of the foil. "I know it sounds dumb, but I'm worried we'll go back to the way we were before I started working at the bar. We didn't talk or see each other as much as we do now."

"You're right, that is dumb." I join her at the table but don't touch the burrito sitting in front of me. "That's not going to happen."

"How do you know?" she asks me around a mouthful of food.

I don't move, allowing the silence to settle between us long enough for her to know how serious I am with my answer. "Because I need you."

She stops chewing and swallows, staring up at me with wide eyes. "Oh."

"Yeah." I sigh, sitting back in my chair the same way I was before Vada knocked on my door. "We don't have to go into it, but I just want you to know. I do need you, Vada."

She sniffs, wiping the corner of her mouth with a napkin. "I need you, too."

"Good." I tap my finger on the table as both our eyes shift back to the guitar. This time Vada brings it up.

"It's been a while," she says.

"Yep." I lean forward and rest my arms on the edge of the table.

"What made you bring it out?" Even though she asked the question, I can see the answer written all over her face. She already knows. She's just waiting for me to say it out loud.

"I figured it was about time."

She reaches forward and plays with the open metal clasp. "I haven't heard from her if that's what you were wondering."

"I wasn't." I deliver a straight lie to my sister. She catches it.

"I know you were because if you weren't, you wouldn't look the way you do right now." She purses her lips and crosses her arms, falling back into her chair. My sister can always tell when I'm lying. I'm surprised she couldn't tell I was hiding my relationship with Sloan from her. Maybe she's been too preoccu-pied with her own life to pick up on the signs.

"I don't look like anything."

"Yeah, you do," she says, picking up her burrito again. "I've seen this look on you before."

"What am I supposed to do, Vada?" I ask her. I run my fingers through my hair. "She ended it, and honestly, I wouldn't blame her if she never forgave me. I shouldn't have lied to her. She didn't deserve it." I slowly nod my head up and down, allowing Sloan's silence to eat away at me more than it already has. "I deserve this."

"I do agree that you shouldn't have lied, but we all make mistakes, Dallas. You shouldn't have to pay for them forever, just like you shouldn't have to live the rest of your life in grief. Hailey wouldn't have wanted this for you, and you know it. She would have wanted you to find love again."

I clench my hands into fists, digging my nails into my palms. My sister is right. Hailey never would have wanted me to live my life consumed by grief, but sometimes we get caught in the riptide of it all. We struggle to kick to the surface for air, suffo-cating on our own pain. We just never know how long it will take to break through the surface, if we ever get there.

I clear my throat. "Do you forgive Sloan for not telling you about us?"

The night Sloan and I broke off our arrangement, I immedi-ately went home. The pain was evident in the way I swerved in and out of traffic that night, my tires squeaking against the wet asphalt. The weather was way too dangerous for me to be driving my motorcycle, but I felt like I had no choice. It was my quickest and only means of putting as much distance as possible between me and Sloan.

Not long after I made it home and changed into dry clothes, Vada was at my doorstep. She quickly forgave me for not telling her about my relationship with Sloan. I was surprised, considering Sloan is her best friend. Apparently, Vada's concern for me overpowered her desire to be angry with me.

I admired her for it.

"I was pretty upset at first," Vada admits, answering my question. "Sloan is the closest friend I have, next to you and Colton. If you even want to count yourselves in that category."

"You can count me in there," I tell her. "Can you count Colton?"

"I don't know." She rolls her eyes. "My point is that yes, I've already forgiven her. Because whether she told me or didn't tell me is irrelevant. This isn't about me. This is about you and her. Sloan is the best friend I've ever had. I'm not petty enough to throw my friendship away just because she didn't tell me. She had her reasons, and I can't fault her for them."

I offer Vada a small smile. It's a small consolation for how I'm feeling on the inside. "That makes me feel better."

It's the truth.

"Are you going to play?" My sister nods toward my guitar case.

I sigh and massage my forehead with my fingertips. "I was considering it." I lower my hand and rest it in my lap. Every part of me aches. It's strange since I run every morning. I'm in the best shape of my life, but I know my aches aren't caused by muscle and bone. Mine are caused by heartbreak.

"You don't have to if you don't want to," Vada says.

I stare at the black case. Her answer is every word I've told myself for the past year. The truth is I want my music back. I just have to figure out how I'm going to do it.

"I don't have to," I tell her. "But I want to."

Vada grins and stands. She grabs the uneaten burrito sitting in front of me and places it in my refrigerator then swipes her keys from the table. "I have to get back to the newspaper. I have an article submission to read over from one of our reporters."

"On a Saturday?" I ask her, looking up at her in confusion.

"Yeah." She nods. "I'm finally going back to full time. There are no weekends when it comes to the news, Dallas."

"Right. Just like the bar."

"Exactly." She points to me then starts to make her way to the front door.

She opens it and stands in the threshold. I look past her shoulder and across the street. Sloan's house still looks empty, and her car isn't parked in the driveway like it usually is. I miss her. I miss the way it feels to have her chin resting on my chest. I miss how it feels to have my face buried into her neck and my dick inside her. I miss how accident prone she is and how she continues with her life as if it doesn't affect her. That's the kind of woman she is. That's the kind of woman I've fallen in love with.

Vada holds on to the doorknob, ready to pull the door shut. "It's okay to love again, Dallas." Her eyes meet mine, and my chest tightens with her next words. She swallows down the tears threatening to spill over. "Hailey would have liked Sloan. Don't you think?"

Vada gives me one reassuring smile before shutting the door behind her.

Once I'm standing in the entrance to my house by myself, it feels as if all the air has been sucked out of the room. I run my hand down my face, letting my sister's words sink in. My chest aches and my head pounds as I try to figure out a way to move on. How do I start my life over when I haven't been living one for the past year? Or at least I wasn't until I met Sloan.

I stand in front of the case and slide one finger in the small open crack. I lift it open and slide my hand across the strings. The sunlight pouring in through my windows reflects off the glossy light-toned wood. The pads of my fingers grate against the strings, allowing them to release a quiet shrill squeaking sound until I stop them at the top of the neck. I inhale a deep breath, remembering every song I've played with this guitar, all the places I've been and the shows I've played.

I wrap my hand around the neck and remove it from the case. I'm about to wrap the strap around my shoulder, but I stop. A small piece of paper sits in the bottom of the case. Its white color is a stark contrast to the red velvet lining.

I place my guitar on the table and slowly reach for the paper. My mind races thinking of all the possibilities. I've never kept papers inside my case before, much less buried them underneath my guitar.

No, this paper was placed here by someone else.

My heart pounds inside my chest, and I hold my breath. When I pick up the paper, I open it with shaky hands, reading the handwritten words on the inside.

CHAPTER TWENTY-SIX

Sloan

Leaving the cool air of Minnesota and stepping out into the sizzling Texas heat is a shock to my system. It's hard to believe you can be in two drastically different places in a matter of the same day. This morning I woke up to the cool northern sun shining down on me in my brother's guest room. Tonight I'll go to bed with the warm white moon filtering through my bedroom windows.

I drag my suitcase up my driveway and to my front door, propping it up long enough for me to fish my keys out of my purse. I fight the urge to glance over my shoulder to see if Dallas is home or working on his motorcycle in the driveway.

My short-lived trip to Minnesota turned out better than I expected it to. Liam didn't press me for more information after our walk along the beach of Lake Superior, and by the time we'd gotten back to the party, most of the guests had already left. Mark didn't ask us where we had gone. The expression on his face when he saw me walk through the door told me he already knew the answer to where Liam and I had been.

Although I enjoyed my time with my brother and his husband, it didn't resolve the emptiness I still feel inside. I still missed Dallas and everything that came with him, like working at the bar and singing up on stage.

The only comfort I've been able to find is knowing the school year is about to begin. I hope once the school calls to tell me my classroom is ready for me to start setting up, I'll be able to throw all my energy into it. Teaching six-year-olds how to read is the perfect distraction I need.

There are still another few weeks before I am expecting the school to reach out to me. Until then, I'm hoping I'll find another task to fill my time now that I no longer work at Dallas'.

I was more than prepared to lose myself in work when I got back home, but plans changed when I finally heard from Vada. As soon as the plane landed, I turned my phone back on to find a text from her. It was fairly short compared to her other texts, but I didn't complain. Her reaching out to me at all was enough for me. In her text, she simply asked if we could meet up at the end of the week so we could talk. I didn't care that it had taken her over a week to reach out to me. I desperately need my best friend, and the next six days can't pass fast enough.

Uncertainty still lingers as to whether she wants to continue our friendship or not.

When I finally unlock my front door, I take a chance and look over my shoulder. Dallas' truck is sitting in the driveway, and his motorcycle is parked beside it. He's home.

I swallow the thick lump forming in my throat at the sight. I start to wonder what he's doing in his house or if he's thinking of me at all.

I quickly pull my suitcase inside and shut the door behind me. I rest my back against the door and tip my chin up. I'm looking at the ceiling when I close my eyes and take a deep breath in.

Once my heart and mind have returned to a sense of calm, I head up to my room to unpack and take a shower.

I stay in the shower longer than I intended to when I first came home. I let the water cascade down my back. The steaming water washes away the aches from sitting on a plane all day, and when I get out of the shower, I change into my favorite leggings and top. After I'm dressed, I sit on the couch, ready for a night full of movies. But once I sit back and cross my legs under me, I stare at my coffee table. The box I found in the attic is still sitting in the center, completely untouched. The strip of brown tape is still fastened down the middle, holding the flaps together.

I unravel my legs and scoot to the edge of the couch. With shaky fingers, I inhale a sharp breath and pull the box toward me. I can't explain it, but a feeling has been buried inside me ever since the day I found the box up in the attic. This box means something.

Digging my fingernail underneath the edge of the tape, I start to pull at it. It comes off easily, the entire strip lifting off at once.

I lift the first flap, then the second. To get a better view of what's inside, I lean forward and pick up the box, placing it in my lap.

I'm surprised when I look inside to find only two things sitting in the bottom of it: a covered photo album and a tape recorder set on top of it. I pull both items free of the box and set them on my lap. I drop the empty box on the floor and run my fingers over the cover of the binder. Confusion...it's the only word I can use to describe the feeling of finding a tape recorder. The object is a small rectangle, a tiny cassette tape shut inside.

First, I decide to open the binder. Almost immediately after seeing the first photo, I gasp, tears already building behind my tired eyes. It's a picture of me from the day I was born. It was taken at the hospital. I recognize it because it's the same picture my father used to keep in our house in Minnesota.

How on earth does my mother have this picture of me?

I flip to the next page to find another picture of myself. This time it's a recent picture of me, one I recognize from my college graduation. I continue flipping through the pages, frantically turning them, one after the next. Some are posed, some are candid.

I quickly flip through, confused as to why my mother has an entire album full of photos of me when I never even knew she was still alive. I pick up the tape recorder beside me and hover my thumb over the play button. I hold my breath and press it.

There are a few seconds of silence followed by a small cough. Then I hear her voice.

"Hey, Sloan." She clears her throat. "If you're listening to this tape, I know my lawyer followed through with giving you my house and you've found the box I left for you in the attic."

A tear slips down my cheek. Not because I'm surprised by what my mother has left behind, but because I'm emotional because I've never heard her voice before. The more I listen to her, the more I notice how similar our voices sound. It's as if all the wind has been knocked out of me, tears flowing down my cheeks.

I keep listening. "I know this is all very confusing. For years, I've never been able to tell my story, and now that I only have a little time left, or so the doctors say, I wanted to give myself the chance to explain. You deserve that at least. I considered writing you a letter, but doing it this way makes it feel as if I'm talking to you in person."

I cover my mouth, my stomach twisting into knots. I keep the album open in my lap to the first page, with the photo of me in the hospital.

"The day you were born was the happiest day of my life. It's cliché, I know, but it's true what they say—having children changes you. You became my entire world that day. I didn't have a ton of money and I was single, working at a diner up in Minnesota, barely making enough to pay rent. Your father wasn't in the picture so I couldn't rely on him for help. It was going to be me and you against the world. That's how I saw our lives working out. Regardless of what my parents told me, I wanted you. I wanted to keep you." My mother sighs. "The day after you were born, I was pulled into emergency surgery from complications from the birth. After it was over, I had a reaction to the anesthesia, which further complicated me being with you. I was left to believe you were safe with my parents, but once I woke up and I was healthy enough to take you home, they told me you had passed away from complications after birth, said your heart had simply stopped beating."

My mother's voice quivers. My throat swells and my stomach turns with her story. It feels as if I'm in a completely different world, listening to someone else's story, not mine.

My entire world is crumbling, everything I've ever known turning to dust on the ground.

"I grieved for you, Sloan. I held you for all of twenty-four hours before we were ripped apart from one another. It was hard to move on after I left the hospital, but I did what I could to live as normal a life as possible. After a few years, it became unbearable to stay in Minnesota. I closed my eyes and pointed to a map. That's how I ended up here in Austin. I spent the next twenty years of my life putting the pieces back together until one day, about two years ago, I received a letter from my mother. She was in hospice care and only had a short amount of time left. I opened the envelope and found a picture of you from your college graduation. In the letter, she said she and my father had forged my signature on an adoption form, giving you up. I was angry...angry because I had been lied to for twenty years."

My mother pauses, and the only sound coming from the tiny speaker on the recorder is her heavy breaths. They're hushed but deliberate, each one slow and methodical. Then her voice cuts through again.

"I wanted to reach out to you, Sloan. But once I considered it, I didn't know how I would even explain. You were living your life in Minnesota. From what I could tell, you were happy. You had someone you loved, you had a family...everything I ever wanted for you." She sobs into the recorder. "So, I decided to let you go, to live the life you were meant to live. But now that I don't have much time, I want to leave this for you, my house and everything in it. Anything I can possibly give to you is yours. You're all I have in this world, Sloan. I'm so sorry the universe kept us apart all these years, and now that I don't have much time left, I wish I could at least get the past two years back."

"Oh my god," I whisper, listening to my mother's confession. I swipe my fingers across my cheek.

"I realize this may seem hypocritical of me, or even cowardly," she continues. "Waiting until I'm already gone before you find out about me. But I didn't want to uproot your life just for my sake. Instead, I leave you my house. Do what you want with it. Live in it, sell it, use it however you please. I may not have much, but I worry for those I'm leaving behind that are closest to me, you and my neighbor, Dallas. He recently lost his wife to cancer, and now with me being gone, I'm not sure he's going to handle it well. If you get the chance to meet him, go easy on him. He's a good man, Sloan. He's going to need someone who's kind and gentle with his heart." She inhales a deep breath then releases it, her cries still audible. They're simply calmer and more measured than they were before. "Well, I need to go since my nurse will be over here soon to check on me. I want you to know I've always loved you, Sloan. You'll always be my baby girl. Don't make the same mistakes I did. Take chances and love with every muscle, bone, and fiber of your being. I love you."

The tape recorder clicks and the cassette inside stops spinning. I release a breath I didn't realize I was holding and stare at the recorder resting in the palms of my hands.

Every bit of my mother's story comes crashing into me at once—her talking about the day I was born, the way I was given up for adoption without her knowing, and then her mentioning Dallas. My heart aches with an echo of pain, the grief of losing people that were never truly mine to begin with hitting me in a wave.

I never knew my mother, yet I still grieve her loss.

I fell in love with Dallas, yet I broke every single rule we laid out between us.

I set the album and tape recorder on the table in front of me and roll to my side. I close my eyes and bury my head into the couch.

It's incredible to me that my father never once mentioned adopting me. That must mean my adoptive mother was the one he was always telling me about, the one who died.

He never knew my birth mother.

It's then I realize my mother and I are similar in more ways than I ever could have imagined. We were both lied to for most of our lives, but we also had the opportunity to love fiercely.

CHAPTER TWENTY-SEVEN

Sloan

I IMMEDIATELY SEE VADA WHEN I WALK UP TO THE COFFEE shop we agreed to meet at. She's sitting on the front patio, scrolling through her phone while she sips on the coffee grasped in her other hand.

When she looks up, she sees me, waving me over.

I can't help but feel a sense of relief when she smiles. I figure it's a sign we might be headed in the right direction and we can salvage the friendship we once had. At the same time, I don't know how deep Vada's bitterness goes. It's been two weeks since I saw her, but it somehow feels like a lifetime.

I sit down across from her and drape my purse across the back of my chair. Thankfully, the weather isn't bad today. The clouds are able to stave off the sharp rays of the sun attempting to shine through them. The light reflects off of Vada's dark curls, which hang loose over her shoulders.

"Hey," I say hesitantly. I'm nervous, mostly because I don't know what types of conversations she and Dallas have been having. My concern about our friendship is the one I try to tackle first. "Vada, I—"

"Wait," she says, holding up her hand to stop me. "I know

you probably have something to say, but I need to get mine out first. I feel like it might save us both the trouble of explaining."

"Okay." I lean forward and rest my arms on the table.

"First of all, I want you to know you're my best friend." She gives me a small reassuring smile then reaches across the table, placing her hand over mine. I truly don't deserve having someone as incredible as Vada in my life.

"You're my best friend, too," I tell her, squeezing her hand. "I'm so sorry for not telling you."

"Stop." She waves me off, pulling her hand away. She sips on her coffee then sets it back down. "I understand why you did it, Sloan. There's no need to rehash everything. But I also want to make sure you're okay. Dallas told me you went to Minnesota last weekend."

I bite the inside of my cheek, resisting the urge to ask her about him.

Dallas has been on my mind ever since the last time I saw him outside his bar, but even more so since last weekend when I found out about my mother. The idea of my mother knowing Dallas and of him losing Hailey settled in the pit of my stomach, causing my heart to pound inside my chest. Every part of me wants Dallas. I knew it then.

Somehow, I like to think my mother knew Dallas and I needed each other. I just don't know if I will ever get him back, or if it's even possible.

"Yeah." I nod. "I just got back yesterday. I was only there for a few days to celebrate my brother-in-law's promotion."

"Oh." Vada perks up. She smiles against the rim of her cup. "Tell him I say congratulations."

"I will." The news of my mother weighs heavily on me as I stare at Vada across the table. I am done with secrets and lies, especially when it comes to those I love. I take in a deep breath and release it. "I found a box in my attic a few weeks ago. I finally opened it after I got back."

Vada's eyebrows dip in concern and she sets her coffee cup down, peering at me with her eyes wide and focused. I start to tell her the whole story.

By the time the waiter brings me my coffee, I'm already near the end. Vada stares at me with her jaw dropped. She hasn't spoken a word since I started, allowing me to tell her without interruption.

"She mentioned Dallas at the end of the recording," I tell her. This is the part that gets me the most. My mother's explanation of her absence made sense to me in a way. Of course, it was painful. She spent twenty years believing she'd lost her only daughter, and I had thought the same, but the wound left by my relationship with Dallas is what hurts the most, and knowing about my mother's relationship with him only made it more intense.

Vada swallows, digesting my words. Tears line her brown lashed eyes, threatening to spill over. "What did she say?"

"She told me she was worried about him since he'd just lost Hailey not too long before she found out she was sick and dying. She said if I decided to move here, to go easy on him and he would need someone who was gentle with him."

"Well..." She releases a small laugh under her breath. "She wasn't wrong."

"Yeah." I nod and take a drink of my coffee. I have yet to drink it since telling Vada about my mother's last message to me. I sigh and give in, asking Vada the one question that's been on my mind since I sat down. "How is he?"

"I was wondering when you were going to ask me." She grins.

"Well, of course I wanted to ask, but I wanted to make sure you and I were good first."

"He's doing good." She looks down at her hands and drags her red nail across the glossy wood-top table. "He and Colton have been working on the bar quite a bit. They've mostly been working on some new menu items. They've hired a handful of bartenders since you and I no longer work there."

"That's good." I press my lips together, disappointment washing over me. It's not that I'm not happy for Dallas' success with his business. I'm just disappointed that he seems to be heading in that direction now that I'm no longer in the picture.

"Oh." Vada suddenly sits up in her chair. She straightens her back and gives me the largest grin I've ever seen on her. "They finally hired a guitarist to perform permanently every weekend. He sings too."

"What?" I ask her, stunned. I'd be lying if I said it didn't feel like a punch to the gut hearing this news. "Really?"

"It isn't Gareth, if that's what you were thinking," she adds.

It wasn't, by the way.

She relaxes and shrugs as if she's talking about the weather or what she ate for breakfast this morning, as if it doesn't affect me at all. "Colton and Dallas posted about looking for a new performer. It only took them one day to find someone."

"Wow." I sit back in my chair and turn to look out at the people walking up and down the sidewalk. The street isn't as busy as I've seen before. Despite the cooler weather today, the crowd is sparse.

"I'm sorry," Vada says, pulling my attention back to her. "I didn't mean to upset you, I just thought you'd want to know. It's a good thing, right?"

I sniff and shift my gaze back to hers. "Of course it is. I just wasn't expecting it, that's all."

"Hey." My best friend reaches out and grabs my hand like she did before. "Would you want to go out tonight like we did earlier in the summer? It looks like you could use a girl's night. Lord knows I need one too."

I breathe in the cool summer air and twist my coffee cup between my fingers. The paper grates against my fingernails, and I remember how it felt that night I went out with Vada. My red dress under the neon lights of Sixth Street...it sounds like a fantastic idea.

There's a glimmer in her eye as she waits for my answer. She's holding her breath as the corner of her mouth curls into a smirk, the same way her brother does.

Yeah, I could use a good night out with my best friend.

"Sure."

AFTER WE FINISHED OUR COFFEES, Vada offered to pick me up at my house. I told her there was no way I'd be willing to go out in a pair of torn jeans and a ten-year-old Minnesota Vikings t-shirt on. She quickly agreed.

I dab the last of my lipstick on when I get a text from Vada telling me she's already waiting outside for me. When I meet her outside, I hop into her car, holding the bottom hem of my dress as I sit down in the passenger seat.

"Shit, girl," Vada says. "You look amazing."

I look down at my dress and blush. I have to admit, it's just as revealing as the last one I wore on our night out, if not more.

The dress is a deep shade of blue, nearly black. The sleeves are long, but the chest dips down well below the space between my breasts, showing a perfect V cut. The bottom of the dress stops at the top of my thighs, and for a brief moment I think I may have gone a little too far in picking out this dress.

"You don't think it's too much?" I scrunch my nose, uncertainty lingering in my chest.

"No." She dramatically shakes her head back and forth. "It's perfect, actually."

"Thanks." I sigh with relief, knowing Vada wouldn't lie.

Her outfit is similar to mine. Her bright purple dress is short-sleeved, and the collar is round, showing just enough of the tops of her breasts. She looks gorgeous.

Vada backs out of the driveway and I quickly try to sneak a glance across the street to see if Dallas is home, but we're already down too far for me to see. She pulls out of my neighborhood and grins. "I figured we could go back out to Sixth Street like we did that night we went out."

"Okay," I agree. "I liked it down there."

"Cool," she says, turning onto the highway. "I just have to make a stop at the bar really quick if you don't mind." She winces, shifting her eyes to the side before bringing them back to the road. "I lent Colton money last week and he said he can pay me back tonight. I'd rather use cash than my credit card."

"Oh." I ignore the way my stomach somersaults at the idea of possibly seeing Dallas. It's been two weeks since I've been at the bar, and I don't know how I'll feel walking into it. "Okay."

"You can stay in the car if you want to. I'll only be a minute." She shrugs and bites down on the corner of her mouth, pulling her lip under her teeth.

I may still be upset about my failed relationship with Dallas, but I don't want Vada to think I can't handle going into the bar. I can handle it. Or that's at least what I tell myself.

I straighten my back and square my shoulders. "No, I'll go in with you."

A short silence follows my words before Vada breaks it. "Okay."

Ten minutes later we park in front of Dallas' bar. To no one's surprise, it's packed. There's a flood of people outside, standing in front of the building. They're blocking the view to inside, but something tells me even if they weren't there, I still wouldn't be able to see through.

I step out of the car and adjust the bottom of my dress. Honestly, I'm using it to buy me a little time before heading in there. I look up at the neon sign hanging above the front door. It's the same neon sign that caught my eye the day I walked in here the first time, the day I literally stumbled into Dallas' life. My heart pounds in my chest and I take a deep breath.

"Are you coming?" Vada is standing in the front of her car, near the outside of the crowd. She sends me a reassuring smile from where she's standing, and it's enough to pull me back from the spiral I was going down.

"Yeah."

I follow Vada into the bar, pushing our way through the crowd.

The second my foot hits the concrete floor, I hear it. There's no country music blasting over the speakers as usual. The sound of a guitar floats above the chatter of the crowd around us.

"Is that the new guitar player?" I ask Vada. She's in front of me and glances over her shoulder long enough to answer me.

"Yep."

I listen to the song as we continue making our way back. It's beautiful, the notes seamlessly played, one after another. I still don't have a clear view of the stage as we move farther back, and I wonder if it's like this all the way to the back hallway leading to the alley.

"I can't see the stage from here," I tell Vada.

"Me either." She grabs my hand and tugs me forward. My shoulders nudge people out of the way until I've finally stepped through the outliers.

I find myself standing in a clearing set back about five feet from the stage. Somehow the bar feels larger now that there's no one in front of me. The entire audience is standing behind me now.

Vada lets go of my hand just as my eyes move up to the stage.

My lips part as I take in a sharp breath. Every nerve in my body tingles, shivers shooting down my spine at the sight of the man sitting on the single barstool in the middle of the stage, a microphone propped in front of him. His black shirt matches the black painted brick behind him. He's wearing his familiar torn jeans, the ends are tucked into his black boots. Everything about him is just as I remember. He's the exact same.

His ice blue eyes have been staring at me ever since I stepped out from the crowd. My fingers tighten their grip on the clutch in my hand, stunned by what I'm seeing.

Dallas playing guitar on stage.

His fingers continue to slowly move along the strings, playing the same tune over and over, the same one he was playing when I walked in. My body heats with the memories of how those same hands have explored my body, searing every inch of my flesh.

He quickly swipes his tongue across his mouth, wetting his smooth lips.

He doesn't stop playing when he leans forward slightly, bringing his mouth closer to the microphone in front of him.

He opens his mouth to sing, and that's when I know I've fallen in love with Dallas all over again.

CHAPTER TWENTY-EIGHT

DALLAS

Fuck if I know if this is going to work.

My palms are clammy, and my throat is dry. I should've had a glass of water before getting up on stage, but I was nervous, anxious to get started. It's been well over a year since I've played on any type of stage, whether it was a park bench or in a venue such as this one. It doesn't matter. The feeling is just the same, and now as I look out at the crowd, it hasn't changed.

The people filling my bar start to blend together, their faces becoming anonymous and blank. The tables set out near the front end of the restaurant are full, several of the new servers Colton and I hired serving them. I scan the crowd repeatedly, waiting to spot her in the faceless masses. Vada swore she would find a way to get Sloan here by the time I got up on stage, but I can only hold off for so long before the audience starts to notice.

I've been playing the same tune for the past ten minutes like elevator music on repeat, only mine is better than that bullshit they play. I'm still plucking away when Colton emerges from the kitchen. He leans against the wall behind the bar and watches me. A ghost of a smile appears on his face. He's enjoying this, watching me do the one thing that's ever made me happy.

I give him a small nod then turn my attention back to the growing crowd. They inch closer to the stage. The lights inside the bar are dimmed, the golden hue casting a warm color over the audience. My chest twists with the thought that Sloan isn't showing up. Maybe Vada couldn't convince her to come inside.

I'm about to give up when I finally see Sloan emerge at the front of the crowd. Her tan skin glows with the amber lights, and I've never seen her look as gorgeous as she does now.

There's a prickle down the back of my neck, and now I'm really fucking wishing I'd taken that drink of water. My throat dries and my fingers almost stop playing altogether.

Her long hair is curled around her face, framing the smooth curves of her pink cheeks. Her full lips are painted a bright red. Her dress is a deep shade of blue, the same as her round eyes. It reminds me of my favorite color, the one I told her about the day we went to the furniture store.

The fabric stops at the top of her thighs and cuts down the center of her chest, displaying the top curves of her breasts. My dick twitches at the sight of her, remembering how my mouth has explored her body, devouring her.

I swallow the thick lump forming in my throat and scoot forward on the barstool, bringing my mouth close to the microphone. I don't take my eyes off Sloan, even when I start speaking to the audience.

"Hello, everyone. First, I want to thank you for coming tonight." I maintain the steady rhythm of the tune I've been carrying the past ten minutes. "My name is Dallas Beckett, and I'm one of the owners of this bar. I recently met a woman who made me rethink all the rules."

The crowd cheers, clapping and whistling. I still keep my gaze on Sloan, my heart beating and thrashing against my chest.

Sloan's mouth pops open and tears line her eyes. One single tear spills over as she blinks, and I wish I could step off the stage so I could wipe it away. It's hard to tell what she's thinking in this moment. Despite the uncertainty, I continue.

"I used to think we are only destined to love one time in our lives, but it's not true. This woman has changed me, in every way possible." I clear my throat and take a deep breath, starting the song I came here to play. "Sloan, I couldn't be more thankful you stumbled into me that day. You not only bent my rules, you also shattered them." I give her a slight nod and briefly close my eyes. When I open them again, Sloan has her hands clasped in front of her, and her stare hasn't moved. She's only focused on me.

I open my mouth and start to sing for the first time in over a year.

I'VE NEVER BEEN *the one who had a way with words*
But here I am now, laying it all on the line
for the last time
You know it all, even when you fall
Take this love you've been given and don't look back
You can love again, even when your heart is guarded
Don't worry, this feeling won't be forever
Always know, I loved you to the end

I LOVED *you to the end*
It may have been the end for me
But it isn't for you
As I've said, you know it all
Even when you fall
You've known it all along

You can love
You can fall
You can fall in love again

MY HANDS QUIVER above the strings as I continue strumming. Sloan's tears are flowing down her face in a way I haven't seen before. She's left breathless, her chest still and her face frozen. I lock eyes with her the entire time I play, trying not to fumble the lyrics. After all, I wasn't the person who wrote them.

The last lyric leaves my lips, and I play a few more chords before finishing on the last note. The crowd is silent, listening to every word and note I've played. Blood is pumping through my veins, and I feel a prickle down my spine.

It's the same feeling I would get when I played before, the rush and the adrenaline of performing for a group of people. It hasn't gone away. The sensation is still there, just like my ability to love again after losing Hailey.

I thank the crowd then leave my guitar on the stand near the edge of the stage. I can't wait any longer to talk to Sloan. But when I step down, she's no longer standing in the same spot. Her back is turned to me, and she's already started to make her way back to the front of the bar.

The usual country music booms over the speakers scattered across the bar, and the sound drowns out the chatter that has picked up since I stopped playing. Everyone has gone back to their seats or original places, moving away from the stage.

I quickly follow Sloan and elbow my way through to catch up with her. When I make it to the other side, I find her standing outside on the sidewalk. She's standing in the same spot where we argued the night she called off our agreement, the night she let me go. My stomach sinks, dropping to a new depth. I'm not sure why she's attempting to leave, and the fear that she's over me starts to settle in.

Maybe I'm too late. Maybe it isn't enough. Maybe she doesn't love me the way I thought she did.

I push through the large glass door and meet her off to the side of the building. She's wrapped her arms around herself, and when she sees me walking toward her, she releases an audible gasp.

The neon light of the sign above us reflects off her skin, giving it a light pink hue. Her tears have subsided only slightly.

"Hey." I wish I was more cavalier in this moment. Of all the words I've imagined saying to Sloan in the past two weeks, *Hey* was certainly not one of them.

"That song..." Her voice quivers and she nods toward the bar. "It was beautiful. Did my mom write that one, too?"

I tentatively take a step toward her. She doesn't move, so I take another one. "No." I subtly shake my head. "She didn't."

"Oh," she says, swiping at her wet cheek. Her eyes search my face as she tries to understand why I decided to play tonight.

"Hailey wrote it." I let my confession hang between us.

Her bottom lip pops out and she searches my face. "She did?"

"Yeah." I grin. It's the first time I've been able to feel this way when I talk about Hailey. "I found it underneath my guitar when I took it out of my case last week. In a way, I think she knew I would need it one day."

"I thought you said you wouldn't play on stage again," she whispers.

"Yeah." I take another step closer, bringing myself within touching distance of her. "Sometimes we can change our mind. And sometimes we can break our own rules."

"Dallas." There's a warning in her voice. She breathes in as another tear slides down her cheek, and I catch it with the pad of my thumb. She leans into my hand before she shakes her head. "We never should have made those rules. I never should have had my rules to begin with."

"I agree." I wrap my hand around her waist and push her back toward the wall of my bar. She lands softly against the brick exterior and rests her head back. She tilts her chin up so I get a perfect view of her dark blue eyes. I was right—her dress is the same shade.

I slide my hand from her cheek to the back of her head, threading my fingers through her long soft waves. "You can't place rules on heartbreak, Sloan. I think both you and I know that."

She lets out a quiet sob. At first, I think she might start crying again, but instead, she lets out a small laugh. "I think you might be right."

"I am?" I smirk, quirking an eyebrow.

"Maybe." She twists her mouth in thought then frowns. "But I don't know if we can do this. I think we both need to figure out what exactly it is that we want."

"I know exactly what I want."

"Maybe we were too naïve to think it could work before." She shrugs. "How do we know it can work again?"

My eyes search her face, my heart thrashing inside my chest then sinking into my stomach. I inhale a sharp breath. "Because this time I know I'm in love with you."

"What?" Her round eyes widen at my confession, and it feels as if I've destroyed the wall I've built around myself for the past year.

"I am," I tell her. "I'm fucking in love with you, Sloan. I was just too blinded before to notice. But I know now that you can't put rules on heartbreak, and you can't put them on love. When Hailey died, I thought that was it, thought there was no possible way I could ever love someone as much as I did her, but you changed that for me. You literally came stumbling into my life, Sloan. You buried yourself into every aspect of my life, and I did the same to you without even realizing it. I fell for you, and I fell hard. It was fast and messy, but you were more than I ever could have imagined. You pieced me back together."

Tears start to fall once again, one after another. She reaches up and places her hand around my arm. She takes in a heavy breath and closes her eyes. I rub my fingers back and forth across the flesh of her back and her head. I feel sick again, unsure how Sloan will react. She looks relieved to hear my words, and from the way she hasn't pushed me away, I think she might feel the same way. But there's always the chance she won't, and I'm very aware of the possibility.

She opens her eyes again and places her other hand on my face, mirroring the way I'm holding her. She stares into my eyes. "I love you, too, Dallas."

"You do?" I'm both shocked and relieved hearing those words.

She nods, a smile spreading across her pretty mouth. "I do. I have this whole time."

"Fuck. I love you. Come here." I breathe out a sigh, still in disbelief. Closing the space between us, I pull her to me without another second of hesitation. Before my mouth meets hers, she gasps, and it's the most beautiful sound I've ever heard.

CHAPTER TWENTY-NINE

Sloan

Loving Dallas hasn't come easy, but now that I'm here, it's as easy as breathing. It's a feeling woven into every fiber of my body and soul.

After I tell Dallas I love him out on the sidewalk in front of his bar, he wastes no time in wanting to take us back to his place. He doesn't care about the crowd holding on to hope that he'll jump back up on stage. He doesn't care that he is leaving Colton behind to deal with the rush they are going through.

His sights are set only on me.

Dallas walks me over to where his truck is parked on the side of the building. It's in a less lit portion of the parking lot, definitely a place I wouldn't normally be if I were by myself, but I'm with Dallas, and I don't want to waste another second.

He opens the passenger door for me then jogs around to the driver's side and hops into his seat. He moves to slide the key in the ignition, but I quickly stop him and place my hand over his.

"No," I tell him. "I can't wait that long. I can't wait until we get home."

His eyebrows dip and his ice blue eyes spark with my words. He lowers his hand and turns his body halfway to me, giving me access between him and the steering wheel. I slide across the bench seat and straddle him, placing one leg on each side of his. He puts his hands on my hips and pulls me closer to him then moves them to my shoulders. He pulls my dress off them, exposing the top part of my chest, my breasts popping out from the top hem. His eyes dance across my body. "You're so fucking gorgeous."

I place my hand on his cheek, the stubble on his jaw grating against my palm. "You're not so bad yourself."

He gives me a small laugh, and the way his smile lifts the corners of his mouth is enough to make me melt.

The bottom of my dress has already slid up my thighs, and once Dallas notices, his hands are on them. His large palms stretch across them, and his fingers grip my flesh.

His hardened cock springs to life underneath me and I moan, feeling it press against me. My chest is in line with his face, and his hands start moving along my body the same way his eyes do. He can't focus on one part of me. He's everywhere all at once.

"Shit, Sloan." He moves his hands farther up my thighs until his thumbs graze the front of my thong. I'm already soaked and ready for him. He slides his thumb under the fabric and finds my clit. He starts to circle his finger around it, and I lean forward, wrapping my arms around his neck. I lean down and kiss him, placing my lips on his.

I moan against his mouth, my body already starting to heat at his touch. He gently bites down on my lip then pulls away, laying his head back against the headrest.

"Give me your hand." He removes his thumb from my clit and wraps his fingers around my wrist. He moves my arm in between us then guides my fingers through the top of my thong. "Touch yourself here. I want to watch you."

With his hand wrapped around mine, I slide my fingers

between my slit, finding my warm center. My fingers are immediately wet as I start to circle my clit. All the air leaves my lungs when I start rocking my hips along with our joined hands. Dallas' hard cock is pressed against me, and I can't help moving against it, feeling his length move in between my legs. He watches me in amazement.

I close my eyes and tilt my head back. Dallas' mouth lands on my chest. He kisses the top of my breast then pulls on the flesh, gently biting down. I hiss as every nerve in my body shivers with tiny explosions bursting along my skin.

"Dallas...I want you inside me."

He removes his hand from mine and slides it underneath me to unzip his jeans. I continue with my hand as he frees himself from the constraints of his pants. He centers himself then places his hands on my hips, lifting me slightly.

"Shit." I groan, knowing if he doesn't slide himself inside me, I'm going to cum before he's even had a chance.

Sensing I'm close to the edge, he wraps his hand around mine and pulls me away. He lifts my fingers to his mouth and presses his lips against them. It reminds me of when he first touched me at the club that night on Sixth Street.

"I love you, Sloan." He breathes out. I can tell he's growing impatient. His dick twitches, and I gasp at the sensation it gives me. At the same time, I know he's trying to savor this moment like I am.

Him telling me he loves me causes my heart to flutter in my chest. I reach down below me, grabbing his length. I lift my hips and center him under me before I start to lower myself back down. "I love you, too."

With my other hand, I grip the back of his seat and slide down. He groans, tilting his head back and closing his eyes. He lifts his hips up from the seat slightly, helping to slide himself in all the way. I groan against him and dip my head, watching as I move up and down. Resting his hand on my cheek, he pulls my gaze back up to his. I lean into him and bite down on my bottom lip, pulling it between my teeth.

"I promise," he says, "to love you and only you, Sloan. No more rules. No more heartbreak. Just you and me."

Dallas grips my hips tighter and moves me over him faster. He doesn't waste any more time as he lifts off the seat, pushing harder every time our bodies meet.

"You have me, Dallas Beckett. All of me." I move my hips up and down above Dallas when my orgasm comes. It's intense and amplified by his promise. My body quivers above his, and I press my hand against his chest as I come down from my high. I keep moving over Dallas, watching as he slides in and out of me.

"Fuck, Sloan. You feel so good, I can't..." His legs tense beneath me as he wraps his arm around my waist, pulling me closer. He orgasms inside of me, and it's an entirely different feeling than before.

When he's finished, I don't immediately climb off him. I stay above him, with him inside, and stare at the man I love. I truly do love him more than I've loved anyone before.

He plants kisses along my neck, his lips lingering across my damp skin. He kisses me on the lips and pushes my hair away from my face.

I give him a smile then glance through the driver's side window, toward the bar. The windows are too foggy for us to be seen or to see through. All I can see are the faint, blurred neon lights from the street. Some of the light peeks through the window, casting a glow on Dallas' skin. I swing my gaze back to him. We're both still taking a moment to catch our breath. I run my thumb across his bottom lip and smirk.

"Do you want to go back in there? Maybe play another song?"

Although I hope Dallas might not want to go back inside, I

still haven't stopped thinking about the song he played inside, and the fact that Hailey wrote it for him. Like my mother's recording to me, Hailey knew Dallas would need that song one day, knew it would lead him to love again.

He frowns in thought, three creases forming across his forehead. He swipes his tongue across his lips and takes in a deep breath.

"No, I don't think so. There's plenty of time for that."

His arm is still wrapped around my waist. He tugs me forward, and I yelp when his dick hardens inside me. He hasn't pulled himself out yet. I clench my thighs around him as it grows inside me.

"For now, let's go home."

Sloan

"I TOLD YOU—YOU CAN'T BE TRUSTED ON LADDERS. YOU'RE going to fall." Dallas stands behind me, watching as I try to decorate our front yard for Christmas.

"I'm going to fall if you keep talking." I groan, trying to reach across the front window. The wreath I'm holding between my fingers swings in the brisk winter air. I sniff and stand on my toes a bit higher.

"This is ridiculous." He huffs. "I should be doing this. Besides, who hangs wreaths from the window? I thought people put them on their front doors or some bullshit like that."

With Christmas only a few weeks away, Dallas and I are behind the rest of the neighborhood when it comes to decorating.

Each of us still has our house across the street from one another. I considered selling mine, but the attachment I've grown to my mother through the gift of her house is too much for me to give up. At least it is right now.

As far as Dallas' house is concerned, he feels the same way. It's the house he and Hailey bought together, and I can't fault him for hesitating to sell. For now, we are splitting our time between them and enjoying being together. If he ever wants to sell, I figure he will do it when he feels the time is right.

"Just so you know," Dallas says, "I don't remember your mother ever hanging wreaths on the windows."

"Oh, yeah?" I ask him, glancing over my shoulder. "What did she do then?"

He shifts his eyes up in thought then grins. "Actually, she never did decorate."

"Well, I happen to think she would have liked my wreaths."

"She probably would have."

Silence follows his words, and my chest warms thinking of her.

The same day Dallas and I made up at his bar, I told him about my mother's voice recording and why we were separated after I was born. It was the first time I'd seen tears in his eyes since he told me about Hailey that night in the rain.

He truly did love my mother.

"Are you still set to perform tonight?" I ask him.

"Yeah, I told Colton I'd show up a little earlier to help him with some of the barbecue."

After the night of Dallas' surprise performance on stage, he agreed to perform every weekend. He still only plays a few songs, and although I haven't returned to work at the bar, I still come in every night he performs. Sometimes he even drags me up on stage to sing with him. Teaching is a joy for me, and I don't plan on replacing it with any other sort of career, but I enjoy singing for fun with Dallas.

"Did Vada say she was coming?" I ask. Vada stays busy at the newspaper, finally fulfilling her role as editor in chief. She actively tries to spend as much time as she can with me and Dallas, a promise she made after quitting the bar. I'm not sure she does the same for Colton.

"I think so." Dallas shrugs. "But with her, you can never tell."

"Right." I nod, pressing my lips together.

"Are you sure you've got it?" Dallas asks. I can hear the nervousness in his voice.

"Just a little more." I stand on my tiptoes and stretch my arm out, hoping the wreath will catch on a nail my mother must have used for hanging plants.

Before I even realize I've leaned too far over, I start to fall. My heart leaps out of my chest just before Dallas steps to his right and catches me. He corrects the ladder and stares up at me in disbelief. His face pales. He's certainly no stranger to my clumsiness.

"This is what I'm talking about." He lets out a light laugh. "Here, let me help you." He moves to pick up the wreath and hang it himself. I climb down the ladder and step back, allowing him to make his way up.

He easily hangs the wreath without any effort then climbs down, standing beside me to study his work.

"Looks great," I tell him, breathing in the cool winter air. The winter hasn't been nearly as brutal as the ones in Minnesota, but sometimes I still catch the same shiver down my spine when the breeze blows through.

"Thanks." He wraps his arms around me, pulling me to his chest. I tip my chin up and look into his eyes, putting my arms around his waist. I slide my hands under the bottom of his sweater and run my fingernails across his smooth flesh. He groans against me as goose bumps rise across his skin.

"I think we should make another rule," he says, twisting his mouth in thought then giving me a devious grin. The golden hue of the lights hanging throughout the neighborhood reflect off his ice blue eyes, melting me from the inside out.

"I thought we said no more rules."

"We did." He grins. "This one is a bit different."

I pause and give him a smile back. "Fine. Let's hear it."

"Rule number one: My wife isn't allowed to use ladders anymore."

"Your wife?" I whisper, a white puff of air escaping from my mouth.

"Yes," he says, his face turning serious. He swipes his thumb across my lips and examines my face as if he's trying to engrain it in his memory. "I love you, Sloan, and there's no doubt in my mind that I want to marry you. I never thought I would be able to say these words again or want the same out of life as before, but you make me want those things again. You brought me back to life, and I want to spend the rest of it with you. I want to be there to catch you when you fall."

He pauses when a laugh erupts from my throat. It's a small one, enough for Dallas' mouth to quirk at the sound. My stomach flutters.

"Marry me, Sloan."

"Okay." Tears build in my eyes, but I hold them back and stand on the tips of my toes. "I'll marry you, Dallas Beckett."

And then without hesitation, under the clear Texas sky, he leans down and claims my mouth with his.

Sneak Peek

Vada

TABLE NUMBER FUCKING EIGHT.

Every time I look at it, my body immediately reacts. What's it called? Muscle memory? I've heard about it before when talking about people learning to walk again or when you lift weights, but could it be true for people you've slept with?

I've never had to learn how to walk again, and the thought of going to the gym specifically to pick things up and put them down couldn't sound any more awful than it already does.

But muscle memory from sleeping with someone? It's a possibility, and if it is, I'm fairly certain that's what I'm experiencing.

It's pretty fucking stupid actually.

Part of me is thankful today is my last day at my brother's restaurant, if only for the sake of not having to look at table number fucking eight every single day.

"Remember, your shift ends at six. After that, we're celebrating."

"It's six right now," I tell my best friend, Sloan, as I fill a few glasses of beer—for table fucking eight.

"Oh shit," she says, spreading her eyes wide. She quickly grabs the beers from my hands and nods toward the computer behind me. "Clock out."

The beer foam spills over her hands, dripping onto the floor. I freeze, my body stiffening in shock at what she just did. She hasn't always been the best at bartending. She's been working here for the past three months. After Colton hired her, she started seeing my brother, and they've been together ever since. I have a feeling Sloan is here to stay since she's the only one who's managed to bring Dallas back from the dead, and he wouldn't take a chance at screwing that up.

She also happens to be my best friend.

I watch Sloan as she puts the glasses down on the counter and grabs a fistful of napkins, hastily cleaning off her fingers. It barely does anything before she tosses them in the trash and picks up the beers again.

She nods toward the computer again when she sees I haven't moved. "I'm serious, Vada. Clock out. I've got this."

"Do you?" I ask her, stifling a laugh.

She rolls her eyes, already heading toward the end of the bar to walk out to the dining room. "Yes. Now go."

"Wait—before you go, I need to close out my tab." I turn around to find Cassidy standing on the other side of the bar.

She's leaning over it with her hands wrapped around the edge. Her mouth is spread into a wide grin, displaying her perfect white teeth. They're blinding, even in the dim lights of my brother's restaurant.

"Fine," Sloan says, stopping mid-stride. The beers are still perched in her hands as she talks to us over her shoulder. "Close her tab and then clock out. You can't be wearing those clothes for your going away celebration."

I look down at my shirt, spotting a barbecue stain near my shoulder and a wet spot on the bottom hem from leaning over the counter to clean spilled drinks all night. "Yes, ma'am." I chuckle as she walks away, all the while keeping a smile on her face as well.

When I turn back to Cassidy, she's already pulling her card out of her wallet.

"Here you go." She holds it out for me. Her long blonde hair is pulled back into a high ponytail, the ends dancing across her bare back. She's wearing a thin-strapped tank top, her gold necklace resting against her chest. Her lips are painted a pale pink, the same shade as her cheeks.

Cassidy is a photographer for *The Daily News*. Our newest hire, she's only been working at the paper for the past month. Even though I've just been popping in every now and then, writing articles whenever I can find the time while working at the bar full time, Cassidy and I became quick friends. She's younger than me and fresh out of college, but I like her. She fit in easily, and I know she's here waiting to celebrate my last night at the bar with me before I go back to the paper full time. I swipe her card for the two drinks she's had since she sat down an hour ago.

By the time I give her card back and she signs the receipt, Sloan's already returning. This time her hands are now full of dirty dishes.

"Did Cassidy cash out?" Sloan asks, dumping them into the bin we keep behind the bar to save us from always having to run back into the kitchen.

"Yes." I laugh, giving Cassidy a side glance in response to how Sloan is rushing me.

"Good. Get out of here and go out back. Colton's taking you home to change while we close up. It'll be an early night for us."

"Why is Colton taking me?" My heart skips a beat. See? Pretty fucking stupid.

"Because Dallas is out grabbing the rest of the supplies for your party," she explains. What supplies he needs, I have no idea. "And I'm here covering the front," Sloan adds. "The kitchen isn't serving food anymore, so Colton's the only one who is free."

I open my mouth to object, knowing full well I can drive myself, but I don't. I can tell how excited Sloan is for this party.

I stop arguing with her and clock out, mostly because she saved me from having to walk to table eight, forcing me to remember how Colton's tongue slid between my—

"Fuck." I gasp when I suddenly slam into a firm wall of muscle. I look up, and my eyes land on familiar ones staring right back at me. Light brown irises narrow as he presses his lips together. Hot breath comes out of his nose as he stares at me, his lips separating just enough for him to blow it across my skin.

I must not have seen him push through the door connecting the bar to the kitchen.

"There you are."

Want to read Colton and Vada's story?
Read *The Secrets to Heartbreak*!
CLICK HERE

You can also read the start of Colton and Vada's story in One-Time Secret.
Grab the FREE bonus short story HERE

If you loved The Rules of Heartbreak, you'll love my upcoming spicy, angst filled, second chance billionaire romance, Gorgeous Lies!
Grab your copy HERE

Thank you for reading Dallas and Sloan's story! There's more to come in The Heartbreak Series. If you enjoyed the book, I would absolutely love if you left a review. Reviews mean the world to us indie authors and it would mean so much to me.

Thank you, again!
XOXO

Want to sign up for my newsletter and be notified of my upcoming releases?

You can also join my reader group, Brittany's Book Lovers

THE WRONG PITCH

Chapter 1

Ophelia

Moving in with my younger brother at the ripe old age of twenty-two isn't exactly what I had envisioned at this stage of my life. I always imagined living in a high-rise apartment in the center of Boston, owning my own fashion design company. I wouldn't rely on anyone other than myself, and my success was all owed to the work I'd put in the past four years.

I was well on my way there. My path was free and clear. Nothing stood in my way.

Until I woke up this morning and my life was catapulted in a completely different direction. It feels as if within the matter of a few words, my life came to a screeching halt, and now I'm left with next to nothing.

I'm walking down a lonely, dark road, headed to my brother's house with nothing but the clothes on my back and the suitcase trailing behind me. The eerily quiet street is deafening, sending chills down my spine ever since I stepped off the bus half a mile back. But I was left with no other options. My life dissolved before I'd even had an opportunity to realize what was happening. Between work and school, I hadn't taken the time to invest in buying a car, which led me here. Forced to book a last-minute bus ride from Boston to the tiny town of Eden, Maine.

My hometown. The last place I ever wanted to return to.

I'm dragging my suitcase behind me, the small plastic wheels beating against the asphalt. Every now and then I run over a few pebbles. My suitcase wobbles before balancing back out.

I grunt in frustration as I march down the long, deserted road. Normally, I wouldn't complain about being dropped off one block away but considering it's nearly midnight and there are only two streetlights on this road, I'm annoyed. Frustrated beyond belief at the circumstances leading me up to this point.

Chills prickles their way down the back of my neck. It's silent. Uncomfortably quiet. Something I'm not used to, coming from a city such as Boston. I pull my phone out from the back pocket of my jeans and call my best friend. At least she can keep me company while I head toward Reed's house.

"Ophelia?" Claire whispers into the phone. Her voice is low and gravelly, as if she's trying to sleep. Or she was on the verge of falling asleep. "What's going on? Did you make it to Reed's yet?"

"Claire, shit." I place my hand against my forehead and wince, remembering the plans my best friend had gushed about non-stop earlier. "I didn't interrupt your date, did I? How did that go?"

"No." She snorts, her voice clearing slightly. She groans. "I'm in my bed. The date was going great until the end when he asked if I was interested in a foursome."

"No," I say, stifling a laugh. It's a contradiction to how I was feeling only moments ago. But this is exactly why I called Claire. "He didn't."

"Hey," she's quick to defend. "Still nowhere near as bad as

the one guy who asked me what wine I drank at dinner, and when I told him I liked white, he still proceeded to order a one-hundred-dollar bottle of red. Then by the end of the meal, claimed he left his wallet out in the car and didn't even offer to go get it. Worst and biggest waste of two hundred dollars I've ever spent."

"Oh my god." I grin. "I do remember that."

"I'm telling you, Ophelia. Dating fucking sucks."

"Tell me about it," I mumble. "At least you're going out on dates. I'm currently walking down a creepy dark road all by myself. Not to mention, I'm moving in with my little brother."

"It's only temporary, Ophelia."

"Doesn't feel like it." I sigh then inhale a deep breath, hoping it'll make me believe my own words. "Or at least I hope it's not."

"It's not," she reaffirms. "Besides, it's a good thing you took that self-defense class a couple years ago when we joined that sorority freshman year. I can't believe you have to walk."

I nod, even though Claire can't see me. She's right.

Claire's been my best friend ever since I met her in one of those speed dating sessions our college organized. I was only nineteen at the time. I didn't have any intention of finding my soulmate or my future husband, but apparently, Claire was. She has been for as long as I've known her.

I don't know where she gets her drive from when I decided to give up a long time ago. Not that I haven't dated over the years. But I haven't been dead set on finding my perfect match.

As far as I'm concerned, love is for the birds.

"It's a good thing I still remember some moves," I tell her. "I guess joining the sorority wasn't completely useless."

"You're right," Claire mumbles, her words dragging into one another. "Are you almost there? Why exactly are you walking by yourself? Reed couldn't pick you up?"

I groan, still trudging down the street. Reed's house comes into view. There's a light turned on the front porch, but otherwise, it looks dark. All the windows are a pitch-black.

"He had to work tonight. Shouldn't surprise me, though, considering he's always working. Working or playing."

"None of his other roommates are home?"

"No." I sigh again, knowing my luck hasn't been the best this past week. "I'm not really sure where they are. Reed told me one of them had to work. I guess the other is out training or something."

"If no one is home, how are you going to get in without a key?" Claire asks. "I'm guessing he didn't leave the house unlocked for you."

I snort. "No, I hope not anyway. Reed told me he left the spare key under the doormat."

"Good," Claire says.

I survey the neighborhood, gauging the kind of environment I'll be living in for the foreseeable future. Well, at least as long as it takes me to find another place to live.

"I don't get it. This is supposed to be a college town," I tell Claire. "The school is only a few blocks away, but I've never seen a college town so... dead."

"Well." Claire sighs. "It's not forever, right? You're only there for a few months."

The hope in Claire's voice is enough to bring tears to my eyes. Warm liquid wells behind them, and I sniff, attempting to keep them at bay. I look down and kick at a few pebbles dotted along the street.

"I don't know to be honest." I bite down on my bottom lip. "I'd like to go back to Boston, but I don't even know how I'll be able to do that."

A silence follows my words, and I know exactly what Claire is thinking.

She reads my mind. "I'm sorry you couldn't stay with me."

"You've already apologized." I shake my head.

"I know, but it still fucking blows that I couldn't even take in my best friend. My roommate isn't moving out for another six months, and there's no room here."

Take in.

Hearing Claire use those words only makes me feel worse. Like I'm some sort of stray begging for a place to stay. As if I have no home.

"Seriously, Claire. I get it. I didn't expect you or anyone else to have a place for me to stay on demand. None of us saw this coming." I pout. I can't help it. I still haven't gotten over how drastic my life has changed in the past three days.

The worst three days of my life.

Day one. Laid off from my job. Day two. Lose all my financial aid, forcing me to drop out of graduate school. Day three. My roommate inexplicably disappears, doesn't renew our lease, and I find an eviction notice taped to my door. I begged my landlord to give me time, but she wasn't hearing a word. She stood in the doorway only long enough to allow me to pack whatever I was able to take with me. My two hands and a suitcase.

She offered for me to come back and pick up the items she was going to leave out on the curb, but at the time, the task seemed impossible. My life was crumbling quickly. I couldn't think straight.

I guess the saying is true. Bad circumstances usually happen in threes. Or I'm at least hoping that's how this works.

Claire's voice softens. "I'm still shocked they pulled the rug out from under you the way they did. Is it even legal?"

"It is." I tilt my head to the side, pressing the phone harder against my ear. "Everyone I talked to says they had the right to shut the whole company down. It was the shareholders anyway. They control everything."

"Shit."

"Yeah, well, money talks." I bite down on the side of my cheek. The familiar sickness I've been experiencing all day returns.

Claire offers me nothing but her silence in response. She knows I'm right and she doesn't bother trying to convince me. My entire situation is bullshit.

"It's fine." I inhale a deep cleansing breath, willing myself to believe the words I'm speaking out loud. So far, it hasn't helped. "I'll figure something out."

Uncertainty ebbs its way into my bones, burrowing deep inside me and making a home there.

"I know you will," Claire reassures me.

I look down. I kick at the rocks again. They fly out in front of me, skittering out several feet.

"Is there anything I can do for you?" Claire asks.

I abruptly stop, leaving Claire's question unanswered. I'm only a few houses down from my brother's but I can't move. I yank on the handle to my suitcase, but it won't budge. The bottom corner is stuck in a small pothole, and the wheel has popped off. It rolls down the street, landing a few feet away from me.

Maybe I'm wrong. Maybe bad circumstances happen in fours. Not threes.

"Shit." I groan, still holding my phone to my ear. "Could this night possibly get any worse?" I let go of my suitcase and walk to pick up the wheel. I want to laugh. I want to cry.

My body can't decide which emotion to feel. My throat swells, yet I find the urge to laugh. At how different my life is in this moment. I swallow down the tears I know are threatening to come and move to pick up the wheel.

"What happened?" Claire asks, but I don't answer her.

I'm mid pick-up, bending down to grab the wheel. An unfamiliar sound stops me. A quick secession of pounding comes from my right. It gets louder as if it's growing closer to me. It's a noise I haven't heard aside from my own feet and the wheels of my suitcase grinding the pavement with every step. It's the rhythmic beat of another person's footsteps on an otherwise desolate street. The air catches in my throat. I look up to see someone charging in my direction. He's running at full speed. Directly at me.

His face is covered in shadows and darkness. The hood of his sweatshirt is pulled up and over his head, hiding himself from me.

My heart races in my chest, and the blood drains from my face. My neck prickles with nerves, and my stomach flips.

His footsteps grow louder. I use every instinct in my body when he reaches me.

I immediately let go of my phone and drop it onto the street. I have no idea where it lands. All I hear is a loud smack, the sound of crushing metal hitting asphalt. I have no clue if Claire is still on the other end. I lift my arm, stopping the man before he has the chance to attack me. He stops, his eyes growing wide, realizing I'm prepared to fight back. I haven't been able to see them until now. Not until he's inches from my face, realization replacing his determined expression.

Not today, asshole.

I wrap my hand around his wrist. With my other hand, I grip onto his bicep and push him backward with as much force as I can muster.

His yell echoes across the otherwise empty street. The deep guttural growl that erupts from his chest as he slams back onto the street shoots straight through me. Adrenaline immediately courses through my veins. I tackled him. I *actually* tackled him to the ground.

I kneel over him, pressing my knee into his chest, holding him there and pinning him to the asphalt. He begs for me to get off him.

"What the fuck?" he grits out.

He tries to grab my knee with his one free hand. I have the other held down on the ground. His hood has slipped back and off his head, exposing his face. The one streetlight above us highlights his features, and I immediately make a mental list of all of them. You know, in case I need to call the police afterward. If my phone still works.

Dark-brown hair cut short on the sides, long strands at the top falling back away from his tan forehead. His thick eyebrows are knitted. He opens his eyes. They're a bright shade of green with golden flecks, igniting with anger. His near-perfect sculpted jawline is clenched tight.

My heart continues to hammer in my chest. I bend my head down, bringing my face closer to his.

"What is wrong with you?" I ask him.

He stops moving, still grunting against my knee pressed into his chest. His eyes spread wide and he inhales a sharp, tight breath.

"What is wrong with me?" he asks. "What the hell do you think you're doing?"

"What did you think, huh?" I ask him, my eyebrows arching across my forehead. "Did you think I was an easy target? Woman walking alone in the dark?"

"What?" he asks, frowning. Shock is written across his regrettably gorgeous face. I hate admitting it to myself, considering the man tried to snatch me off the street. "I wasn't trying to attack you."

"Yes, you were."

He groans, squeezing his eyes shut before he opens them again. "I was not," he insists. "I was running. Like I do every night. *You* were the one who attacked *me*."

Normally, I wouldn't pause to consider an attacker's excuse. But the softness in this man's eyes urges me to listen. It's not that I immediately believe him, but I take my chances anyway.

Aside from the fact that his skin is covered in a thin film of sweat and his hair is equally just as drenched, there is one white earbud into his ear, the other sits on the concrete beside his head.

The distant, faded sound of drums and guitar flow from the one small plastic bud. I don't move my stance, but I glance over my shoulder at his feet. He's wearing a pair of worn running shoes. Printed in the corner of his black t-shirt is a baseball with a patriot hat on top of it. The same logo as my brother, Reed's, baseball team.

I realize none of this equates to proof he wasn't intending on attacking me. The man was clearly headed in my direction, but my intuition urges me to give him the benefit of the doubt.

He rests his head back on the concrete as soon as I loosen the pressure on his chest. I move my leg and let go of his arm, pulling myself to a stand. I'm cautious, moving slow. Just in case.

The man bends to pick up the lost earbud. He fishes inside his pocket and grabs his phone. He taps the screen, stopping his music.

My heart is still pounding and my cheeks warm. The man catches my eyes with his. He hasn't changed his expression. There's a permanent scowl written across his impossibly gorgeous face. If we didn't meet in this way and if I didn't think he was trying to snatch me up on the street, I might have immediately fallen for him. It'd be impossible not to with a jaw cut like his.

I don't let my guard down. Even if I might catch myself staring at him longer than I should.

I swallow the heat in my throat and take a moment to steady my breath.

"What?" The man asks, impatient with my silence. The anger inside him is now spread across his gorgeous face. "Are you going to tell me why you thought I was attacking you? I think you at least owe me that much."

I place my hands on my hips, biting back the tears behind my eyes. I can feel them, swelling and threatening to spill at any second. My chin quivers. Today is quite possibly the worst fucking day of my life.

"The wheel to my suitcase broke off."

Want to read more of Ophelia and Hunter's story?
Grab your copy of The Wrong Pitch HERE

ALSO BY BRITTANY

Standalone

What are the Chances

See Through

Paper Hearts

The Wrong Pitch

Without You Duet

Without You

Without Me

The Back to Me Series

Dissipate

Mine

Back to Me

The Heartbreak Series

The Rules of Heartbreak

The Secrets to Heartbreak

The Troubles with Heartbreak

Harding Brothers Series

Gorgeous Lies

Pretty Heartache

Sweet Sorrow

ACKNOWLEDGMENTS

If I were to thank everyone who had a hand in helping me create Dallas and Sloan's story, I would never finish typing. For now, I'll start with this.

Writing *The Rules of Heartbreak* has been different than any other book that I've written. I started writing Dallas and Sloan's story not long after I released my standalone *Paper Hearts*. The premise and start of the story for *The Rules of Heartbreak* came easy for me. Sloan with her silly rules and Dallas with his short, yet deeply emotional set of two. The story flowed for a while, and I thought I was headed on a great track to publishing the story quickly. That is, until health issues had landed me in the hospital for two weeks, causing the book to come to a screeching halt. This stay in the hospital was scary and unpredictable, leaving my family and friends wondering what the future held for me. Thankfully, after a week on a ventilator followed by a week of physical therapy, I was healthy enough to go home. But even after being released from the hospital, it took countless weeks for me to recover and get to a mental and physical state strong enough to get back to writing Dallas and Sloan's story. Thankfully, in time, I did. This story may have come a few months later than expected but at the same time, I believe it was meant to be. In a way, Dallas and Sloan saved me and reminded me of why I love writing books.

With that, I would like to thank first and foremost, my husband. Words can't even accurately express the love I have for you. I'm convinced we'll be together forever, even after this life.

Wherever that may be. From the beginning, you've been unwavering in your support of me and everything I want to accomplish. Thank you with putting up my incredibly tight schedule as I finished this book. All the late nights and days where I tried to fit in as many words as I could. As I've said before, in a room where the world is out of focus, you're the only one I see. You're my best friend, my biggest cheerleader, and my soulmate. I love you.

To my two boys. You are the reason I push through all the self-doubt and endless nights. Thank you for being my light. Always.

Dani, I don't even know where to begin with you. You're my sister and best friend. You lifted me up when I was at my weakest. You're an amazing Aunt to the boys. The only issue now is that we need you closer. But we'll save that discussion for another time. Thank you for being the first to read Dallas and Sloan's story and thank you for encouraging me to get through it.

To Tiffany. Oh my goodness, where do I even start with you? Like this story, you came into my life at the perfect time. The gratitude I have for all you've done for me this year is endless, especially when I physically could not work. You kept my life together and have opened so many opportunities for me. You have made me a better author and I don't know what I would do without you. You're the friend and assistant I never knew I needed.

Caitlin, my editor. You never fail to amaze me with your incredible edits. You always polish my books and you've made me a better writer. Thank you.

My designer, Amanda. I seriously think you were meant to design the cover for this book. You came into this project when I was lost on what to do. You took my ideas, graciously (and effortlessly) made it happen. Thank you so much for making this cover incredible.

To Ashley for always having my back and for your unwavering support in every part of this author world.

My beta readers, Amy, Ashley, and Dani. This story would not have turned out the way it did without your honest and positive feedback.

To Shauna and the Wildfire Marketing Team. Thank you for all that you've done for me from the start. It's been amazing to work with you and I can't wait to start on the next one.

And to you, the reader. Thank you for always being by my side. I can't wait to share Colton and Vada's story with you.

ABOUT BRITTANY

Brittany Taylor grew up all over the world including places such as California, England, and Texas. Her love of reading started at a young age. Finally deciding to fulfill her lifelong dream, she took the plunge into the writing world and published her first book when she was twenty-eight. Today she resides in Connecticut with her husband, two sons, two cats and one dog.